The Chip Shop Crew,
Last in the

2nd Edition.

STAND UP AND
BE COUNTED

I take no responsibility for anyone's interpretation of this book. I know my sense of humour is a bit warped. Yet I mean well. So writing this book. And wanting to actually depict football hooliganism. Yet at the same time. When you are playing out a character, and you realise that. The football hooliganism era. It was in relation to 80's street fighting. Yet a lot of people took it on board, and just used it as an excuse to mess around. When in reality, when you realise the social values of this book. When the fights started and ended. And then you would understand the context behind this. If you really want to understand the context behind this. This Is England, is one of my favourite movies. And you then realise. That by depicting these things, you are not glorifying them, yet highlighting them.

I have proof read this myself, and I know you have to get other people to proof read things. Yet that's how it is. This book was designed to highlight the football hooliganism era. That still continues to this day.

Highlighting it, brings awareness, and change. It allows people to have more knowledge about what football hooligans do. And the firms they have.

Motivation of this book is to bring awareness of the football hooliganism era.

(c) Copyright protected, under copyright laws, it's a civil offence to copy any of my work. Without my permission.

Chapter 1

You feel grounded. With your back against the wall. With double edged swords. You walk, alongside the Yid Army. Shrapnel being thrown, coins being thrown. This was against The Seaburn Casuals. Sunderland. Yid Army through and through. We ran through the lot of them out of the concrete ground. Twenty of us, and twenty of them. With a thin layer of police.

50P's being tossed at the Seaburn Casuals, putting in a good fight with a good few crossed the line. One smacked me in the face. The horrible bastard. I said to him, "you are gonna pay for that'. I smacked him back. And it was me and him, as I threw him on the fence. As everyone else was oblivious to it at first. Police saw it. Marko saw it. Two police officers tried breaking up the fight. I shoved Marko away. Laying into this Sunderland Seaburn Lad. Punch, punch, right hook jab, punch. On the fence. Broke his jaw. Broke his teeth. Pushed him against the fence, as he dropped. Like a sack of potatoes onto the floor. His eyes were blurry, he was unconscious. The two officers now who are with me, chase after me. I trip one up. Punch the other. Grab the other one with his helmet, push him across the barrier. As Marko and the rest of us, put me behind them. The Police unable to get me as we keep throwing shrapnel. Pieces after pieces, bits of shredded down bricks, layers of rocks.

An ambulance arrived for the bloke I knocked out. As the Seaburn Casuals now wanted revenge, all 4 of them on me, punching them. Kicking them. Marko was getting involved. Throwing them to the

ground. Putting them on the floor. The aggression. The aggression on the right hook, as I knock one over, as he trips.

Regan has his work cut out as more casuals walk up to him and he's battering them bloody and blue. And I get involved, and I am the one getting the beating now. With two Seaburn Casuals trying to knock into me, as I square up to both of them. Knock both of them out.

Marko starts punching some more Seaburn Casuals. One of them shouts. "Yeah, what you saying' lad, do you want a piece and all do ya?" He hit me in the stomach, as I knocked into him. A real skin head. He was. 6 foot 3, kicking him, tripped him over, right hook. Left hook. Jab to the face. Jab to the abdomen. Tripped him over. Punched him in the balls.

Regan said, "let's go, old bill."
We legged it over the fence, denim jeans, white jacket, threw myself over. With no escape plan there was more throwing of rocks. Old bill scaling the fence also, as we sit there, and rattle the fence to knock them over. As they find their way in through a cut bit of the fence.

We run towards this field, and the Seaburn Casuals, and The Police want us now. Firmly and solidly out of breath, fuming. The sight of me. My hands are bloodied. My face is bruised. My knuckles are torn.

I said, "Regan, you muppet, are you going to let the police catch us you prick?"

Regan said, "We're lost, and it ain't up in deep south. We're in fuck off north of England. And pigs swarming us like flies mate."

I said, "you dim low, why did you insist we scaled this fence."

Regan said, "because what other options did we have?"

I said, "we're running out of them." Seriously, what else do you want to do on a Saturday? Go online, and surf the dark web, or eat cheerios out of the packet? Not that I didn't do that. But with police officers swarming all over us. And we had to run. So we legged it towards this field.

The same field we were in, so that was the reason why I smacked Regan and said, "you piss artist, why did you make us go all the way up here?"

Police swarming us, batons at the ready, and peppers sprays also. This one police officer ran towards him. I kicked him in the teeth, and punched him in the nose. And steal his wallet. Could do with some McDonald's vouchers.

His name was PC Rick, I said, "Listen mate, jog on you muppet."

He said, "I'm the one with the pepper spray, and handcuffs you daft idiot. You tried out running me."

I said, "lost in the middle of the north, what are you going to do in your spare time? Go on tinder, only to get matched with that nurse at the hospital. Who stood you down on that date because you wouldn't buy her a big mac meal. You are getting it right in the teeth mate."

He said, "nothing wrong with McDonalds son. Better than you spending your time in KFC, and inviting people over. Who don't give a fuck about you."

He starts wrestling me to the ground.

I said, "do you know PC Townsend?"

He said, "yeah, why?"

I said, "because he's run out of options and so have you. You're too busy watching the grand national. Dim low."

I punch him in the face, and steal his pepper spray. Pepper spray him in the eyes and he's screaming with pain.

Regan said, "let's go."

The police ran over him, we legged it towards them only to find The Seaburn Casuals wanted a piece of us also. Not much publicity about them lot. So will give you the large truth. With me and them. And with Tottenham, Yid Army and them. It goes back a hundred years. The Sun just won't have it on the front or back pages. We get on the coach. All thanks to Ian, and he's now giving me lemon for being late. The sad act, wouldn't be lying in bed with a cigarette, only for him to miss his wedding.

Regan said, "come on, over here."
Just to let you know, we were running around in circles. Seaburn Casuals had us surrounded. Even though I beat up that police officer. The pigs had us surrounded. The fence, had us. And yeah. I work, sometimes at the Chip Shop. This is The Chip Shop Crew. You know that. You see it with your eyes feller. That is what is happening and it ain't changing.

With your back against the wall, you run out of options. And you run out of them quick. With no get away car in sight. And this fight was before the game. It just goes to show what you gonna do, with life. As you wake up in the morning, all blurry eyed. Forgetting about the game. Because it ain't even on yet.

Sunderland away, a real chance to meet some classy birds. Meet them anywhere, but with nothing else really to do.

Marko was with us, we managed to run towards some more Seaburn casuals, and Danny boy was driving the jeep. We get into the jeep, but rocks are being thrown at us, and I swerve out of the way. Police try putting down a road block. As we have police on our tail.

I managed to get on the motorway. The others managed to get on the coach. Nobody was willing to engage with Ian. Needed to meet him at the hotel. Wanted to watch the game and now I am on the motorway. With Ian begging everyone to go back to the east end. With me in the Jeep on the motorway. Went back to the Sunderland ground.

The game was still on, and I wasn't going to miss it because of the piggies. Too busy wasting their time. All I did was knock three geezers out, and Regan is looked defeated.

Chapter 2

I managed to swerve back to the Sunderland ground, lost The Police. This is the concrete jungle. This is what we are living for. Sniffing cocaine, and selling each other viagra.

Whilst Danny starts saying we ought to have another round with The Seaburn Casuals.

As they are looking bloodier than ever.

It never made TV, our time fighting, and it never made it because it wasn't what the fight was for. I had served in the marines. Most of us in the firm had. Used to confuse me sometimes, because I did my service. I came back a changed man. Yet never could get a match on Tinder.

Then I started hanging around with Regan and Marko. My best mates, and they taught me that living. Was like sniffing powder up your nose, and watching the game was when you were pissed out your skull.

Confused and rattled. I still remain strong as the leader of the firm. And that isn't going to change. I lost sight of it really. The things you see. The people you meet. The journey you won't forget.

Seaburn Casuals were looking to fight, throwing flares at us. We couldn't resist but throw flares back. Throwing rocks and coins.

The Police thought they had us because they had helicopters in the sky. What they realised was there was 50,000 fans, and only around 300 of them. And that was on a good day. Because they were the thin line. That stopped the fights turning into brutal murders. What I could see as something quite tasty as a fight. As I knock this Seaburn Casual down and it's too easy for me.

Looking over my shoulder, we still have a long way to go until the game is on. And I don't want to go back to the hotel. Ian parks up, and we all get out, and start throwing

rocks.
    This fight was probably one of the biggest ones in my life. This was a friendly. Before the season started. Backs against the wall. Tinderless dates, cocaine, broken season tickets, and the daily mail stuck to your arse cheeks. If only it was that easy to find your balls in the morning. You would run a few quid down market stalls.
    The fish bar was safe, and that's all that mattered. But right now we had more pressing business to attend to. Pure carnage. And it ain't hate that's glueing these fans together. It's pure fighting.

Chapter 3

    The police were still looking for us whilst we were watching the game. I said to Marko, "been a while since we've been up north, not many seagulls around."'
    Marko said, "you daft prick, just watch the game. Why are you talking in that muggy little voice for? You got a game to watch."
    I said, "oh yeah, so how does it feel getting arrested in the cells and crying your eyes out. Later to be found bollocks naked. Tied to a railing."
    I hated Marko at times, that pure passion for football, fighting, and booze. Anything. Just was something that we craved. With him just running his mouth. It was time to seek advice from Regan
    I said, "listen mate, long time no see, you

enjoying the weather?"

Regan said, "you've lost your touch, when Sunderland are looking like the winning team."

Jordan Jones, Sunderland, scores a sitter. And right now, it's going to get even worse when he nets another one in from close range. With 2-0 to go and 70 minutes on the clock.

I said to Regan, "it's strange up north, get a different buzz from it, but don't get lemon with me. Because it ain't working out for you. You are going to end up chucked out of the jeep."

Regan said, "we're getting the coach dim low. The jeep was just on hire. Danny boy is outside, just keeping things casual. No more of this talk."

With the game ending 2-0, and us losing 2-0. The Tottenham fans were still going to shout, "Yid Army!" All of the way.

Carnage at the end, fighting, and breaking some of the Seaburn Casuals jaws. Yet one of them comes at me with a right hook, and I throw him off balance. Another one tries upper cutting me to the face, and I block it, and kick him in the nuts. Bollocks to him, I am going home.

So we all head to the coach, Ian was waiting for us. One of the people I would knock out if he wasn't a coach driver. Saying that. What is he doing just driving all day.

We walk up to him all bloodied and bruised, he's looking for an argument. And I am not having it.

I said, "Ian, what you doing, falling asleep. Time to drive now pal."

Ian said, "what do you think I am going to do?"

I said, "you've been driving this coach, you haven't been drinking have ya?"

Ian said, "listen mate, and listen carefully, you are a snake in the grass. I drive this coach. Now you sit down."

I said, "I caught you in buying Nuts Magazine in brought daylight you SI. You're a stupid cunt who doesn't know the meaning of football. That's why you're stuck in this coach, driving."

He was right, he did drive this coach, and I was just the passenger. It reminded me of the days. When I used to get the bus home. Only to get flooded in rain.

With the Yid Army and The Chip Shop Crew finally as a firm. It was time to snore on the coach. Remember the good times in life. Yet that came to a halt, as the dim low driving it seems to be drunk. And has a flat tyre. Called out the RAC.

I said, "you're going to get nicked if you don't watch out."

Ian said, "leave it out, only had ten beers."

I said, "you dim low, I will cut you. I have busy things to do though."

RAC came and didn't take notice of the drunk driving, replaced the tyre, and we were on our way. *Mind you, with good chance come to reason. It was only a matter of time before the piggies pulled us over. With Ian driving on the motorway. Hard shoulder. This was bandit country, everyone was right. And I was doubting my own sanity, as Ian, managed to get into lane one. With police vehicles behind him.

Now he's getting pulled over, by PC Townsend, with only 13 miles to go until Tottenham. I didn't know what to do, walk from there. Or catch a black hackney cab. All of us were sat there. Looking pale, as pale ale.

PC Townsend gets Ian to blow into the breathalyser. Obviously Ian has failed the breathalyser test, because he's blown 1.3 on their machines. And you wouldn't think that was much. As I see him getting handcuffed and taken away in a patrol car.

I shouted, "well who the fuck is going to drive our coach now then?" With it on the hard shoulder Luckily, our mate Dave. Has a HGV licence, and since the coach is thirty party insurance. He manages to drive it all the way back to Tottenham. We all waved to Ian. "See you later Tubs." He was going to have a good meal in the cells. Pasta, they used to give him. Used to give him 5 of them to shut his noise of complaining.

Chapter 4

With your back against the wall. Some times you don't know what to do. Knowing Ian, the soppy prick was going to get done drinking and driving. Finally home in my flat

11A. And Regan and Marko over. Getting annoyed with life. Fucking hell. Every things a mess. Maybe it's me. Maybe I need to change. I keep telling myself maybe snort less cocaine. Call the officers police officers "piggy" less often. But it gets stuck in your brain. And you can't get it out. Like wasps, fucking animals. And the longer you think, the worser it gets. Knowing the cocaine gave you a buzz, but I had to sort things out with Regan and Marko. Because I was still running from The Old Bill. For that shooting. To be fair. If I had known he was a Chelsea fan. I probably would have nutted him one also and kicked him to the floor. And then used my pistol.

For all I knew, that was it, with Tottenham losing 2-0 away at Sunderland. You got used to the Yid Army. Like on repeat, you always knew they had your back. But that was the trouble. Always knowing. Not quite knowing what's gonna happen.

Going to be a long time for the season to start, in my mind, only gonna bee a few days in reality.

I was connected with skinheads who used to literally follow the bible and kick two shillings out of people. Used to have a bible in the glove box. When I met Danny and he introduced me to Daniel, and Rick. When we realised that every hotel room they stayed in had a bible. In the draw. They used to nick it and put it in the glove box. Read it. And I am not joking or saying the bibles wrong. Yet they used to read bits to me, as they were driving.

Read bits to me, and some of it stuck in my mind. Like 'Disciples, Shepherds, Serpents, Snakes." It all followed a pattern.

Life isn't a game of poker, knowing full well that bad luck followed me around. Like a cat chased some milk. But I didn't know why. Maybe it was my negative attitude and my longing willingness to fight. Maybe it was that reason. Mind you, I always found positivity a bit too much. Almost like if there wasn't a fight. My mind wouldn't be buzzing. And you wanted to see a fight.

Our firm never prearranged fights, some firms did. Our firm just went into the crowd and it was pure, and still to this day. I know. The Yid Army. My respect to them, and what they have done for Tottenham. Being a part of that firm, and being aware. That I can get a text, and I know the games on. The fights are on. The Seaburn Casuals left me with a sour taste in my mouth. Some people said, "leave the fighting out, grow up, don't be an animal." Yet it wasn't for the buzz like some firms fought for. I am not saying it didn't give you a buzz. Yet the fighting was pure passion for the club you were supporting. It went into over drive. When a team, you don't even know. Shouts, "Fuck Tottenham" You know the fights going to end up in casualties And I don't mean the TV Programme.

And that is just the beginning. I knew some people liked a laugh, and my lucks running out all of the time.

It came to reason that I was going to take that killing of that Millwall fan to my grave. Unless they could get me in jail without me chatting up, I ain't confessing. The worst part is, is having to put up with Marko and Regan And you know what they're like. When they're backs are against the wall. If you put too much sugar in their coffee. They're animals. They'll fight you.

With my head spinning, I didn't even know what to think, except I knew that everyone has a negative side to them. And I knew that I had that in me also. Seeing the women outside. You paid them respect, and the older we got. The more we realised that. 30, almost 31 now. Things change and times change.

With my back against the wall. I was

going to need some viagra to get myself to sleep. Stare at the wall and wander which models in nuts magazine would date me. Probably not many.

Chapter 5

I need to listen to my instincts, I need to law low, and just remain calm. Yet I knew that the piggies would be around me. Sooner or later. The Chip Shop Crew larger and larger. We had around a hundred members. I was still in charge of the firm.

I said to Regan, "today isn't it."

He said, "I feel like snapping someone's neck in two. fuck sake."

I said, "mate, I wouldn't lie to you, but there's fighting outside now. Some pikie called Sarah, and she was running her mouth. Claiming someone had nicked her phone. Bearing in my mind she had one in her hand. So I was not believing this bullshit. So I walk on the balcony, and I shout. "fuck sake, stop making a fuss over nothing, you haven't lost it. What's that in your hand then?"

She replied, "er it's my work phone."

I said, "you don't work."

She said, "yes I do, I work."

Are you on Adult work?"

She said, "no."

Judging from the fact that she just said no. There was no evidence to conclude wether she was a prostitute with Adultwork or not.

I said, "so what do you do then?"

She said, "I'm a hairdresser."
All of the women chavs say that on the local estate. Even if it's picking one of their nose hairs out. They claim they're a hairdresser.

Regan wasn't buying any of the bullshit either and he said, "love, I ain't being funny, but you ain't a hairdresser I shaved my pubes this morning, does that make me a hairdresser. Who else is gonna do it for me eh? fuck sake."

Sarah said, "I need my phone, I need it."

I said, "alright, well not my problem."

Regan shouted, "you can come and do my pubes loves. I'll pay you a fiver."

In the end Sarah left and we thought that was the end of the interaction. Only for her to leave with her middle finger up. A signal we always remember as a hate signal. But coming from one of the birds on the estate. We just went online to see if we could book her on Adultwork.

Regan said, "I ain't dealing with Alex, for fuck sake. It's one of his women."

I said, "might not be."

I scroll online and can't find her, but I am only on the first page.

Regan said, "fuck sake, she's got into my brain, that lady has. We'll see if we can book her later. You coming for a pint down the Cheshire?"

I said, "yeah, going to, got to be done, need a break from the estate."

Things were not looking up. I can have my good days and my bad days. Going down The

Cheshire, was supposed to take my mind off things. I am going to have a chat with Rachel.

So me, Danny, Regan, and Marko all walk in The Cheshire. We all have a pint of Stella Each. Fancied a change from the carling.

Rachel was serving. I said. "Alright Rachel, long time no see."

She said, "alright, if you lads don't mind, I have work to do."

And she did, because it was Saturday night, and I don't mean the song. I mean bouncers on the door, and cash out of her pocket.

A big, fuck off massive guy, who was 6 foot 6, muscles like bricks. Stone henge look on his face. Was placed by the door. Almost like he could blow down the whole of London, by one whistle. Geordie bloke.

I said, "Rachel, that cost you an arm and a leg, that bouncer."

Rachel said, "yeah, but so did the broken windows, that the insurance refused to claim."

I said, "who's been breaking the windows?"

Marko said, all cocky but chilled, and stood at the bar. He said, "chavs have been breaking the windows."

I said, "how do you know?"

He said, "just can tell these types of things. That's the main point of this isn't it. Figuring out how we are in deep south right now."

I said, "nah I don't think so."

I spoke too soon, and six Chelsea fans walk in. This was going to end up in murders. As they walked through the door. The bouncer just standing there.

One of the Chelsea geezers, sat at the bar said. "Alright, Tottenham lads, bit of a surprise, we are playing you on the first game of the season. At home you bellend. Like it always is."

I said, "what's your name, you soppy streak of piss?"

He said, "Jack."

I said, "well have you heard of me, Steve Smith, then have ya?"

He said, "yeah you make the news all the time you daft twat. If I wasn't so drunk I would smash you."

I said, "with what, your lager bottle, simmer down."

He said, "they won't give us lager bottles you dim soppy streak of piss. It's plastic. The bouncer at the door confirmed it. That's why the bar lady has taken your glass bottles. And my glass bottles. So we have nothing to smash around now do we feller?"

I said, "well come over here and I'll knock you one, you silly little cunt."

Jack walked over. The soppy streak of piss. And he said, "if I wasn't so drunk, I'd open you up."

I pushed him to the floor, the door man. He bounced forwards. He shouted, "Oi fellers, fellers, fellers, stop getting involved." Never heard a Geordie sound like a Londoner so quickly. Within the blink of an eye. Just from being on the front entrance of a London pub. The accent catches on.

The bouncer, Steve, he said, "right you

two, I want none of this again. Otherwise I am throwing you out."

There was silence. I had shares in this pub, this was my local. And the bouncer winked at me as I went and spoke to him. I said, "Alright Steve, I am ex military by the way."

He said, "Ex navy me."

I said, "what, swimming and stuff?"

He said, "yeah, and diving into a deep sea, a lot of training involved. I did my service there. Got an SIA licence, and I have punched more people in the face. Than obese people have had mot meals."

I said, "so you are trained to fight?"

He said, "yeah, the only reason I didn't knock you two geezers out is because I know you. But seriously mate."

He starts to whisper, he said, "seriously mate, don't cause aggravation in here. They are just trying to wind you up."

I muttered, "well it worked." Under baited breath.

He said, "well don't fall for it then, you silly bollocks, you need to prove yourself when you meet them next. Tottenham away at Stamford Bridge mate. Yid army will be all over them like milk over cornflakes. You take it easy, have a cornetto or something."

I said, "alright mate, by the way, you from Newcastle?"

He said, "yeah, well I am from Newcastle, moved here two years ago. So enjoying the scenery, of the chavs walking around smashing things up."

I said, "you speak to many police officers?"
He said, "yeah."
I said, "anyone in particular?"
He said, "oh PC Brian Townsend, he's a good laugh."
I said, "his wife chucks him out the house, did you know?"
The bouncer replied, "yeah, I am aware of it, it's hilarious mate. He came around mine the other day. Bollocks naked, rang on my doorbell. I had to let the poor fucker in."
I said, "so are you mates with him then?"
He said, "well kinda, yeah, wouldn't say best mates, but he's alright."
I said, "me and him have got history."
Steve the bouncer said, "yeah, he's told me."
I said, "about what?"
Steve said, "well, about everything really, the pepper spray, the Millwall fan that he thought you killed. All of the people you knock out, and don't look the other way, until he arrives."
Steve started to laugh and said, "oh you're a good laugh mate, but seriously. That guys got issues."
I said, "haven't we all."
Haven't we all got issues, haven't we all got problems. Haven't we all got things we hate about ourselves. Haven't we all got insecurities, weaknesses. We do. All of us. The greatest weakness, is thinking you are invincible. I know for a fact that I'm not. The Chelsea fans simmered down. I walked right

back up to them, and Jack said, "sit down mate."

I said, "you're lucky we've got a good bouncer, he's put things into perspective. Are you going to the game?"

Jack said, "probably."

I said, "well when I see you there. You're going straight on the concrete, you streaky streak of piss."

He said, "oh I am scared."

The Chelsea fans started laughing. There was no chance, me and my firm were going to scrap. With the bouncer at the door. But I had an idea.

I said to the bouncer, "do you fancy a McDonalds?"

He goes. "Yeah could do."

I said, "here you are, here's ten quid, there's one right around the corner, get what ever you fancy."

He said, "cheers mate."

He walks off.

Rachel shouted, "I paid good money for him to stand there, not for him to take breaks like that. Every ten minutes."

I said, "he's a smoker, he takes breaks all the time."

She said, "really?"

I said, "nah he don't smoke, well he does with bacon."

I walked right up to the Chelsea fans, it wasn't personal, but I slam right on Jacks hand, as he crunched to the floor. It was like he just slammed forwards, as I broke his hand."

Another geezer lunches forward, and all of my firm and the Yid Army get involved. Danny boy is the one with the top off, and the slim appearance. Who don't take bullshit from anyone who can throw people around like dices. Takes one of them. Tears them a new arsehole. I waltz into another three of them. Crunch them to the floor. Broke another geezers hand, and Regan gets involved. Smashes another one. The rest run off. Rachel has to close the bar because she's had enough. The funniest thing, and as funny as in the context. Of strange funny. Not ha ha, funny. Is there wasn't a McDonalds around the corner. So soppy bollocks is going to be asking for directions for an hour before he cottons onto. The fact I've taken him for a mug. He knows PC Townsend. What a streak of piss,

Rachel screams, "this is my pub, I run this pub, and I know you're a local, but you do my fucking head in."

We all leave and head back to mine. That fight was good and everything. The fights always turn ugly. But Jack that geezer, 40, apparently he's in University. Studying football. Actually studying the subject football. You would think I was joking. Well actually he's studying sports education. But the geezer only has an NVQ in door opening, but he's coming out of there. Like he owns the place. Jack Paul, his name is. Big massive bloke. A ladies man. When he can find them.

But I ain't getting personal, because

fighting for us. Was like taking the lid off a can of carling. It was like yawning. Or opening a door. It became a habit. Good or bad, not up for me to say. I mean, if it wasn't for the war that I fought in Iraq. They would have more oil. So to be fair we got the petrol prices reduced. So I ain't that fucking worried if I am being honest.

Chapter 6

I am feeling small, because you know we live in the Tottenham estates. And you know all of the cockney rhyming slang. So I know what is going on, and I am buzzing because it's Chelsea away tomorrow. Tottenham verses Chelsea. Next. Which means bring everything in. Get everyone involved. I want to know how many people are going to get involved, because I got Marko and Regan with me. We are just getting ready.

Regan said, "listen, don't mess with me, you you dickhead, you know what you are. A nob-head. Like you know. What you are going to do?"

I said, "you're mugging me off with that cockney rhyming slang. Go out in the balcony and come fight with me then!"

Marko said, "I want to order a Chinese, but you have me laughing."

I said, "come on Regan, outside on the balcony."

So I bring him out on the balcony, and I said, "you better be in this firm for the right reasons, because I run this firm. So you need to be on this. You aren't allowed to be just jogging along like you in the background. You are in the front line. Stand up and be counted. Knock horses out, when the police mount on it."

He said, "we ain't knocking out horses, we kick them in the ankles, and we sprain the ankles of the plods. How many dogs barking right now. I want to know. Because I am going mad. Going out of my head. With madness."

That is what I want to know. But it was like the resources were running low, and there wasn't much time to do things. And it was the day before the game. We don't hurt the animals. That is what you are under the impression. I am talking and trying to scrap, so that is what we are going to say.

We are not going to stop, and stomp on Chelsea. Get the whole of Yid Army involved. Because Tottenham had suburbs, this is where we grew up. This is where we got educated. But now there are so many dickheads roaming the streets. And I am not trying to get involved in things that I can't handle. I have so many spams on my phone from Alex. fuck Alex, the pimp. That was on Adultwork, trying to get me these prostitutes.

I want to get into the fight, and we know that we are going to cruise into Chelsea, and it's going to get messy. So we know what's happening. This is The Chip Shop Crew. The salt and vinegar of the fighting, the sour taste in your mouth. The Burberry cap, and what I am saying. This is how I roll, and I reside in. so recognise this right now.

Marko said, "all you lot do is chew on biscuits and it's old news."

I said, "I want to hear that attitude man, because you ain't going to be saying that tomorrow. So think what you want about me. So we are going to get into Chelsea. And remember. This is The Yid Army, Chip Shop Crew. This is the best, and nobody else has taken my place. So I am the best out there. So I am going to have to speak to the feds in the future, so that is something we are going to do. But listen, right now. The police are going to try to break the fights up. So we are going to start knocking into the police officers if they do that."

Marko nodded, and sipped some milk and said, "yeah, that is the thing, the piggies try to break us up, this is not like it is mate. This east end, this is Tottenham. Yid Army. Like an arrow and a dart. And get things twisted, nobody getting this wrong."

I said, "yeah exactly, we are just going to charge at Chelsea, they are not going to know what's going on. They don't even know our tactics. Our tactics are going to be on point. Charge right at Chelsea fans."

Danny boy enters the room and said, "yeah, respect, and remember, allow the haters man. Because they talking too much and I can't hear them. So we are going to be breaking into people."

I said, "yes exactly, this is what is going on. My Uber driver was an alcoholic, he was the victim of a mugging the day before he drank a bottle of Jack Daniels. And I don't know the rest of the story."

Marko said, "you need to switch Uber drivers man, I have sympathy for the mugging. But then you are chatting about drink driving. Like that soppy sack Ian. Getting pulled over by Police. 1.2, on their score. Getting in jail. Now he's drinking orange juice in his boxers. Watching Redtube."

I said, "he is actually, he texted me, he's all hype, he doesn't do anything. He ain't going to get lemon with us. Because this is not going to work like this. We are going to get lively."

I know things are going to get lively, because this is what is going to happen. So I am going to know. I am going to realise. That we have a plan. And the Yid army know. You know how we crashed into the Seaburn Casuals. I knew that. And that's exactly what happened. Yid Army, can't fuck with us.

So I go on the balcony, I am bouncing like a bumble bee. So many thoughts in my head. And I know what it's like. So have to understand these things.

I didn't know how many people want to get involved in this. This is going to be ruthless. Come on let's fight. This is not Strictly Come Dancing, this is the fighting, and I am getting annoyed. And riled up. Because some people get lemon with me. For this. And I had my eyes all over the flat, and it was not going to be as lively. I am bouncing. I smoke a cigarette. And then I go to bed early, and I forgot to set my alarm. But I don't mind, because Marko usually wakes me up. By throwing milk on my face.

Chapter 7

I am woken up by Marko, and we are going to scrap, and we are getting involved. Everyone gets involved. I get ready first, and I am just chilling. Just having a smoke, and I am just putting things into perspective, but understanding. What's going to happen, as we march towards the tube, hundred of us. And we get the tube. Yid Army, all of the way, more join in. we have a thousand now, and we manage to mount over the terrace. Where Chelsea were. And we manage to start fighting them straight away. And the only Police officer in sight. Was ordering a beef burger anyway. So we start mashing into Chelsea. And I knew this is going to sound brutal. But I am going in. I get a tooth knocked out. But just having a scrap, and pushing people back, just to scrap. Punches flying, and kicks flying. Yid Army are literally fly kicking people in the face. As there is a semi kind of crush, where people push forward. And I lose sight of Yid Army for a bit, but I catch up with them. People asking if I am okay. As Chelsea march forward. And it's getting bloody, bruised. And I am feeling swollen already. Fight fights. This is what is happening. The brutal fighting, of the east end. This is the fighting. That we have to get involved.

Marko said, "charge."

So we all charge towards the Chelsea fans, and this man called Stan. Chelsea fans walks forward. And tries to act like he's acting the best. I tell him to fuck off, and I punched him in the face. Then I have Chelsea on me. Like they want to punch me in the face. They did before. More punches being thrown towards me. And punches towards Marko. And Marko is getting involved. Regan is also, and it's getting intense, and it's not stopping. Nobody is stopping. This is the war on the streets. This is the serpents in the bible. This is what is happening. I am not the serpent in the bible. Not the dishonest. People ringing me on my bluetooth, and I am smashing more people out of the way.

Of course I am angry. I am angry because Chelsea think they can make themselves noisy. And I said to Stan, "listen, you better take a step back, otherwise you are getting smacked up. You twat."

He wasn't taking a step back, so he was getting snapped up. So I smash him, and I attacked him. I punched him multiple times. I was losing it. I was an animal the way I was going. I am saying, it's not just for the buzz of it. It's for just getting people involved.

Marko said, "you are letting this guy go." Marko is piling into this guy, literally jump kicking into this guy. And knocked him unconscious with one punch.

With your back against the wall, you don't know what to do sometimes. That was the essence of fighting. And even though I had served overseas for four years. This was a different battle. A war on the streets.

At this point, it all gets blurry, and I start to realise. This firm, it was built on respect. Yet when I am scrapping. It means something to me. I am nervous, biting my nails. Everyone around me nervous. I have to fight my way throughout Chelsea firms. They are tougher than expected. And some geezer runs with a crowbar, and almost knocks me out. As I dodge him out the way. Feeling disorientated. And realising something. When you are alone in this concrete jungle. Then you know when this happens. When I was Iraq. It was different. Because it was a different war. Yet this war on the streets. Is making the adrenaline rush through my bones and muscles. Ligaments. And the smoke flares run through my mind. Delirious, and not thinking straight. If only I had a plan out of this. But it wasn't that straight forward. Running this firm was taking it out of me.

This is east end and when you realise what you are dealing with, if it isn't the local police officers around the corner. Then they can creep up on you, and before you know it. They have used the element of surprise. Yet that was the tactic I used. As I dodge smoke and I knock a copper in the face. As I walk back, I fall onto the fence. And then I realise. Listen.

This is serious. I am the guy, that is living through this. My life is not a musical. I don't need a stereo, and you realise that things get really heated. It doesn't stop, and even though the adrenaline could make me angry. Like a bulldog without a chain or a leash.

If you knew what I meant. I had to fight my way out of The Chelsea firm. I was getting angry. Because they know I am the toughest fighter of the Chip Shop Crew and The Yid Army. The firm was getting tough with me there. As more smoke flares were fired towards the enemy. This was a civil war, and the police were just eye witnesses.

There was no news of PC Townsend, or what he was doing. I mean, his Mrs hasn't kicked him out of the house in a long time, which is good. But it's just embarrassing having him around because I know what he's like. He fishes for information.

Regan said, "come on mate, what the fuck are you doing?"

I said, "listen, this fight is going on forever. This war on the streets. So many geezers trying to knock me out."

The geezer with the crow bar, was arrested by Police. And I was running from the police, as they charged in full riot gear. I under estimated Chelsea. They were ruthless with their hits, and their punches. It was leaving me bloody and bruised. And as much as I like to joke about the local police. Getting flashbacks of the time at Millwall away. Was playing on my mind. And it was making me feel worried.

Chelsea Headhunters arrived, and were making a noise. This is when it really dawned on me that they meant business. All I wanted was fish and chips. Now I have to fight for an hour, with riot police trying to stop me. This was the battle that you would expect. Deep south, soppy streaks of piss trying to push me out of the way. As I was knocking them away.

Deep south was closer than you thought. Staring you right in the face. The gruesome attacks of Chelsea Headhunters. Wanting me dead, and leaving me dead threats in the mail.

I am not trying to say it's easy, of course it isn't. Being part of this firm changed my life. In ways you never would have imagined. Tottenham and the Yid Army, knowingly. Deep down, that the players out there. We will all be cheering on Harry Kane. And there will be hooligans who don't even know where the toilet paper is whilst they are sitting on the bog. That they sit on at half time, waiting in line at the pie stand. To get bovril, and slip drugs in there. Of all kinds I can't even imagine to describe. The way they were getting mixed around was extraordinary.

But right now Regan was facing unrest, he was facing challenges, none any other men had faced. Chelsea Headhunters had him by the scruff of the neck. And one of them had a knife pointed at his eye. If only I had skipped today, taken the day off, done some painting. Maybe gone to get cod and chips. This might never have happened.

Yet the Pukka Pies tell you something

that no other man can tell you. And this is about knowing. Where Regan is right now, I don't want to talk about pies. I want to help him.

I said, "Regan mate, I got you."

I smashed the headhunter, but he didn't fall to the ground. Just me and him scrapping, and now it's my eye. That's under attack as I give him a few right hooks as the knife falls on the floor. Everyone scrambles. I pick the knife up. Now *I am in charge*. This is The Chip Shop Crew. This is what I am saying, alongside the Yid Army right now.

I said to him, "give me one good reason why I shouldn't stab you right in the eye."

He said, "this ain't question time, you can't ask me questions like that."

I said, "well maybe it is question time, because you are hanging around. What the fuck is this knife made of anyway?"

He said, "I just come out of jail."

I said, "you hand crafted this knife, in jail, it's solid, it's got metal on it. Good shape. Why are you doing this fighting and all that?"

He said, "why not?"

I said, "you need to stop this bullshit. You are in deep south. This is what I am going to do. I am going to punch you in the stomach. And I am going to throw this knife in the bin."

I jabbed him to the stomach and threw the knife in the bin. I said, "how do you feel?"

He said, "how the fuck do you think I should feel? You just punched me."

I said, "Yid Army, all the way, your crew

are not with me on this. Join me on this adventure."

He said, "no thanks, now get the fuck out of my way."
Being on the front line was scary, and it wasn't something I would always recommend. In some ways though. It started to make sense. Out of all of the fighting that was going on in the streets. This fight had it's purpose. Because it was a rival gang we were fighting against. And I knew that time almost stood still at first. Almost like in a James Bond movie, where the actor. Just stands there, looking around. Yes that can be counted, things we see on a daily basis.

Yet this wasn't a James Bond movie, this was reality, and Regan started to shout loudly, "are you going to fight me or not?" As I just stood there.

Chapter 8

Everything seemed dull at first. You would forget about life itself. You would forget about the meaning of life. You would ignore all of the geezers request to leave it.

I said to Regan, "listen, let's take a break from fighting."

I wasn't scared of the Chelsea headhunters, I wasn't scared of them. They didn't have enough clobber. I had clobber. And I realised something. I hated the Chelsea firm, upper class, posh nosed, idiots. And to be honest with you. That was how it was. Yid Army, was the place to be. Yid Army, was the place, was the ticket. This was a vacation for us.

Yid Army meant something to me, we are in collaboration with them. It's on like Donkey Kong. And I know what a lot of people have been saying. I know what it is. About wearing the right clobber. About doing the right things. Yet I wasn't taking a break from fighting. Smashed two guys faces in. Then PC Townsend turns up, and it gets kind of weird. Because I was expecting him to be kicked out of his house. From his Mrs. In a thong. His mrs had kicked him out, and finally, after all of the brainstorming he had done. He had managed to find some boxers.

I said to PC Townsend, "we are making some progress aren't we, your mrs has chucked you out of the house. But you have managed to find some boxers."

He said, "yeah, and what's your point, you are one swear word away from getting arrested"

I said, "I haven't sworn."

He said, "well who the fuck was calling me an idiot back there then?"

I said, "there's over 70,000 people turning up to this game, could have been anyone, maybe the fact that you are all stripped down. Don't take it personally. You still in the police?"

He said, "of course, and is that of embarrassment to you?"

I said, "of course not, I just wanted to know."

At this point in time. I didn't know how to feel. I felt sorry for the guy, that he had been kicked out of his house. That he owned. I was kind of happy to see him again. That was the ticket, that was what it all meant. And that was what it was like. Just trying to make ends meet, taking things day by day. And you realise something. All of this fighting will be worth it one day. Except, he is going to challenge me, on the offences committed

He said, "So, sir, have you committed any offences?"

I said, "No."

He said, "We've found a suspect for the guy who killed Lee, also known as pale ale."

I said, "who's that then?"

He said, "the landlord of this pub that we drink at."

I said, "How do you know it's him??"

He said, "fuck knows, he makes good beer though, and why the fuck are you still around. Soppy bollocks. I will open you up like a cannister. Haven't you got a game to watch?"

I said, "Yeah I have actually, but it was good seeing you again"

He said, "Seeing me? Okay, fair enough, listen. I only slept 2 hours last night. I have a headache. And my mrs, kept talking to me, telling me about things. That I should be aware of. Telling me about things I should know. Like how many tigers there are out there in the jungle. It was crazy. Listen. I will leave you to your game. Remember. Remember something, this is the wild wild west."

He did a little fake shooting thing with his arms, and hands, and did a "pow" sound. And he left.

He was then to get an egg thrown at him by a guy driving a black Audi.

Yet, we were making progress. Because last time. It was a disaster. And for once in my life. I forgot about the fighting. I forgot about it, and I remembered a time. When things were different. You know, when bread didn't have seeds in it. When machines weren't manufactured. When silence would hit the planet.

Chapter 9

It goes quiet for a bit, you forget about everything. You forget about the fights, yet, the police as we know them. Kept hounding us. Every day, knocking on my window. Every day. "Can I have a word?" So finally, in my boxers and my dressing gown. Because that was all I was wearing. I answer the door.

PC Rick is there, looking a bit gormless. He said, "Alright chap, just a social visit." I said, "It's too early, what do you want?" PC Rick said, "There was a hit and run here a few weeks ago, did you witness anything?" I said, "I don't want to talk to you on my door step, come in if you want. Do you want a brew?" I made him a coffee. And sat down with him. Now PC Rick said there was a hit and run. Apparently a prostitute, was run over and killed by a Jeep. He wants to know which fucker had done it. I am looking surprised because I have no fucking idea.

I said, "I have no idea, I don't know who did it, it could be anyone. You roam this estate. I am telling ya. These prostitutes have been ruining our estate. You should lock *them* up."

PC Rick laughed and said, "Do you own any Jeeps?" I said, "Yes I own three of them." PC Rick said, "They're popular, sure it wasn't you who ran her over?" I said, "Do you think I would remember if I did?" He said, "I don't know, I don't know your state of mind. The only other person I know with a Jeep in your estate is Fat Tony.

I said, "Well it must be Fat Tony then, is he the pimp?" PC Rick said, "Yeah he's the pimp, but why would a pimp want to run over one of his own?" I said, "Nah it doesn't work like that. The hookers are not owned by one pimp, there's a dozen pimps. It could be that he doesn't want other pimps dealing on his turf."

PC Rick said, "So the pimps are fighting each other?" I said, "pretty much, they use the women, sell them out. It's like a post code war basically. They have a patch of land each, and if they cross over. I see them all the time saying. Oh you are on my street, and this and that."

PC Rick said, "Fat Tony, right, he lives in privately rented accommodation, I know the guy well." I said, "So it could have been him." PC Rick said, "Well we need evidence." I said, "Yeah we do, we do need evidence. I never liked the bloke."

I go into the kitchen to drink some whiskey. Even though early in the morning. I am feeling sick. I return. I said, "PC Rick let me explain something to you. All of this aside, everything I have done here on this estate. It wasn't me. So I would appreciate it. If next time you come over. You don't insinuate it's me. I own three Jeeps. What do you want to do next. Go and search them if you like. You won't find anything. Because it wasn't me." PC Rick said, "I never said it was you." I said, "you insinuated it was, you said I have three Jeeps. So what? So fucking what? Why does it matter?" PC Rick said, "Just trying to connect the dots." I said, "Well fucking connect them but don't go on a witch hunt." I said, "how long have you been in the forces anyway?" PC Rick said, "11 years." I said, "So the job's like a marriage to you?" He said, "Yeah you could say that." I said, "Well fucking hell, do you hit snooze in the morning. You been sleeping on duty. I have seen you."

PC Rick said, "I don't know what you mean. I haven't been sleeping on duty." I said, "Yeah, I have seen you, by the petrol station, filling up on petrol. I have seen you."

PC Rick said, "Hang on a minute, you have seen me sleeping whilst filling up have you?" I said, "Yeah". PC Rick said, "Sounds like you are spreading rumours." I said, "'Spreading rumours pal, nobody else is here." PC Rick said, "Call me sir, everyone else does, I called you sir, have the respect to call me that." I said, "I could call you worse than 'sir' pal, trust me on that." PC Rick said, "So, was it you who ran over that hooker in your Jeep?" I said, "No." PC Rick said, "So will you mind if I take a look around your Jeeps?" I said, "if you want to." So PC Rick strolled around my Jeeps, checking the tires. Checking the windows. I said, "you satisfied now?" PC Rick said, "satisfied of what?" I said, "that it wasn't me who ran over that hooker. I don't dabble with hookers." PC Rick said, "do you ever drink and drive?" I said, "no." PC Rick said, "you sure?" I said, "yes I am sure, if I am on the piss, I take the train. Now can you please leave." PC Rick said, "oh it's like that is it?" I said, "well yeah, because this is the type of stuff which does bother me, being accused of running over and killing hookers." PC Rick said, "so it wasn't you?" I said, "no."

PC Rick said, "you sure?" I said, "well if it was me, then I don't remember doing it." PC Rick said, "alright, I believe you. I have to go to do some paperwork now. You keep your nose clean." I said, "I would say the same to you, looks like you are on the fucking gear." PC Rick said, "excuse me?" I said, "you heard me, it looks like you are on gear."

PC Rick said, "be careful, I will have you locked up for public order." I said, "what for?" PC Rick said, "for saying I am on gear." I said, "that ain't offensive is it, just expressing my opinion." PC Rick said, "well to be honest with you buddy, one more word out of your mouth, one more word. And you're nicked for public order."

I didn't say anything, he just stood there

smiling. Got in his car, did a wheel spin. And drove back to the nick. Where I am thinking. "For fuck sake, I know I killed Pale Ale, and all that. But I ain't killing any prostitutes."

If anyone knew the meaning behind what happened with Pale Ale. It was a no-nonsense, a local Derby game. And to be honest with you. I get my 9mm gun out. But I thought the gun wasn't loaded. Was just trying to scare him. This was Chelsea vs Millwall Next thing I know, I am running for my life. It was chaotic, and listen. I am not over it yet. The irony is, is they think I killed that hooker, and they ain't even talking about Pale Ale anymore. I've even forgotten his name, he was so insignificant. So the twat in the high vis celebrity costume. Has left. Threatening to lock me up for public order. And I return home. Speaking to Regan and Marko.

It's me Steve Smith for crying out loud. Thought everyone had forgot about me. I can't remember everything that has been happening. I just had a police officer at my door threatening to lock me up for public order. All I did was give the opinion he was on the fucking gear. Fuck sake. And listen, this ain't stopping. The fights on the streets don't stop. That's the whole purpose of this.

Chapter 10

His name wasn't really Pale Ale, it was Lee. He was nicknamed Pale Ale, because, actually. I don't know. And part of me doesn't want to know.

We went to the same football matches, the same cold winter nights. The same cliched comments calling the police piggies. But this was getting boring. Stood in the cold, ordering a burger. Tottenham were playing Chelsea in the FA Cup, 3rd round.

But for one in my life, we weren't there to scrap. We had business, you know. Now we are the chip shop crew. We had business to attend to. Paperwork and all of that. So we are all ordering our paperwork at Stamford Bridge. The agreement was we wouldn't wear any Tottenham gear. To an outsider, we could have been Chelsea.

We sat down on the wet grass. Police above us on the terrace. This one large chap, with a truncheon the size of two cocks put together. I am not even exaggerating. I looked up at his miserable face. You could see his high vis, and he looked back at me. He looked back, and he kept looking. At this stage, I went over and spoke to him. He wouldn't give his name. He wouldn't even give his shoulder number. It wasn't even on display. I went over and I said, "taking an interest to me are ya?" He said, "yeah because you were staring at me, and I wandered why." I said, "is staring at people a crime?" He said, "no, but murder is." I said, "wait, that was random, who says I am murdering people? We are eating burgers." He said, "cut the crap, CID have enough evidence to charge you. We know you killed Lee." I said, "right, so you have a team of monkeys on the third floor trying to manufacture some evidence. Okay then, where do we start. It wasn't me." The Police officer said, "If I had a pound for every time I heard that. I would be able to quit my job, buy a mansion. And have holiday shares abroad. I know you're bullshitting me."

I said, "but buddy, you are not CID, why are you getting involved?" He said, "I work with CID. I don't have to be CID to work with them." I said, "What do they stand for? Chronic Idle Dickheads. Come on man, you know me better than this. We had an agreement. That if I gave you some information. Some intelligence. You would go a bit more slow time on this whole investigation."

The Police officer, turns out his name is John. Because I hard his mate holler it just now. The Police officer, John. He said, "if you give us intelligence, every week, at the station. On paper. We'll whitewash the whole thing. We'll frame someone else. But we need the intelligence. And right now. You ain't giving us anything."

I said, "okay, I'll start." He said, "for the rest of your god damn life, you start giving us this intelligence man, this ain't no Christmas party or anything. This is real business. I know you, and I think you're a bit of a cock. In all fairness. But if you give us intelligence. We will go easy on you. May even give you a day in the Bahamas."

I said, "I find it hard to believe you have evidence. Lee was shot in the head. Do you have a confession, no. Do you have CCTV? Probably not. So what evidence do you have, before I start doing work for you?"

He said, "we have you on CCTV you dickhead."

I said, "how clear is the quality?"

John laughed, he said, "we have facial recognition, it's in HD. It was a covert camera set up, and it's worked a treat. The CPS say they have enough evidence to charge you. You have been on bail for murder, for two years. Man that is a long ass time. You are being a cock. But listen. I am good friends with the DC who's speaking to the CPS. So I can get an agreement sorted. But I am going to need the intelligence. And no fake bullshit either"

I said, "what's your collar number?"' He said, "it's fuck off." I said, "...*you're funny...*'" He said, "Just give us the intelligence, enjoy the game. Your fate, your future. Lies with you. You dug your own grave when you shot Lee. The coffin is waiting for you. But we have enough time to exonerate you and frame someone. Someone else's coffin, someone else's mistake. Hey, if you're giving us intelligence, if we put you in jail. You ain't gonna talk. You know what happens to police informants, rats, and snitches in jail?" I said, "yeah I know what happens to them." He said, "Don't let me down, and next time you come over, don't compare my truncheon to two cocks put together. I heard that. That was stupid." I said, "okay, well I am going now."

John said, "look, if it's any consolation, I

hate my job. Can't stand it. Wanted to work in security. You get more time to sit on your arse cheeks in that job. This job, if you ain't moving every second, the Sargent gets in your face. And yells at you. Man, fuck this."

I said, "so why don't you just quit?"

He said, "and become what? A G4S security guard? Looking after drunks?"

I said, "the police work is dealing with drunks, is it not?"

He said, "to less of a degree, now fuck off."

I walked down the street to meet the others. Marko, for one. For the first time in my life. I had a mixture of emotions. I knew my boys had my back, but this deal. I am not sure if I wanted to do that. Or not. I spoke to Marko and Regan, wanted to express my concerns with them.

Me, Steve Smith, going to a football game, just to get that bullshit. All I was doing was looking at his truncheon but he's bought me some time. I tell Marko and Regan what I am required to do. And they are supportive, and don't want me to go to jail. Yet, I was going to have my work cut out.

Chapter 11

Regan and Marko were going to take convincing. Wind up someone's bitch in prison or wind up the Police's bitch. Giving them information. It was a lose lose situation, but I would rather be outside of jail. Regan and Marko were drinking Stella, in my council flat.

And were upset. Marko said, "let the piggies think what they want. What do you expect them to do? Get information from ya? Who the fuck do they think they are? Casanova or some shit?" Regan said, "fuck this, let them do what they want. It doesn't phase me one bit. We always tell them about the hookers on this estate. Do they do anything about it? No of course they don't. Bunch of wind up merchants. Fuck them. Seriously."

I said, "well I have told them about the hookers on the estate."

Marko said, "yeah but they want to know about the pimps, and shit." I said, "they know who the pimps are." Marko said, "who are they looking for then?" I said, "I don't know, probably County Lines drug dealers." Marko said, "That's the price you have to pay. For killing some geezer. To give information on County Lines." I said, "it's either that or jail." Marko said, "well let's get to work then." I said, "we start right away."

We login to Facebook, and Marko asks around for some crack. Eventually we get a runner at the door. A young lad, around 17. He stands at the door nervously. Legs like jelly.

I said, "nah we ain't after you, we know these games." The boy just stood there. I took the crack, I juggled it about. I gave it back to him. I kept the money.

Marko gets out a pistol and says, "come inside now."

I said, "oh dear, shit has hit the fan now." So this nervous lad. Was sat on the chair. And

Marko was spilling his guts out in anger and phlegm. Ranting and raving. Shouting, "you fucking stupid cunt, you tell me who is pushing you into this." The runner, Gary, said, "I'm dead if I tell you." Marko said, "you're dead anyway if you don't tell us. I will shoot you in the head. Who's pushing you?"

Gary said, "Mike Dustbin." I said, "you trying to wind us up you fucking SI, you expect us to believe his second name is Mike Dustbin?" I said, "Who do you take us for, a couple of mugs."

Gary said, "That's his name." I said, "yeah maybe his street name, what's his real name?" Gary said, "I don't know." I said, "look stop pulling our chain, we wanna know, who this Mike guy is. His second name. And I don't know any surname, called Dustbin."

Gary said, "that's his fucking name, for the last time, that's all we want to know." I grab my gun. Pistol. Works as a semi automatic also. I said, "I wanna know more about this guy, where is he?" Gary said, "London." I said, "yeah no shit, which post code, you turnip." Gary said, "Kensington." I said, "Which part?" Gary said, "North Kensington." I said, "Give us the address, or I am putting a bullet in your head."

Gary said, "46 Prescot Road, Fairfield, Liverpool, L7 0JA." I google it. I said, "Kensington Kebab House." Gary said, "yeah." I said, "let me guess, upstairs." Gary nodded.

I said, "we ain't letting you go until you give us the real surname."

Gary said, '"Mike Daniels." I said, "next time, don't try and lie to us." My semi automatic pistol. Regan has a gun pointed at him. Pistol. Marko, loads the gun. Grabs his shotgun and shouts. "Hello." Sarcastically and abruptly.

Gary said, "I have given you all of the information. Can I go now?" I said, "no, we're turning you into the Police." Marko said, "Dude, we need Mike Daniels, not this snowflake. Chuck him out." I said, "If we chuck the snowflake out, then Mike Daniels will get a whiff of what's going on, and leg it. From now on. Gary. You're our hostage."

Gary said, "fuck sake.." I said, "I have a deal worked out, now send a text to this Mike Daniels and tell him you're going to be late. Say the train is cancelled, do it now."

Marko yells, "Oi, fucking oi, do it now feller!"

I yell, "Oi Oi!!"

Gary sends the text. Marko whispers to me, "we can't hold him here forever."

I said, "We won't."

I dial up 999, give the location of the address, of Mike Daniels. I get a text from PC John Ricks. He texts. "fucking hell mate, we hit the jackpot." I said, "Are you ordering food in there for fuck sake, or are you trying to find this guy." PC John said, "both of you, shut up." I phone PC John Ricks up, and I can hear lots of Proactive CID units shouting. "Sit down, shut up, sit down, Police, tazer, tazer, tazer." Next thing you know Mike Daniels hits the deck.

Struggling to get up, one of the kebab assistants, burns his hand on the frying pan, and tries to retaliate As the police are trying to taze him. As more units arrive. Riot squad enters, and there's a stand off between the workers and the Police.

The owner of the kebab shop is really angry, and says, "what the fuck is going on?" Fat Phil. That was the name of the kebab owner.

Fat Phil reaches for a butter knife, Police try to taze him, but he's so fat it doesn't work. Next thing you know armed Police shoot him in the leg. The worker with the frying pan knocks himself out with the frying pan, accidentally, whilst slipping over on the geese on the floor. Mike Daniels is in cuffs.

Meanwhile, at my estate, I said, "Well Gary, you are here with us now, and we are handing you over to The Police." He said, "what for?" I said, "drug dealing." He said, "I was forced to do it." I said, "yeah I know you were." Police enter, and arrest Gary. Seized his cocaine. The police officer arresting him shouts, "you got licences for all of those guns you fucking nob heads?" I said, "yeah we have." The officer shouts to Gary. "Listen, you fucking wrongun, I couldn't care if they forced you into it or not. You have 20 kilos of coke on you. You fucking liability. Come with me."

Handcuffed, hands behind his back. Shoved over. The arresting officer accidentally slips over and hits the deck, and Gary is wrestling like a worm on the floor. I kick him in the stomach. More Police arrive.

Eventually he's taken away. Next thing you know. Me, Marko, and Regan Are putting away our Arsenal of weapons." Into the cupboard. Regan said, "long day's work." I said. "let's go to bed."

Chapter 12

I feel different. I don't know why. County Lines gangs were growing, and I was now their main target. Disrupting their entire operation. Came as no surprise.

Now, I wander, why all of these movies, and TV Shows. And things, just kiss the police's arse cheeks. And think they get a slice of the action. The Police were nowhere to be seen today. I was in a bad mood.

I kind of felt that, you can be your own worst enemy sometimes. Yet, apart from all of the wise words being quoted. What do you think The Police do? Just sift randomly through libraries, reading book after book. Trying to find the golden nugget of information. I have never seen CID at a library.

It's because the cops think books are bullshit, just made up conspiracies. Junk, but deep down. Whilst I was reading Orwell, 1984. I felt kind of relieved. His pain was my pain. I felt, some similarities. Yet, I couldn't wander why. Why John Ricks, this cunt of a police officer. Is making me read Orwell. That's part of the deal. He's fucking with my head.

Making me read this shit. He's trying to make me love Big Brother. That's the whole point.

But seriously, fed up of this crap. I get a knock at the door. I get a cage of frenzied rats. Outside. All bloodshot. It must have been from John Ricks.

I dial his number, no answer. What the fuck is his fascination with Orwell? I have the cage with me. What the fuck am I supposed to do with this now?

Marko said, "dinner has arrived." We took the rats in. 20 of them. All in this cage. And Marko says, "sounds like that copper loves Orwell a bit too much, what do we do with these things?" I said, "have to kill them humanely..." Marko said, "Okay, well I will feed them rat poison then, but we might have to wait a couple of days." I said, "we have semi automatics, rifles, and pistols. Yet you want to kill the rats humanely." Marko said, "yeah it's the law isn't it." I said, "stop contradicting yourself, but okay, what ever floats your boat." Marko said, "I don't have a fucking boat." I said, "you do." Marko said, "how come I don't know about said boat then, you idiot." I said, "I have just bought it for you. Turns out the information paid off. I get a cheque. He tells me to buy you a boat. It's in Southampton. Brand new."

Marko said, "I appreciate the offer, but I don't really like water." I said, "it's the copper, he's just fucking with our heads. We are giving him intelligence, what more does he want?" Marko said, "sounds like he's bored, and he's using us for entertainment." I said, "A new boat isn't cheap." Marko said, "maybe he's won the lottery. He cashed out." I said, "maybe he put a bet on the football..'" I was interrupted mid sentence by Regan With the shot gun, and he's pointing it at the rats. He said, "right all these fuckers are going to die." I said, "we're killing them humanely."

Regan said, "that means waiting two days. I mean, we have that long to wait." I said, "it's the law." Regan said, "we have guns." I said, "we have a licence for the guns." Regan said, "well I don't like rats." I said, "for fuck sake."

Next thing you know. John Ricks. PC John Ricks. Enters the house. In the house. He says, "did you like my presents?" I said, "nah a bit too creepy for me, you fucking psycho, what do you expect me to do with a boat in Southampton and a cage of rats. And a George Orwell book. You fucking nerd. We had an agreement, and you are pushing it." He said, "fine, one call to the CPS." I called his bluff. I said, "if you call the CPS. I'll rat on everything you've done. Everything. Every final thing." He said, "they don't believe you." I said, "well call them then. Jail's better than this kind of bullshit."

He picks up his phone, it's dialling You can hear someone answer. "Crown Prosecution Service, how may I direct your call?" John, Ricks. PC John Ricks. The biggest dickhead you can imagine. He stutters. And he said, "nothing.." and hangs up. I said, "you're a piece of shit, you know that. I am quite happy to give you intelligence, but don't send me any more gifts. And another thing. This is every month, not every fucking week. I am not your bitch."

He said, "forget it, you go down, I do too. You're a free man."

I said, "the County Lines gang?"

He said, "this is my job, not yours, you just carry on smoking your cheap tobacco and living in this council estate, I don't need to bury you, your conscience, will do that for you."

He left without a trace, never to be seen again, and Marko is freaking out with the rats. And to be honest with you. I was starting to like them. I called the RSPCA. I said, "yo, I have these rats, that someone has left outside my property. We are killing them humanely." The RSPCA officer said, "where are they?" I said, "in a cage." The officer said, "well take them out the cage." I said, "hell no, I don't want them running around."

The RSPCA officer said, "look, just go to the nearest bit of land, and release them, you fucking drama queen." The phone hung up. So I did as I was told. I walked down to the bit of land. Outside the building, and released them. Ingested with poison they were going to die anyway.

But it didn't work as planned as they scurried towards the nearest bins. And were eating on this mouldy pizza. And it was just crazy.

I walk back up to the third floor. I said to

Marko. "That police officer is one sick and twisted vile man." Marko said, "he's not a cop." I said, "what?" Marko said, "we've done a background check on him. He was fired from the force three years ago. Never handed in his badge." I said, "and they still let him enforce the law." Marko said, "yeah."

I said, "nah there are some inconsistencies in that story, what about the drugs raid?" Marko said, "was him and his mates with a shot gun, it was a whole set up."

I said, "right, I am sick of this. I am going to hand myself into the police station for merger."

I walk into the police station, and I said, "I would like to hand myself in for Merger."

The custody Sargent said, "Do you mean murder?" I said, "Yeah." He said, "come right this way."

He pushes me into the interview room, strips his trousers down, and he's wearing a pink thong. And his meat and veg is pretty big also and I can tell. And I said, "please, just calm it down a bit." He said, "listen here you punk, this isn't a police station."

I shout, "no........" I wake up, in my sleep. Dreaming. John Ricks is real, the agreement is real. But him making me read Orwell, the rats, and the boat. Was a dream.

Fuck, what had I been taking, the night before to dream of this!? Maybe things were looking better. But with Tottenham – Chelsea, ending 1-1. And a lot of explaining to do to John Ricks. I phoned him up. I said, "man you are giving me crazy dreams." He said, "That guy, the guy who you ratted on us, he's been charged." I said, "the runner?" He said, "charged also, claimed duress, but it's down to the court." I said, "So I can put my feet up and just wait until next week, and do another sting." He said, "maybe, I don't know, the police always tell members of the public not to get involved." I said, "so why are you getting involved then?" He said, "because I am a police officer." I said, "I am getting involved." He said, "yeah well with you we made an exception."

    I said to him, "these hookers, some of them, it's hard to describe, but some of them smell of BO, and cheap perfume." PC John Ricks said, "mate, I am getting fed up with all of this, we are told by the fucking liberals at the fucking top of the tree. Not to nick them. But I would nick them." I said, "alright calm down, have you had your morning bistro yet?" He said, "no." I said, "well go and have it, crying out loud mate, have some bovril for fuck sake. Have a cup of tea, have a biscuit, eat a tangerine. Do a dance. fuck sake man, you can do better than this. You are acting crazy." He said, "I am the one who is acting crazy? You are the one who is acting crazy. Mentioning these hookers all of the time. All of the time. Fuck you, fuck you to high heaven." I said, "I would rather not, thanks." He said, "listen rude boy, there comes a point in time where we start to understand things okay. fuck you."

    I said, "what's with all the passive

aggression?"

He said, "I had a bad experience with a prostitute once."

I said, "what happened?"

He said, "went to this brothel, wife wasn't giving me any. I pay my money. I go inside. And she refuses, I ask for my money back. She declines. She then tries to accuse me of making off without payment."

I said, "this is crazy, did she smell of cheap perfume, and BO?" He said, "yeah, listen, just try and reign it in a bit mate." I said, "where did that come from?" He said, "listen just try to understand where I am coming from. Back in the day, boys will be boys, ladies love a man with confidence. Boys will be boys. Then you reach a stage in your life. Where some random man is idly staring at you in a random shop, and when confronted, he acts like it was nothing. Like he let out a fart or something."

I said, "Nah, it's not that, it's women."

He said, "what about them?"

I said, "I don't know, I mean, in the 90's, it was good, we were allowed to have sex with them. Now, in order to have a woman now. You have to go along with all this feminism bullshit. And watch them grow their arm pit hair and dye their pubes. And talk about Jon Bon Jovi."

He said, "I wouldn't know mate, my wife keeps me happy, been with her for 20 years now."

I said, "is she a feminist?"

He said, "every woman is a feminist, you

mad dog, do you expect me to believe anything else. What do men have to do wear pink thongs and bullshit. Just to fit in, with this fucking crap."

I said, "This is getting nowhere."
It wasn't. The tectonic plates were shifting. Life was changing. The gun I used to kill Pale Ale. It wasn't a real gun, it was a blank firing gun. Yet it still did the job.

I look at the world now. It's different. Things change. fuck, you know. Time and time again. And you look back and you wander. Why all the hatred. Why all of this. Was it worth something way back then. Maybe but now. This, four times a lady, and a pink dress. Not much else to say. Felt like flying to Kazakstan, felt like moving abroad. Felt like being the geezer I always wanted to be. Wanted people to admire me. Yet, you get to the stage now, where. I am staying out of the firing line. Ironically, with an arsenal of weapons in my cupboard. PC Totsworth arrives, and inspects the guns.

He said, "your licence please?" I showed him my licence. He said, "you do know, that semi automatic gun is illegal." I said, "how did I get a licence for it, it was granted by the superintendent." Totsworth said, "gun laws, weapon laws have changed now. You are going to have to contact the super again and unfortunately. Surrender it, and we will dispose of it."

I said, "if I wasn't a police informant, you'd nick me." He said, "if you weren't a police informant, you'd be doing jail time. But we know how hard it is for people in prison to talk. Without getting "snitch", tattooed on their forehead. So we look after you, we do patrols. We turn a blind eye, to the fact you killed Lee, and you have an illegal firearm."

I said, "this is what it comes to now. I am a police informant." Totsworth said, "mate, we have lots of informants, you are just one of them." I said, "yeah like I had a choice." PC Tetsworth said, "why did you have to pull that trigger, you could have just knocked him out." I said, "he said I was Millwall I am Tottenham through and through. Yid army. And I am not a fucking police informant. Maybe once, but not twice, you can go fuck yourself. I'll do the jail time."

PC Totsworth radios into control. "Yeah Steve Smith has a semi automatic weapon in his cupboard." Control pick up. Control officer says, "Right, well, the super said he's got a licence for his guns, so what do you expect us to do?"

PC Totsworth said, "Get armed police over."

Superintendent James Jones, intervenes "You can all fuck off."

PC Totsworth said, "right."

PC Totsworth read me my rights. I put my hands out. I am placed in cuffs.

Armed police arrive, and it's the anti terrorism unit. The armed police said, "right, Steve Smith. You fucking wrongun degenerate."

We sat down. I said "So you are just going

to detain me here?" One of the anti terrorism officers said, "yeah." More armed police arrive. Just normal armed police. Back up, riot police. I am sat down, in cuffs.

Detectives walk in. DC Bill Bailey. He said, "right, Steve Smith, what's going on?"

I said, "PC John Ricks, blackmailed me into giving information on County Lines. In order for the murder evidence to be whitewashed."

DC Bill Bailey said, "yeah I know, we all fucking know you bellend." All axon cameras are off. They knew, they had a chance of getting me. They knew they had a chance of me doing their dirty work. But I wasn't having it. I said, "no fuck this. I gave you evidence once, now fuck off. You have the evidence to put me in jail. Then go and do it."

James Jones the Super arrives, with his mason ring on his finger. He said, "look, we can make this work. You did good the other day. You gave us vital information. You single handedly gave us information to shut down an entire county lines. Drug gang. They are doing 150 years between them. Don't let that intelligence go to waste. Yeah it was a shame about Lee. But you weren't to know were ya?"

James said, "I hate to say this also, but Lee is my son. Hated him. Kind of glad he's gone. If you hadn't have shot him. I probably would have done it. He was a right wing extremist."

I said, "I can hear crickets, everyone likes the union jack, you bellend."

James said, "Well he was a nob head, why

did you shoot him though, in all fairness.."

I said, "your story keeps changing, maybe it was you who shot him."

James said, "nah we got you on CCTV."

I said, "does the CCTV have facial recognition, because I'll just say.."

James laughed and said, "say what, it's your identical twin." James burst out laughing. We have you in HD. It's clear as day. It's got audio too. You're banged to rights. But I think I want to keep you as an informant. Since we have let Totsworth, run a bit wild here."

The superintendent kicks PC Tetsworth in the balls. Now, *PC TOTSWORTH HAS HIT THE DECK.* Marko runs up with a baseball bat and hits Totsworth over the head. Riot police stop him. I stand up looking confused. Regan grabs a butter knife, and throws it in Totsworth's direction.

The superintendent said, "look, nobody in the force likes PC Totsworth, PC Townsend actually, to be fair, but it's a nickname, he's a prick. He cheats on his mrs." The riot police burst out chuckling, and were doing fist bumps.

I said, "look, what happens now, we just sit here."

The Superintendent crouches down to my level. He said, "Look, give us more information, we need to shut County Lines down." I said, "I ain't giving you anything."

Regan said, "mate it's better than jail, I think it's a good deal."

I said, "fuck sake."

The super said, "look, okay, let me make it even more easier for you to decide now. How about we get something sorted, you want a new house? You want a Role? We can get you anything you want. You want cash?"

Regan said, "sounds good."

I said, "nah I don't want to take the money like that, you're bigger than this man. Seriously doing my head in.

Regan said, "It's a lose lose situation, but you don't want to end up in prison."

I said, "alright, I'll do it."

The super radios into control. "Oh hello, yes, he does have weapons, but, he has a licence for them." Control said, "listen we know what's going on." The super said, "what's that?" Control said, "you're off your fucking head you mad cunt, what do you think you are playing at?" The super said, "right, you're sacked." Control said, "Was going to quit today anyway."

I said, "listen, lads, this is getting out of hand. This whole thing. What if I told you, that I didn't have any weapons." All of the weapons were gone. Lost. In oblivion. All the police officers looked shocked. I said, "it's an optical illusion, I didn't kill Lee."

The Super said, "who did it then?"

I said, "Lee, never existed, he's a figment of your imagination."

Super said, "and yours."

I said, "look, show me the CCTV then."

Super James Jones, showed me a picture killing Lee, in the head. With a pistol.

I said, "it's funny that."

The super said, "damning evidence, don't you think, and stop talking bullshit about having no guns. We have just seen them." I said, "they disappeared." The super laughed and said, "yes because Regan put them in the cupboard, and closed it, you fucking mad cunt. Who the fuck do you think you are? David Blaine or some shit? Do we have a deal or not? One last time. Stop testing my balls. You in or not?"

I said, "yeah alright, better than prison, but listen. County Lines. We aren't talking a small fish pond. You know the Atlantic Ocean?"

James said, "well, yeah, I have swam in it, been to the USA on holiday."

I said, "well, that ocean, that's how big this whole thing is. It's not a pond."

James, the super said, "can you stop making these stupid fucking analogies you mad cunt, and get to the point. You're in, that's all that matters. You give us the information. We keep you away from prison. But listen, any more cock ups like this today. PC Townsend is a dickhead anyway."

PC Townsend wakes up, from his coma of getting knocked over by the Super, gets to his feet. Charges towards me, armed police shoot him down.

I shouted, "TOTSWORTH!!"

The Super said, "now you know how fucking ruthless we are, we don't fuck about, you don't want that to be you, do you?"

I said, "how are you going to explain that to the commissioner and the Chief Inspector?"

The super said, "everyone's in on it, and nobody likes him."

I said, "this is just more shenanigans I can't handle right now."

He was lying dead next to the union jack cross. I couldn't fucking believe my luck. I thought he was a prick, but we got to know him. Now he's dead. And I am stuck, with these officers. In this room.

Super James Jones said, "listen mate, don't fuck about and stop acting so sensitive, broaden your shoulders and fuck off."

All of the police left along withTotsworth, they framed an elderly lady for the killing. From the block of flats opposite. Said she had a rifle and got angry, because she was anti police. Put finger prints on her, locked her up.

I said to Marko, "that old lady, what a surprise." Marko said, "she was 66, not really old, but what ever, a big fucking fat lady. Looked crazy enough to fit the bill. So fuck it. Let's get on with County Lines intelligence work."

I said, "well we know that they operate out of kebab houses. Usually the first floor. As in, the ground floor is where they serve customers. The first floor, as in the first floor. Is where they hide the stash, the drugs. The money. Kensington, it's all chained together in there. Linked. That fish bar. Just one out of many."

Regan said, "fuck this. I can't believe

what's been happening. What have we become." I said, "shut your mouth, I know a way to get out of this."

Regan said, "what?"

I said, "we're moving abroad."

Regan said, "yeah give me one second, whilst I sell my adidas watch for 10 quid. We could move to Ibiza." I said, "mate, that's perfect."

Regan gets The Sun newspaper. We get a cheap holiday to Ibiza for 50p. The flight was a grand."

I said, "we're moving to Ibiza."

Marko said, "no, I say we stay here, fuck travelling abroad, what sleeping with one eye open? That's not freedom." I said, "and you call this freedom, doing all of this intelligence work." Marko said, "you are over reacting, it's just bread and butter intelligence, it's not going to do any harm."

I said, "okay, fine."

Marko said, "no trips to Ibiza please, what, you think the police are stupid enough not to tell border control?"

I said, "listen mate, just shut up, because this is getting out of hand."

Chapter 13

My mind just froze, and with it, the council estate had never been the same. Calling the Police piggies had never been so fun. I was going to wind them up. And still give them the intelligence. Tottenham were playing Millwall, in a friendly, it was international break. And none of their football players were called up for international duty. So they had an agreement.

It was at Tottenham, but I hate Millwall with a passion. Pale Ale was Millwall. Cannot believe the pain he put me through that night. All I did is put a bullet in his head. I mean what does he expect?

I was feeling tired, very tired. Didn't know why. We were at the hot dog stand. The lady serving looked overworked. Marko couldn't resist taunting her. "I want my sausage in those baps please love."

It was going to start all over again. This whole thing. Which in all fairness was why I loved going to the games. But it kind of fizzled out a bit. I look back you know, I look back at life. And I wander. You know, some people blame their upbringing, their parents, for the problems in their life. I blame the gun that I had that day. The trigger was so sensitive, and I didn't even mean to fire. I mean, I meant to fire, but, it happened so quickly, and to see him go like that.

Marko is still giving the lady in the burger shop some aggravation. "Mayonnaise squirted all over the sausage." I said, "Marko leave it out." Marko gripped me against the van. He said, "you wouldn't be meddling in my affairs would you, you stupid prick." I said, "yeah but aggressive flirting mate, it ain't on is it."

Regan said, "how come you are so sensitive all of a sudden now Steve. You've killed someone." Marko said, "to be fair we all went to Iraq and killed people, but Lee didn't deserve to die like that."

The lady in the burger van, was getting annoyed and shouted, "£10.50 please" as her tits wobbled, as she was having a small panic attack. After the psychological damage Marko had done to her. I said, "Marko you idiot, pay her then." Marko paid up. And we left.

Meet PC David Lee Jones, riot, gear. Inspector. Kind of a nob. He said, "Ah Steve Smith, what a surprise." I said, "I go to all of the games, this ain't a surprise."PC Dave Jones said, "PC Totsworth is brown bread now you fucking cock sucker." I said, "don't fucking act the hard man. You are the one that is the cock sucker. You and your entire family." David Jones said, "the guy was a prick, used to harass everyone on the estate, he was one of our own, and we killed him to prove a point to you. That we can do the same to you. As ruthlessly. So don't fuck this up. You owe us information this week." I said, "The match is on, I can't do anything now." He said, "you better come up with something good when you get home. Otherwise you will be eating prison food, for the rest of your life. We will do you for every hit and run dating back since 1899." I said, "I will shag your mrs." He looked outraged and legged it towards me. I punched him in the stomach. He wobbled over. Marko got involved. Punching him to the ground. The inspector was lying on the floor. Like you know, I don't know, fuck sake. Just wobbling and shaking his hands and his feet. I said, "not so hard now are ya?"

Police back up arrived. PC Sarah Jones, ironically not related to him. Plus 20 coppers behind her. She attempts to arrest me. I said, "he fell over himself, you dickhead."

Marko said, "we have an agreement, it was play fighting, now go back to your police officer sty, and fucking stay there."

PC Sarah Jones said, "do you want to watch the match, or do you want to go to jail?" She points to her handcuffs. As PC David Jones rises to his feet. Sorry, inspector. What ever. Inspector David Jones punches me in the stomach. I hit the deck, and fall over Marko. He hits the deck, and we start throwing stones at the police. As one hits Sarah in the tits.

I said, "Sarah, why the fuck do you get involved in these match days. You belong in a fucking psychiatric ward. You deserve to be sectioned. You grade A cunt." Sarah said, "listen, at this moment in time you are under arrest for public order and assault on police." Marko was mocking her, and was copying her voice and was saying. "*oh public order and assault on police.*"

I said, "Public order, there has to be a complainant. The police can't be complainants. But I will happily take the other charge. Assault on Police. Even though I know it will get NFA'd at the station." She said, "how the fuck do you know that?" I said, "Two words, County Lines." She said, "oh right, you think you are running this show now do you? Just because you're giving us intelligence. We're taking you in, and you will be charged." I said, "I ain't giving you information on County Lines then." She said, "Then you're going down for murder." I said, "well fucking do me for murder then, I don't want to end up your bitch anyway. And for the record. Listen. Your tits don't even add up, ones bigger than the other. Let me guess, you did some waitressing back in the day. Used to serve customers. Joined The Police, wanted to throw your cock long clitoris around in people's faces. "Oh look at me, I can police the streets."

Marko said, "mate, no woman has a cock long clitoris, that is just wrong on so many levels." I said, "you trying to ruin my insults, you prick." I punched Marko.

Sarah said, "I am speechless." I said, "yet you are still fucking talking aren't you, that's the problem with you pigs. You keep talking and whinging. And expecting the public to comply with your petty demands. Go home." Sarah said, "Oh gosh," As someone throws a pebble at her, ends up hitting her on the head, not hard enough to knock her out. I am stood there, as riot Police trample all over her, and she gets involved in the fight. Two big burly police officers, arrest me, Mark, and Regan, and we are in The Police van. And it's driving to the local nick.

Fuck, just for a couple of pebbles. This is the thanks I get. Straight in the cells, and you know what. Better than some hotels. I keep thinking about what I am going to say in the interview room.

Sargent Mike Price, custody sargent. Says, "right, you can go, no further action, you've got homework to do." He gets right up to me, and says, "don't act so fucking smart, you work for us, remember that, not the other way around." I said, "Alright gov." He said, "listen mate, I know Sarah has made a few enemies with the Police lads, over her wonky tits. But don't come insulting us like this. You fucking dickhead." I said, "mate, I wanted to watch the game, that's all I wanted to do."

Mike said, "then you shouldn't have got involved. Saying and doing all of that nonsense."

I said, "because in all fairness, it's getting boring now. Half the time I travel to a game, I get nicked, before the game starts, you needle dick." He said, "you are the one with the needle dick." I said, "look mate, just fuck off back to your clan, I am tired of doing your dirty work." He said, "County Lines intelligence. I want you to set up a line, tomorrow. A fake line. We'll give you the equipment. CID are working with us on this. This is where it gets interesting." I said, "no, setting up a fake line. That's fucked up. You have to pose as drug users, buying off them. Not the other way around."

He said, "oh right, you still think it's the Kebab place." I said, "I know it is." He said, "your balls, it better be the kebab houses, otherwise I will come down on you like a ton of bricks." I said, "alright, quit the tough guy act. I have met County Lines dealers in the past mate. It don't always go to plan. You have to trip them up."

Sargent Price said, "listen, just fucking get us some suspects, and stop pratting around." I said, "oh it's like that is it." He said, "yeah, now fuck off."

I walk out, fuck knows where Marko and Regan are. fuck everything man. Having the worst day. Got a headache. Don't feel too good. Grinding my teeth. Bloodshot eyes. I am delirious. Keep seeing snakes in the background. Wandering where my life has become. Marko and Regan are at my place. I walk in. I said, "I can't do this man, when people find out we've been snitching, it will go bad very quickly." They both laughed. Marko said, "grow a set of balls." I said, "fuck you dude." Marko said, "look, I think we have a sweet deal, now check this out." Marko is on the computer. He points to this one Facebook profile. Some dickhead.

I said, "What are you doing looking these people up mate, they don't deal over Facebook." I said, "How do you know?" Marko sends him a friend request. I look a bit perplexed. I said, "alright, well fuck this, I am making a brew, does anyone want one." Both declined. And I am starting to hate The Police more and more.

But we have work to do. So after some digging. Marko pretends to be this drug user. Wanting some cocaine. The guy he's talking to. "Dave Jones." Is saying he has the gear. Marko has arranged for him to knock on our door, with the gear. We have the cash. We can't be arsed to go outside. It's too cold.

Marko said, "this is getting old. This whole thing feller. You know. What happened. The Chip Shop. Yeah it used to make sense, and now. What's going to happen? Nah I can't do this anymore." I said, "The irony is, is we started off at the chip shop, and we are investigating the kebab houses." Marko said, "they ain't the chip shops though are they?" I said, "similar." Marko said, "fuck this crap man, fuck all of this. I can't face Jacky in the eyes again..."

I said, "I love Jacky, she wouldn't want me doing this." The doorbell rings. Dave Jones. Wearing a balaclava. 6 foot 8, massive guy. Man tits, the size of volcanos. Muscles, biceps, the size of mountains.

I said, "Well, Dave, I think you belong in Iraq mate." He said, "why's that?" I said, "you're a tank, look at you mate. Let me guess. You have 20 protein shakes a day. What gym do you go to?'" I say this sarcastically, and he's picking up on the sarcasm. He said, "nah, feller, I have a condition, that makes me put on weight." I said, "oh right, why didn't you say that in the first place then?" He said, "you didn't give me the chance." He starts welling up and crying on our door. We stop laughing at him, and Marko says, "mate, it ain't that bad feller, it ain't that bad bro. You are acting a bit rude with that balaclava, but apart from that. Go on, where's the cocaine?"

Dave Jones, with a fake Deliveroo bag. Reaches for the cocaine. You can see tin foil. I said, "Dave feller, do you want to join us for a coffee, we are having coffee, tea, and maybe some small chocolates. What do you say?" Dave said, "alright, what chocolates have you got?" He comes steaming through the door, and he sits down. I said, "we have lots of things bro, lots of things."

He said, "do you have Terrys chocolate orange?" I said, "yeah." He said, "can I have a whole Terry's chocolate orange please." He starts crying on my sofa. I look at Marko and I nod, and I said, "yeah go and give it to him."

The rude boy, is just sitting there, eating the chocolate orange, and we hand him over the cash. We have the cocaine. Next thing I know. I lock the door. He said, "what's going on lads?" I grab my semi automatic pistol, and I said, "just sit the fuck down." He said, "I am sitting down." I said, "well shut the fuck up. Police will be here any minute."

He said, "it's only a chocolate orange." I said, "not the orange you tit, this is a set up, we ain't drug users man, we are working with the police." I get some rope, and tie his hands together. I said, "police will be here any minute, and I know you ain't one of the runners. Let me guess, they all noticed what was happening. They legged it. So you decided to act rude and deliver yourself big lad. I have caught a big one here." Marko said, "in more than one way, fuck, look at the size of this rude boy." Dave said, "alright lads, just would rather wait for The Police in peace." I said, "What ever mate, you fucking nob head, let me guess. You go to Primark, and chat up the employees there, rude boy. You are old news." He said, "not anymore." I said, "because you're in jail now." He said, "not quite." I said, "Police will be here soon." Dave said, "you keep saying that mate, you don't recognise me do ya?" I said, "who are you?" He said, "I was there when you shot Lee, Pale Ale. I'll tell.." I said, "The Police already know."

He said, "so how come you ain't in prison then?" I said, "they said if I catch one county lines drug dealer a week, I am out of prison." He said, "what happens when you have caught them all?" I said, "it's not Pokemon, ah, I don't know. I think we are moving onto other crimes." He said, "like what?" I said, "don't know, I have just been assigned this task, now you would keep your mouth shut if you knew what was good for you buddy." He said, "Alright, but the police ain't here yet." I said to Marko. "Put a gag on this man." Marko gags the man with a rope.

Police arrive, DC Paul Davis, arrives. He shakes his head. Grabs a knife, cuts the ropes loose. And he said, "Dave Jones, at this moment in time, you are under arrest on suspicion of drug dealing." He said, "right." DC Paul Davis said, "hands in front of you." Cuffs him. With his arms twisted. The dealer said, "can you loosen them?" DC Paul Davis said, "no."

I said, "should have thought about the consequences, before you start dealing mate. You are going to prison." He said, "this ain't fair, he killed Pale Ale, and he's getting away with it." I said, "the gun was faulty, didn't mean to fire it." He said, "well tell that to the judge not me." I said, "there is no judge you fucking idiot, not for me anyway. Good luck inside big lad. That Terrys Chocolate Orange is the only good meal you are gonna get for weeks. It's porridge now rude boy." He said, "you cruel bastard." DC Paul Davis said, "right that's enough, don't antagonise him."

I said, "yeah, right, okay."

The rude boy of a drug dealer was put in a riot van, too big for a prison van. Driven away, in a police escort. Sirens, lights.

I said to Marko, "it's all changing now, let's get the police to issue us with some better accommodation"

So with a bit of communications. I spoke with DC Paul Davis. We manage to get a house. A mortgage. I said to Paul Davis, "this is good, and the Mercedes." He sighed and said, "right with you sir." I said, "I'll let you know when I need some more goodies." He said, "we are only doing this because it will help your operations. Now, we have a whole room set up in your mansion. It's an intelligence room. It's equipped with all kinds of things." I said, "right, okay, double oh seven."

He said, "nah nothing like that, we need you on this case." I said, "I am working on it here. But listen, that big rude boy we just caught. Let me guess, he's asking for three ready meals, pasta meals in custody is he? The fat bastard."

DC Paul Davis, "You are good."

I said, "Well good luck with him, he'll be drinking your coffee in no time."

DC Paul Davis said, "There was no need to say Sarah had a clitoris the size of a cock. Firstly it's not true, secondly, she has filed a complaint in about you." DC Paul Davis said, "maybe".

I said, "the football gets boring, it's all the same, sitting down on those seats, freezing your balls off. I can't think straight some times just watching the game."

DC Paul Davis, "I am not a therapist, stop with this whinging nonsense, now fuck off."

He leaves in his private Jeep, and me, Marko and Regan Are just stuck there. Just waiting.

Chapter 14

Living in this mansion, paid by the state. What am I supposed to do now? With no prostitutes to solicit, and with Reegans balls hanging out. That rude boy Dave Jones knocks on the door. Out on bail. He shouts, "you fucking stitched me up." He is wearing his balaclava, and is banging on the door. I said, "Dave feller, they've bailed you." He grabs hold of his crotch and he said. "Bail this you fucking cunt, you put me through hell, putting me in with all those piggies. fuck you." I said, "when's the court date?" He said, "stick the court date up your balls, you daft twat, you going to let me in for another Terrys Chocolate Orange?" I said, "I have run out." He said, "A cup of tea, something man, I am thirsty." I opened the door and said, "sit down." He said, "my intentions was to sit down, fuck, my trousers ripped in custody, and they gave me some spare trousers. But didn't leave enough room for my giant balls." I said, "That's too much information feller, are you going to tell me how big your cock is next? You fucking lunatic." He said, "No that's private." I said, "fuck you, you cunt. Look at all of the trouble I am in now. Because of *YOU*." He said, "Because of me, you think this is funny? You lunatic. Coming out here, trying to act the big man. With all of your jeeps. fuck you."

This guy, this Dave Jones. Man he was crazy. Surprised he made bail. Must have bribed the police. I am speechless.

I said, "right, well just sit down for a bit feller."

He said, "alright."

I said, "you know how much trouble you're putting me in, you better fucking behave yourself, you lunatic. And take that ski mask off man. You are acting rude all of the time man. There is no need for it..."

Marko charges in, and shouts, "fucking take the ski mask off you bellend, what are you trying to achieve?"

Regan charges in, accidentally knocks Marko to the floor, runs after Dave Jones. And he does, he takes the ski mask off. He's just still sat there. IC2 male, IC3, I don't know. I said, "listen feller, you got involved in County

Lines." He said, "that's all you talk about isn't it. County Lines, County Lines, County fucking lines. You want to scrap? Listen, you can fuck off. Fuck County Lines. This is bigger than you feller, you want to fight, then let's have it out then. Less bullshit from you mate. I have had enough of your cheap talk mate. Ruck you. Wind your balls in mate. Getting me irate like this."

I said, "come on then, let's fight then." He swings the first punch. I dodge it. I punch him to the stomach, he doesn't flinch. Then out of nowhere. He's having this anxiety attack, and he's just like a bumble bee, just going in all kinds of directions. He falls over and breaks the cabinet. He's rolling around having a panic attack. And I am stood there. Over him. Saying, "are you on gear? Yes or no?" He said, "yes." I said, "no wander you are getting into panic rude boy, you on cocaine ain't ya?" He said, "yeah." I said. "This is getting out of hand. You come in here, and try and disrupt our operations." He said, "oh you are acting the big man, just because you done a few errands for The Police? You rude lad. You want to get things sorted. Because you ain't no saint, and I know what you did. So keep your mouth shut, otherwise I am going to kick you in the balls. You are acting rude. Fed up of this."

Marko runs in and screams, "Fuck THIS, Fuck EVERYTHING, WHY IS EVERYONE GETTING RUDE!?"

I said, "I am getting fed up of this, eject Dave from the house man, eject this guy. He's on bail anyway, fuck him man."

Regan said, "it's cold outside man." I said, "oh come on." Regan said, "Listen, Dave, do you want a place for the night." He said, "yeah." He said, "Terrys Chocolate fucking oranges too." I said, "fuck." Regan said, "you are pushing it bro. How many?" He said, "12". I said, "well at least it's an even number, I think we can accommodate that kind of request."

I go online. I order an online Tescos, same day delivery. It arrives. Low and behold. The oranges are there. The chocolate oranges are there. The delivery guy is standing there with his balls hanging out. Acting rude and talking shit. I said, "listen, just bounce man, we got to put these things in the fridge." He said, "I am a health and safety expert, and your house ain't safe bro. Those steps are too big bro." I said, "listen bro, listen to me carefully. I will put a jumbo sausage in your mouth, and smack you across the face. You cretin. Do you want to get in trouble?" He said, "no not really." I said, "well kiss my arse cheeks then. Because we are going global, fuck you, fuck your arse cheeks, fuck your health and safety report. And remember something. I rule London, all of this. This is my district. Kensington."

He said, "mate, why are you getting rude?" I said, "because you have come in here, acting rude man, it's that simple, you can't expect me to be cool with this." He said, "all I said was your door wasn't safe.."I said, "it's a different excuse all the time rude boy, go back home, before you get hurt."

He said, "is that a threat?" I said, "nah, threats are usually empty. Now fuck off."

Regan and Marko walk up to him, Marko shouts. "Listen, we, want, you, to, fuck, off, and, go, away. NOW." The Tesco delivery driver leaves, and crashes into a lamp post, whilst trying to leave. This is when it gets serious.

I go outside, his name is Ian, the delivery guy. Ian said, "going to have to wait for the AA." I said, "going to have to fuck off out of here man." I start pushing his van. He said, "it's not safe to drive in this condition." I said, "you will fucking reverse and drive out of here." I pull out a pistol, and I said, "I don't care if your penis and balls is hanging on by a thread, and you need to go to A and E. Fuck OFF. NOW." He drives away, with the engine rumbling, and I have never seen someone drive so fast. Marko said, "what was this all about?" I said, "fuck knows, I like Tescos, think this guy is new." Marko said, "I don't give a fuck if he's new or not, he's seems like the kind of wanker we knock out at football matches. Now listen silly bollocks. We have work to do."

Chapter 15

Dave Jones, IC2/IC3 male, sat on my coach, eating these Terry's chocolate oranges.

Things seemed settled, I said, "Dave Feller, you want to stay here, full time man, you haven't got accommodation have ya?" He said, "how did you guess?" I said, "you wouldn't be knocking on my door begging for food if you was sorted, stay here bro." He said, "nah man, don't want to be a burden." I said, "mate, stay here feller, I'll take care of ya." He said, "cheers." Regan said, "what are you doing?"

I said, "I feel sorry for him, he's got kind eyes." Regan said, "yeah well alright, when is his court date." I said, "how the fuck should I know when his court date is? Do you want me to measure his ballsack? Do you want me to tell you the measurements of that also?" Regan said, "no, fuck you man, taking this way too far in this mansion bud fuck you, getting heavy for what reason dude. We rule things around here. But you are taking things way too seriously ain't ya? Well you can go and fuck yourself." I punched him in the face, he punches me back in the stomach. We wrestle for a bit. Regan, 6 foot 1, black dark hair. You know, the usual imagery you are going to get in these things. And listen, this rude boy, is taking the piss. I said, "mate, you chatting so much shit, and what about Dave man?" He said, "what about him, he's safe bro, just leave him to his own devices man." I said, "alright."

Dave is still eating the Terrys chocolate oranges. And I am walking up the stairs. fuck sake, this wasn't ending well. I was getting so many crazy thoughts in my head. It was going to stop. I just felt like, life was not going in the direction I wanted it to go in. I wanted out, out of this mansion. Out of this. But in a way. Dave Jones, became one of our best friends whilst he was on bail. Staying with us. The stories he would tell. This guy had a lot of stories. He was telling us how even though the dealers are on the same side. They get into arguments galore. This other dealer threatened to cut his ballsack off, and had the Stanley knife. Right by his ballsack. And Dave had to grab a cucumber and knock the guy out.

I said to Dave, "cucumber." He said, "Fresh out of the freezer, best thing to use." I said, "what about a baseball bat?" Dave said, "I don't play baseball feller, what you chatting?" I said, "I don't play golf, but I have got golf clubs if you know what I am saying." He said, "oh you are trying to act the hard man, you wouldn't get anywhere with a golf club."

I said, "then what do you suppose we do then rude boy? What do you suggest we use?" Dave said, "cucumber, frozen." I said, "okay, well glad you knocked the guy out, what happened then?" Dave said, "fuck knows, he woke up, he kept saying I was on rotation to deal. All of our runners kept going missing. Went into the kebab shop. Got a meat slicer, cut off his hands." I said, "then?" Dave said, "punched him in the face, but the runners, they went on strike." I said, "but you threaten them rude boy, you threaten them that they need to deal otherwise you are going to slice them right?" Dave said, "yeah but it went badly once. We get a wrap of cocaine and heroine. Gets plugged. The runner is running down the street. Next thing you know, the police behind him. Do they stop him, no. Then he starts spamming my phone, in Belgravia. Starts saying he ain't doing this anymore. How can I slice him, I was in Margate."

I said, "you could have got in your car." Dave said, "no, you're acting way too big for your boots. It doesn't work like that. It's more complicated than it looks. He comes back. We slice his neck. He grabs a knife. We had so many knives. I have forgot what he grabbed. But it wasn't a small one. Pointed it towards my fingers. Stabbed me in the hand. I got a nasty infection, and obviously we do our own medicine in the yard like. So got one of the boys to stitch it up. And was just waiting for the infection. The infection kicks in. I go to the hospital. They give me penicillin" I said, "what happened then!?" He said, "I go home, and after a few weeks. I have this scar man." He shows me this ugly scar on his hand. I said, "a runner did this, you reprimand him." He said, "he's six feet under right now as we speak, but that's the problem we have, they lash out. So we have to treat them differently now." I said, "as in, not threaten them. Give them presents, and shit." He said, "well yeah obviously, but we are strict on them, that they have to sell, a certain amount of kilos." I said. "How many kilos?" He said, "I ain't' talking about how many. I have a court date coming up, and I know you work with the police." I said, "I am not arsed to be honest, sounds to me like a lot of Kilos though." He said, "stop fishing man, you've been good to me. You put me up in this house, you've been really good. You cook me a fry up every morning, and give me chocolate. Don't ruin this trust we have man." I said, "but you don't know when your court date is?" He said, "no." I said, "well sounds to me like your trial has been suspended because the CPS have got bigger fish to fry." He said, "I am a big fish." I said, "nah mate, you're a gentle giant. Once we're done on County Lines. We're going in hard on the other geezers."

He said, "you trying to say I ain't hard and ruthless, that hurts my feelings rude boy, you can't speak like that. You make fun out of my belly also the other day. You can't be doing these things man. Fuck this. I thought you were all about going to the football anyway. You haven't been to a game in months." I said, "Yeah because we have to go to jobs now, because of this agreement we have with the police." He said, "jobs, hand jobs." I said, "mate, to be fair, I don't like The Police. Never liked Totsworth, thought he was a cunt. Glad he's dead." Dave said, "nah man, you can't be saying that. You can't be talking that way bro. He was good for us man." I said, "he used to harass us." Dave said, "it's what the police do man, they do it to everyone, not just you bro, he had family, and they shot him dead." I said, "yeah to make a statement, that I could easily go like him."

Dave said, "but they need you for intelligence, don't they?" I said, "yeah." Dave said, "so they ain't killing you." I said, "To be honest. Totsworth, didn't give them much intelligence. Probably why he's dead. He just used to draw tits in his notepad." Dave said, "wow." I said, "I think the guy had issues, nice guy. Gave him some bovril once." Dave said, "what type, chicken or beef." I said, "Beef, dude, beef is much better, get with the programme feller." He said, "yeah man, sorry I was out of line. You got any beef bovril?" I said, "yeah bro, one minute."

As I am walking to the kitchen, Regan said, "what the fuck are you doing, this geezer staying here indefinitely? For what reason bro? This ain't good." I said, "why man, he's a nice guy." Marko said, "haven't heard from the police in days. When's our next sting?" I said, "tomorrow." Marko said, "I can't go on like this man. Next sting, always a next one. Bro, we are not like Dave man, we can't go in ski masks. It's good to have the geezer on board. Maybe he can help us with intelligence."

Nothing seemed to be working, Dave wasn't compliant. Didn't even feel like going to the games. I just kept getting flashbacks of the good times you know. The times where people meant well. Meant good on this earth. It seems to me, like you try and take control of a situation. It doesn't always work as planned. Tottenham game was on today. Verses Chelsea. I had to go. I had to. I was fed up of babysitting Dave anyway. Fed up of it. Every day. Fed up of all of this. When I was in Iraq, I got a bad case of the shits. Whilst firing at the Taliban. My drill Sargent said to me he "DIDN'T GIVE A fuck" and to "GET BACK TO WORK." So here I am, and I still have the fucking memories.

I walk over to Dave, and I said, "have you killed anyone?" He looked nervous and he said, "no." I said, "not even yourself?" He said, "I am alive fool." I said, "Nah this ain't cool. You can't be in my house no more." He said, "I don't have anywhere else to go." I said, "I missed the part where that was my problem, fly like a butterfly out of here." He walks towards the door. Puts his ski mask on. He said, "hey, fuck you, where am I going to sleep tonight?" I said, "no fucking idea, actually that's a good point. One I don't have the answer for." He said, "you trying to make me out to be a fool man, you are a dickhead." I said, "You are the dickhead with the small penis, it's you at fault. You're a cunt. Always have been a degenerate. Now act lively or I will open you up like a cannister. And hit you with a cricket bat."

He said, "Hey fuck you, come here, and say that bro, I can't cope anymore with this. I got my trial. It's in a months time. And now what!?" I said, "fuck knows man, you are the one facing time."

Dave said, "so should I hate the police now, is that what you are saying? Because obviously selling drugs, you make money from it rude boy. What would you rather I did. Worked in McDonalds? Come on man. Cut me some slack. Just trying to make a dishonest living." I said, "at least you're honest about the dishonesty, but not honest about the drugs man. You could have got people killed bro." Dave said, "you've killed someone, we don't kill people man." I said, "listen man, you can talk the talk and all of that, but the bottom line is, you were pushing drugs man, that ain't cool."

Dave said, "what are you going to do? Get off your high horse you numpty, you killed a guy," I said, "yeah the gun was faulty though. I just wanted to caress the trigger to act hard and that. And the trigger was way too sensitive." He said, "yes mate, but your argument ain't gonna hold up in court, do you think it will?"

I said, "ur, I have no court date, I have no prosecution, and there is a tonne of evidence against me. That is why, I am working here. Prosecuting you." He said, "so you are a wannabe gangster detective cop or something, fuck you man. I am ringing your Sargent" I said, "bro, I don't work for The Police. Ring whoever you want."

He said, "then I am dialling up 101." I said, "dialling up 101, hahaha, seriously man, that's enough to give you a headache for a whole day." He said, "why?" I said, "bro, that number's a waste of time. It's just there for people to bitch and moan. And shout. It's a passive aggressive form of 999." I said, "so 999, less bitchiness." I said, "yeah." He said, "I am going to phone up 999, and report you." I said, "for what man? I have done nothing wrong. I have put you up in my house. I have bathed and showered you. I have given you food. I have treated you nicely. Given you water, coffee, McDonalds. I have given you everything. We have treated you like a God. Because we know when you're inside, you ain't gonna have that life. It's going to be porridge, it's going to be a piece of wet bread, with a small amount of margarine It's going to be bovril in a small cup. Carrots in another cup, and there will always be someone stealing your dessert. You don't want that." I said, "I am going not guilty." I said, "do what you want, but as far as I am concerned. You do more time with that if found guilty. Best to go guilty." He said, "you're my solicitor now? I have a solicitor, I don't need you whispering in my ear. Oh it's this, it's that. It's the other things. Fuck your reports."

I said, "I don't work for—the—police." He said, "yet you work with them." I said, "yeah." He said, "I am reporting you to the Daily Telegraph." He has an anxiety attack and starts dialling the number. Meanwhile Marko and Regan bounce in. Marko, the shorter version of Regan like. Marko is fuming. He said, "put the phone down now."

Dave said, "and then what?" I said, "look, what do you want for dinner man, we can order Deliveroo McDonalds dude. Come on, don't be so disheartened." He said, "okay man, I am sorry. I am messing up. I just am worried about spending time in jail." I said, "it's prison, jail is what they call custody. Listen. If we get you a McDonalds. What else do you want?"

Dave said, "a hooker." I said, "you cannot have a McDonalds and a hooker man, now that is pushing it bro. That is more shenanigans that we can't tolerate right now."

Dave said, "pole dancer then." Marko, skinhead, chimed in. Said, "we got no poles fool." I looked over to Marko and I said, "dude shut up man, shut the fuck up. This ain't cool man. This ain't cool." Marko said, "this is the chip shop crew, we order McDonalds, we spam Jacky's phone with cock pictures. But you, you are taking things too far." I said, "mate, I am just trying to help." Marko said, "oh right, so inflicted in this game. Trying to play the sympathy game with Dave, and by the time you wandering. We have more suspects to catch. But that ain't up to us no more."

Next thing you know Dave makes towards the door, having another anxiety attack, and shouts. "I want to be free." He collapsed, and he hits the deck, and me, Marko, and Regan, pick him up. Dave punches me in the balls. I fall to the floor. Marko and Regan are trying to restrain him. Dave reaches for the door again.

Marko said, "you got nowhere else to go fool, where else you gonna go?"

Marko shouted, "WHERE ELSE YOU GOING TO GO!?" Dave said, "fuck man, just cut me some slack, I am having a hard life." I said, "man we are going to have to handcuff you now boy." He said, "you serious?" I said, "No, but do that shit again and I will. Now just wait for your McDonalds. Stop doing this shit man. You're playing the victim. Stop doing that. Who cares what people think?"

Marko said, "the curry I had last night made my anus red raw, like I think a whole chilli pepper came out man." I said, "Marko mate, listen, listen, man just chill, just take it easy. Nobody is going anywhere." Marko said, "did you hear what I just said. I have a complaint about the curry I had." I said, "well take it up with them, not me." He said, "I have bro, they're going to give me another one." I said, "is it the chicken vindaloo?" He said, "yeah." I said, "no wander you got an arse like a fire cracker mate, you need to go mild like Chicken Tila Masala, or maybe something a bit more mild." Marko said, "okay bro, i'll phone them up now and change it." This is all done on Deliveroo. Next thing you know. There's a knock on the door and John Ricks, the legend, the man. He runs towards us. PC John Ricks. He shouts, "for fuck sake, I didn't give you permission to have HIM there." He points at Dave.

I said, "he has a name, it's Dave, show some respect, show some fucking respect dude."

PC John Ricks said, "right, he stays here, on one condition. We want two county lines drug dealers a week. Not one. Now get to work."

I square up to John Ricks, look him in the eyes. The temples. The eyes. He said, "how's Jacky?" It's my mrs by the way. I said, "she's alright, why do you ask?" He said, "I shagged her last night."

I phone Jacky up, and I said, "Jacky...you been shagging police officers now? That's cheating." She said, "nah it ain't cheating because he came on my tits." PC John Ricks said, "to be fair I did." I said, "you horrible bastard, that's my wife." He said, "yeah well she took her wedding ring off when she was with me. I was going to use it as a cock ring. But got too much girth." I said, "you're an animal." He said, "get to work, two county lines suspects a week." He taps me on the shoulder and he said. "And also I get to have a go with Jacky whenever I please." I said, "what ever man, I haven't shagged her in months, go for it."

He said, "WILL DO", he does a little dance. It's strange. He turns his axon camera off. And does a little dance. And Marko and Regan flip out, and run towards him and me also. All shouting. "What the fuck are you doing? You are trying to take the piss."

I said, "I will be requesting that Axon video, you muppet." He said, "go on then, do it, oh and by the way, listen. Whilst this is happening. My inspector had a go on Jacky too." I said, "fuck YOU man." Regan punches him in the stomach. I punch John Ricks in the face. He pepper sprays us all. Gets his baton out. (not his cock). His asp. And starts hitting us. Dave flushes the toilet. Comes out of the toilet after washing his hands. Walks down the stairs. And said, "PC John Ricks. I expect better of you man."

PC John Ricks said, "sorry Dave won't happen again." Dave said, "PC John Ricks...this is not fair, these guys are trying to help, and all you are doing is sleeping with their wives man. That ain't cool. Show some respect." PC John Ricks shouts back. "Oh I will show some respect." He undoes his fly, and shows his 9 inch cock, and said. "How about this for respect. Now get to work." He forgets to put his cock back in his boxer shorts. And he gets in his car, and an old lady hits him over the head with what I presume was a walking stick. He shouts, "fuck sake." Does the zip up, gets his cock caught in the zip. Next thing we know. We have so many people outside the house. The fire brigade, ambulance service. The Deliveroo guy, recording. It was going crazy. I shout to the Deliveroo guy. "Just give me the food man, stop recording this." He said, "public place." I said, "yeah but it's my house you're recording, I don't give a fuck about PC John Ricks over there. Think he's a idiot. But thanks for the food." Meanwhile the fire service, and the ambulance service. Are applying some kind of liquid to loosen the zip stuck on the cock. And it seems to be working. And finally, after a bit of that liquid. (Fuck knows what it was). Could have been KY Jelly for all I cared. He was all zipped up and ready to go.

    The paramedic said, "you okay, do you want to go to hospital for a check up?" PC John Ricks said, "hang on, can I get in my police car, and assess the damage man." The paramedic. George. He said, "jump in the back of the ambulance, and I will have a look at it, and tell you if you need to go to hospital or not." One look, and it ain't good news. George the paramedic said, "mate, this needs treatment bro, you need stitches. There's a chunk nearly falling off man. I am going to apply tape. Stand still."

    I am videoing the whole thing because it's funny, and George shouts, "wind your neck in pal." I said, "it's cool man, it's cool. I will wind my neck in. But in the mean time. This is funny." George said, "show some empathy man, how would you like it, if you caught your cock in your zipper?" I said, "it happened once actually, and I didn't make the fuss you were making. So a chunk almost fell off. Seriously getting to me all of this is"

The ambulance drives off, flashing lights, no siren. Until the end. The fire service, tow the Police car back to the depot. I walk inside, and Dave is eating his McDonalds. Naïve to the whole thing. He said, " man, that guy is ruthless. He's been sleeping with your mrs, behind your back." I said, "not for two weeks, hows your McDonalds bro?" He said, "it's good bro, just a question though, but what do they put in the secret sauce man?"

I said, "don't know." I said, "cum probably." He said, "that is just a lie man." I said, "no it's not."

Things weren't getting better, things were getting worse. Day after day. fuck this. Time to watch Eastenders. Time to relax. You know. What have I got to prove to anyone. I am my own wolf. That is what I am. I am tired of this. People can go and think what they want. Yeah, and the fact of the matter is. The chip shop crew. Still remains strong. Well, I say that now. But things aren't the same. You think this adventure is easy. It's tough. I can't be going outside all of the time anymore. On my travels. And heartbreaking news of PC Totsworth, and his demise. I wasn't going to be scaremongering anyone. I was fed up of John Ricks. Fed up of the bloke. What's worse, is I wasn't thinking straight. Not one bit. So it was getting to me a bit if I am being honest. Time went on, but my mind was blank. I just felt insecure and restless. I couldn't carry on making the same mistakes.

The streets weren't the same anymore. It got to the stage where we stopped watching the football. We stopped. We refused to engage. We had business. With The Police, and time, and pressure. So in the house, I am looking for a reason. For some reason. For any reason, just to wander. Wander what was going on. Wander what was happening. This wasn't what the chip shop crew was about. Honour and respect. But it all went wrong. Fuck were we going to be police informants. So I leave him a couple of weeks. Because I know what he's like. I go up to him. John Ricks. And I said, "listen feller, you can do me for murder, I ain't doing this anymore." He said, "well that's a shame." I said, "there is no CCTV is there?" He looked blank, and he said, "no." I said, "thought as much, besides, even if there is. I'll find 20 people that look like me. Put them in court. You do your own police work. No wander you got your cock stuck in your zip."

He punches me in the stomach. PC Ricks said, "listen, you fat bastard, you will do as you are told." I said, "suck on my man tits, you bellend, what do you expect? All of this is alright is it. I am going back to my council house." He said, "it's been sold." I said, "well I will buy it back." He said, "It's not for sale, an old lady lives there." I said, "well I will go around there and start shagging her then." PC Ricks takes his sunglasses off, he looks around. He said, "you nob head, you taking the piss?" I said, "no." He said, "it seems to me like you're taking the piss. I am not having that." I said, "not taking the piss, listen rude man, you have got to be serious. CCTV, yes, CCTV, no. Make your fucking mind up you sausage. Which one is it?"

(Even though we were away from the fighting, and away from the games. We were still thinking of the bloodshed. We were still thinking of kicking two shillings into someone. The Yid Army was far from collapse.)

PC Rick said, "how the fuck should I know what's going on." I said, "well I am getting tired of you acting the big man." He said, "I am getting tired of your lack of intelligence." I said, "have you got CCTV footage or not?" He said, "yeah but you ain't seeing it."

With your back against the wall. There is only so much you can do. With your back against the wall. You want to seek counsel. You want to seek something. But the fear keeps adding up. And I was not going to be the *police's bitch anymore*. Stick to the game, do the right thing. Follow the rules. Not this.

I go back to my council flat, obviously an old lady lives there. And I ring the buzzer. 10th floor, I was in. So I ring the buzzer, and I hear, "hello", in an elderly woman's voice. I said, "alright beautiful." I then just cringed, and ended up kicking a fire hydrant. And I know they are underneath the ground in the UK. I mean the sign, the yellow sign. DAMMIT. fuck. Why am I going 'back in time' to speak to someone senile. Over something that could have been avoided. Next thing I know the police arrive. Two women. And to be honest with you. They walked towards me. Saying, "what are you doing, Steve? You don't live here anymore." I said, "I know that, hush your gums."

PC Sarah Smith, said, "you need to wind your neck in." I said, "oh yeah, I miss Totsworth He's dead. HE'S BROWN BREAD." PC Sarah Smith said, "yeah, and what's your point. He's dead, and you're next." Their body warn cameras weren't on. I said, "go on then, because I am as good as dead. I am as good as dead. With you piggies chasing me around. Little piglets." Sarah said, "comparing us to animals, not very nice." I said, "a lot of people are animals, squawk, be a parrot, fit in with the world. I hate you for being here. I hate you for arriving like this. You fucking twat." Sarah said, "swear again, and it's public order." I am filming on my phone. I said, "nobody is around dim-low."

Sarah said, "then shut up." I said, "I will tell you the truth. I buy this Audi, and I drive it around. And I go to the local police station. Where were you that day?"

She said, "I wasn't working." I said, "well let me tell you something, and to be honest. I don't like your banter." I said, "yeah but it's Britain, that's the whole point of this. Why are you getting involved?" She shouted, "learn some respect! Why are YOU getting involved?!" I said, "why are you getting involved?" The old lady opened her window, and shouted, "Why, is everyone getting involved...??" Next thing I know, a jeep full of Albanian people arrive. Four of them, and they get outside, and starts yelling. Start saying they run the district. So PC Sarah Smith. She said, "fuck off."

Four Albanian people get out the car. I don't know what the fuck is happening. I am getting on the bus, and going home. Fed up of this crap.

PC Sarah Smith said, "what the fuck," She's new at the job. I said, "ah you're a rookie." She said, "I am the law bitch." I said, "listen, I am not your bitch. You talk some sense into me. We go for coffee. But not like this. You actually are scaring me." She said, "why?" I said, "It's hard to explain. Really difficult to. You reach a point in time where. Things become myths. The legends, the myths. The oracles. You get lost. Now I am not saying it's easy. Especially in these circumstances. Yet, there has to be some kind of way out. Policing by consent gone out of the window. Alright pipe down pork chops. And I am still going to the game on Saturday." She said, "I am not stopping you, but you shouldn't be outside this elderly ladies house." I said, "Are you married? Because if you are. I feel sorry for the husband."

She said, "alright calm down." I said, "listen,

you want to speak to me. I will talk. You nut case." Next thing I know I am in cuffs. Being dragged away. Dragged to the cells.

Fuck this. Being dragged to the cells. With my balls hanging on by a thread, and I am good once I get going. I am a god damn train WRECK. I am fed up. I want my phone call. I walk in. Fuck knows where this police station is. Because the vehicle had black tinted windows. Or maybe it was dark. The officers were snorting cocaine, and taking viagra onto the way to the police officer station. I was in cuffs. I was shouting. "I WANT MY LAWYER, I want my fucking lawyer, you halfwits. fuck." Sargent Thomas, big guy, think empire state building plus what ever they got in Paris big. Big man tits. Like you could squeeze juice out of those fucking things. I said, "I want my lawyer." He said, "listen mate, we will get you a solicitor, what ever, stop jerking our chain." I said, "listen bro, you got me twisted. You know who I am. I am the real deal. I am the geezer that gets things done. My balls will be shining of gold in no time. Now this. All of this stuff. Meet him again. Sargent Thomas. You make me sick. Ever heard of a carrot stick and a treadmill. You lard ass."

He said, "have you ever heard of a job, and a brain, you two faced idiot." I said, "not very professional of you to say that." He leans in. All aggressive, and he said, "in this custody block, you don't have any rights, you don't get a solicitor You don't get a phone call. You don't get to piss in our toilets. You can wait and piss all down the walls. And we are going to keep you here for days."

Then some inspector walks in. Inspector Humphries. Now he is a bit more experienced and he has over heard this conversation. Inspector Humphries said, "THAT'S ENOUGH THOMAS." Really loudly. Whilst there were twenty officers in the canteen, just eating chips, and baked beans. All in some kind of baggy trousers." Inspector Humphries, now he is 6 foot 6, build like a brick nonsense house. And he puts the fear of god into Sargent Thomas. He shouts, "you say that again, you're fired."

I interject, because I am feeling a bit nervous about this arrangement I have a lot of nervous energy you know. And I want to say something. So I say this, "cock, and balls, to all of this. I am standing my ground. You moved me to a fucking mansion geezer. Now just because I won't comply. This is my hotel suite. Let me tell you something. You wanted me as your informant. Kiss my arse cheeks. Because you can kiss them all day. Now if you want to talk business. Let's do this another way." Inspector Humphries takes me into a private room. He said, "listen, it's not so bad being an informant, you know. It's not so bad. If you work with us. Sure, we don't like vigilantism. Whatsoever. But join us." I said, "become a cop." He said, "yeah I can make it happen, we've done dirtier things here than you can imagine. We once employed a dustbin man because we couldn't be bothered to throw away the trash. It's a circus in here, but it's my circus. So how about it? Police constable Steve Smith. fuck the rest of the geezers." I said, "Regan, Marko..." Inspector Humphries said, "let me tell you something. All of this nonsense aside man. They're dead weight." I said, "they are my pals, they need to be with me on this."

Inspector Humphries, a full grown man. Now we are talking body builder. Juicer. Protein shakes. Rumour on the street, is he injects steroids into his arse cheeks. And snorts cocaine, because it's a short cut. If you know what I am saying. In more way than one. When he's cutting, the fat. In his cutting phase. Now this guy can bulk. But whilst he's on his cutting phase. He snorts cocaine. Takes viagra on the bus. And he loses a few stone. And that's not the end of the matter. You know. These cops. You get on the wrong side of them.. You're eating porridge for the rest of your life. You give them a slice of the good stuff. They'll give you a slice of the good stuff. You know.

So I don't want to go down the road, of battery with this guy. This inspector, he assaulted and battered someone The case was dropped, because he had reasonable excuse. Because he hit someone with a battery by accident. You know one of those big batteries. And he has salt on him to grit the road. So they were saying, assault and battery. It went to court. And he said. It was salt, and a battery. The judge was so confused, he waved the whole thing out like he was swatting a fly.

Inspector Humphries, was new to London. But he wasn't new to the force. The big burly guy. The tanning salon he goes to. His dark hair. He was the definition of an Alpha Male. The ladies loved him. But he wants me of all people to join the cops. *Could do.* The whole point of the Chip Shop Crew. Was to nail the cops. Get under their skin, call them piggy, and rile them up. Now, all of those police officer insults. They are going to come back towards me. Maybe this was punishment.

Inspector Humphries said, "make up your fucking stupid thick mind you idiot, are you in or not?" I said, "and leave behind Regan and Marko? Not a chance. I am politely declining."

Inspector Humphries hasn't given up. The Chief Superintendent. Ricardo walks in. He's Spanish, and he's only doing the job for two years. Because he's managed to secure a job working in border control. And his fiance and wife to be. Works as an air hostess at the same airport. So he wants to be closer to her. Because he misses her, and she misses him a lot. With their work patterns. Sounds crazy. Maybe a conflict of interest. But it wasn't just that. She was going to later quit her job, and start prostitution.

And meanwhile, he was going to end up in an underground basement. With Romanian and Albanian men, demanding he gives them cash. Or they slit his throat. Yet, he doesn't know this is going to happen yet. But it does. And you think back, and you wander why this is fucked up. What I am talking about... So let me give you some context. Now Ricardo, he's not clean. He's a drug dealer. And a police officer. Now, Inspector Humphries gets high, steals cannabis out of the evidence room, and rolls spliffs. And meanwhile. The Chief Superintend Ricardo joins him.

I was getting tired of people saying. "Oh the police, they can handle themselves." Maybe, but they have insecurities. Just like everyone else. They have weaknesses, you can exploit. And that's exactly what the Romanian and Albanian gang were doing. Next thing you know. His fiance is prostituting against "her will", whatever the fuck that means. And she's getting cash, but the pimp is getting half. Meanwhile Ricardo, ends up being blackmailed to meet the pimp. And they hold him in the basement.

It all happened so fast. "All units, all units, Stacey has been abducted." Now everyone knows Stacey. Because Ricardo talks about her non stop. So Ricardo. Trying to be the alpha male, but doesn't quite match up to Inspector Humphries. Ricardo goes to look for Stacey in his own private vehicle. Breaking the speed limit on the motorway, and stopping at McDonald drive thru, and shouting. "JUST GIVE ME THE FOOD, I'LL GIVE YOU THE CASH." He follows Stacey. Right into the trap the Romanian gang set up. They trap him in a basement. With rats crawling around, and with prostitutes tied up, he gets gagged and tied up against the floor. This all happens whilst I am in custody. And the worst part is. Is that

Inspector Humphries. Doesn't seem to care. He leans in. He says, "we want you on board, it's either that or jail.." He shows me the CCTV of me killing Lee. I couldn't give a fuck if he was Millwall, or West Ham. Or what ever team he was. Low and behold. They have me. Hidden CCTV camera. Square around my face. Facial recognition. In HD. It wasn't just HD, it was almost like some blue ray, multi media. Expert CCTV, 3D nonsense. Except it was 2D, but the graphics were good."

    I lean over and I said, "okay, I'll join you, however, it's sad leaving Regan and Marko behind." I get angry. I smash the place up a bit. My handcuffs are released. Now inspector Humphries. He is a bit naïve because he's too busy body building, and he gets caught in sex videos. Watching them online, and keeps getting caught. And he's a wild canon. So anyway. I take the job.

    OUT OF DURESS. I said to him, "listen, all of this nonsense aside. You want me to wear a fancy dress also?" I was over thinking this. He was getting my suit ready, and I was struggling to think. Kept smashing up his office, but he didn't seem to mind. Eventually. After some hard work.

    I spat in his face. I said, "no, this ain't gonna happen." Now before, the former. I know it's not good to spit in faces or anything. But he was spitting in my face. And singing the national anthem. For ten minutes. All I did was retaliate I threw him to the ground. I said, "pork chops, 101, go figure. This is your private jet out of here. Say goodbye to your cash cow, because it's leaving the pasture."

I smash him up. I kick the door down. I smash two rookie police officers in the corridor Bam. The ridges of my shoes. I punch the desk Sargent in the face, and he rolls his eyes. Whilst he faints. And I run. I hijack one of their private vehicles. Hot wire the fucking thing. I drive all the way back to the mansion. I said, "Marko, Regan, let's go." We drive, all night. Raining. Wind screen wipers galore. Kept going, kept going. We weren't going to the service station, we were getting the fuck away from London. We were heading north. Behind us, police are on our tail. Three police cars, with sirens, and you know all of that stuff. So I start to think outside the box. I start to think. "You know. In all fairness. I have an escape plan."

I drive off randomly to the service station. One of the cars hits the side of the metal bit of the barrier. The other two cars behind me. Trying to T-Pac me in, or what ever the fuck that manoeuvre is. But I am not having it. I shout outside the window. "COME WITH ME, HAIL MARRY, COME QUICK SEE. WHAT HAVE WE GOT HERE NOW. LA DA DA, RA LA DA DA DA DA DA. Come with me. Hail Mary! Come quick see." And I am playing it on the stereo system. And one of the police officers. He gets so absorbed in the tune. He actually turns his lights off. And he thinks. "You know what, I need to go to church. I have been cheating on my mrs. I need redemption."

Fuck redemption. That was what it was about. So he ends up bailing. I have one car left. It's a police car, a jeep. I was like. 'I didn't even though the police had jeeps." It was one of those proactive CID "undercover vehicles." Yeah good thinking. Had the flashing lights and the siren. The geezers in the front, looked like nob heads. And I was getting tired of this. So I shouted outside the window. "Listen, this all has to stop." Now it gets interesting, because I have never seen this in the UK before. It must be something new they have been working on in training. Out comes a speaker system. And a shout. "CEASE AND DESIST FROM DRIVING." I was driving an Audi, silver. It was in good condition. Automatic. I was enjoying driving so much. I shouted, "it has to be an official letter." The jeep got right besides me, and the officer said. "I"ll give you an official letter. I will spunk in the letter and hand it to you. You twat." I elbow him to the face. He swerves off the bridge. No cops following us for the next hour. Double bluff. We hide in a chip shop. Because let's face it. The police aren't going to think we'd be so stupid to hide in there.

    Marko said, "right I am getting the cod and chips." It was this little welsh Village. We had gone a long way. And this fat welsh lady. With tits, that looked like you could milk the cream, yoghurt, and milk out of them. She stands there. She shouts. "WHAT DO YOU WANT TO EAT." I said. "Cod and chips, please." Her name was Raquel. A quarter

Spanish. Marko takes me aside, and he said. "This has to stop." Next thing you know. A Mexican gang arrive. And I thought we had made peace with them. They come in. they are our associates. They mean well. This one dude. With high white socks. Obviously a bit of darkness in their skin. This one fat Mexican guy. Not very fat. But slightly. He said, "listen, we can help you evade the cops." His name was Ricardo.

I said, "we got it covered, here, have some chips." He said, "we didn't come here for chips. You owe us money." Regan squares up to Ricardo. Regan yells. "We don't owe you anything."

I said, "yeah that's right. We don't owe you shit. Quit playing around."

Life is short you know, very short, and we often wander. Wander why things happen or wander why these things/scenarios happen. On the run from the police. It didn't bode well with me. And for once in my life. I wasn't scared.

Traffic, cars, with their red and blue lights blurring passed. Underneath the belly of the beast, the big Silicon valley of disappointment, beneath my chest. I felt nothing but surprise. The crew had been diversified. But there wasn't peace on the streets. Not anymore. We had vigilantes roaming the streets. Me, Steve Smith. On the run, it was either that or become a cop. Who do they think I am? David Blaine? The fuckers. And trying to find a woman these days, was trying to find a hooker without a sexually transmitted infection. It was tough. Besides, I am just trying to think outside the box here. You know. I said to Marko, "do all hookers have STI's?"

He said, "ur, it's a stereotype mate, some do I guess." I said, "I just don't understand it you know." Marko said, "get a Fleshlight" I said, "might do." Marko said, "man, your head is wired funny, you are talking all of the time about hookers and women. And no wander you don't have a girlfriend. Man you are talking about all kinds of nasty shit." I said, "and then what happens?" He said, "it's how society is nowadays man, men's masculinity is taken away, by a feminist notion. That it's okay not to have a cock, you know. Or if someone has a small cock, or men have emotions. And all that nonsense. It's pathetic, teaching men how to cry and shit and now this.

On the run, man, listen. fuck this. I am not going to say this so perfectly right now. We are on the run. We have hookers, we are not going to buy. Because..." He paused, mid sentence. I said, "because what, dick hole, what is there to be confused about? Everyone wants to make vogue magazine. Everyone wants to read the top shelf porno collection in the corner shop. The story goes on and on. It doesn't end. And as well as that. We come to some point in time where we look at things. Most importantly. We look at issues surrounding life itself. Being on the run from the police. *All of this*."

Marko said, "man, fuck the police, do you see me crying or shedding any tears man. We end up in some prison, and then what bro. Then what happens. The whole system collapses. It's just us now."

It was just us. The whole world. Now nothing, you know. I never trusted anyone. Life was short and I was running out of time and running out of options. That's the problem we have. Running around like a headless chicken wasn't going to solve anything.

With nothing to leave behind, all of this aggravation. Just something in the air, and it just felt surreal you know.

I was talking in my sleep again. Apparently I was singing, 'police officer, police officer, police officer, piglets and pork chops." With snores in-between obviously, I am not an animal. You know. So that is what is happening. I wake up. There's a police officer at the door. He's unarmed. He walks in to speak to us. He says we are all arrested, and he gives this long rap sheet of offences.

So I said to him, "you want to hear the rap sheet of 2Pac, his rap lyrics?" The officer said, "are you intentionally trying to be racist?" I said, "no." He said, "you like his lyrics?" I said, "yeah hello?" He said, "hello." No I said, "for fuck sake, you don't understand do you, all of this bullshit about who is left wing, right wing, and all of that bullshit. And you come in here, all 'tazers' blazing. And you start rapping. He said, "mate, these are criminal charges." I said, "now you're being racist, because 2Pac wasn't a criminal. He was criminalised by the system." That is when my Mexican brothers. Who we made peace with. Because they had been working out from the east. And we had respect from them. And Ricardo said, "hey man, listen, you come to this chip shop, threatening us with arrest. I am going to cut your balls off and fry it. You dumb fuck." The police officer, who failed to identify himself. However was wearing a pink thong. He said, "in all fairness, you need to stop all of this."

I get my pistol out, and I said, "listen, you idiot sit down. Put your tazer on the table." Marko shouted, "do as you are told bitch." So he sits on the table. And I said, "look, how long have you been on the force?" He said, "well ten years." And I said, "and that's it, is it? What else have you done. Scrubbed toilets?" He didn't reply. PC wankstain, I called him. He said, "that's not nice mate." I said, "listen, you come into our chip shop, and threaten us like this man, this ain't fair bro." He said, "I am not your bro." I said, "right I have had enough of this. You go and sit down, what's with the thong?" He said, "I am sat down. My mrs has thrown me out the house. It's all I could find."

I said, "PC Totsworth?" He said, "He's dead mate." I said, "well he was the only officer I knew who got kicked out of his house by his mrs." The Police officer, who is called PC Piles. Real name. And I am starting to wander if this is a real cop.

Chapter 16

I wake up. Waking up has never been the same. Never. Being in Wales. In this kebab shop. Having to listen to this welsh ladies voice. It was going through my skull like a drill. Like I was being lobotomised with her voice. It was killing me. I was getting a headache from listening to her. I said to Marko, "look, I don't give a fuck what is going on in the news right now. I want that woman gone." Marko said, "Okay, with PC Piles, Mr wankstain tied up over there. What's his real name? You have all of these nicknames. What's his real name?" I said, "PC Piles." Marko said, "that's not a real name..." I said, "it is, I have checked. I have checked. I have seen for myself. It's a real name." Marko said, "You gonna call him PC Plywood next? PC Prick? What is it going to take." The poor officer. Was gagged. With duct tape. Hands behind his back. Curry sauce all over his head. Burns on his face. We even put an apple in his mouth and then gagged him. Because he was trying to chew through the tape. Like a god damn rot Rottweiler.

At this moment in time, with your back against the wall. You don't know what to do. Of course I missed Jacky. But there were things. That I had to take care of. I had business to attend to, and for once in my life. I was not scared. Not scared, because deep down. I knew I was going to die rather than be incarcerated. Enter, the cyanide pills. I am not joking either. And if you think I am joking. This is where Marko comes in. He orders a batch online. I take one. Put it in my wallet. He takes one. Regan takes one. Ricardo, the Spanish and Mexican crew. They take one each also.

I said, "if we get close to being caught, we take one. You're dead before you know it." Marko said, "okay, what is this really. Sugar tablets?" I said, "no." Marko said, "the pistol in your pocket, you think it looks good on you, bigger than mine right." I said, "mines 9mm, yours is a snub nose." Marko said, "yeah..." I said, "who the fuck carries a snub nose? What are we doing, shooting elephants!? It's us verses the cops. You don't use that."

I hand him an AK47, fully loaded. I said, "you use this, and you know. They know, you mean business." He said, "there's just one." I said, "we are on the run man, I will get more later." Marko said, "man this is not good, what else have you bought?" I said, "hookers."

Fuck this, this was not going anywhere. I was getting confused. Little things. Keep toppling over. My chest, felt like a burning inferno. I felt vacant. Like my head was full of bricks. Like a brick building. THIS CAN'T CONTINUE, it's a load of balls. A load of bollocks anyway. They can go and chase me, and chase my crew. But with me. With what I do. Who the fuck knows? The less I knew the better. That was how it was. The welsh lady. Turns out her name is Irene, she is getting arsey with me. Keeps shouting, "we need more cod." I should back, "I don't fucking work here." I hijacked the place. She's too naïve, she thinks I am a co worker. Fucking hell. Look at the view. The welsh sea side. The waves crashing against the bricks.

Marko was getting paranoid. He shouted, "this can't continue." I said, "you know what happens to rats, and snitches in jail, I can't do it man, I can't. Even if they paid me. Maybe at first. But not anymore. I can't do it, because it's high risk bro. Street code, never snitch. Because if you end up in jail. You get stitches.

Marko said, "listen, enough of this crazy talk, I can't stand being upstairs to Irene. Who is she to bark orders at us?"

I said, "she thinks we are co workers, she's delusional." Marko said, "no sign of police." I said, "putting us in a false sense of security. Plus, this guy. PC, come on, enough of this amateur hour. What the fuck is his name? PC Piles!? Marko said, "apparently, I mean that's what it says." I said, "unfortunate name." Marko said, "you can get names changed, legally, you know." I said, "doesn't change the person. Besides, it's like having an alias. You know."

Things were getting bizarre. I didn't know where to start really. It was almost like I was going back in time. Out of all of the work, now this. Not really knowing what's going to happen next. It all comes down to this day. Maybe, you know. Or maybe not. I mean, I don't know how long we were going to keep PC Piles hostage. And for a few days there was nothing. No police, nothing. It was just the weight of this whole thing. It was getting to me. The whole thing was. You just decide where your life goes. And some times there is no turning back. You think to yourself all of the time despite problems. And then there's nothing. Obviously, there had to be something. But running away from the police. Not something I was good at. Since I had one of the doughnuts with me. Not really talking, and then nothing else. Comparing an officer to a doughnut. It felt weird, but we were in a volatile situation.

It was just this feeling you get underneath your skin. Like something bad was going to happen. Yet, it just wasn't like that anymore. I would like to explain that it's just injustice. Justice, you name it. I didn't want to be a police informant anymore.

Chapter 17

Things change you know. Things change, and the more I think about it. The more I realise. I was not cut out for this. This was killing me. The whole thing. And how much time I had on my hands right now. For what exactly. Just to run from the cops? Having PC Piles, on a chair, gagged with an apple around his mouth, and duct tape? And that welsh lady doing the cod and chips. Whilst I was just wandering. This is what I would rather do. So rather this, than anything else.

I don't know what it is. Sometimes you can't think straight. People kick you when you're down. Or you end up kicking yourself when you are down. People work jobs they hate, and put with shit from their employers. But this. Running from the cops. I would rather that. Than being an informant. Everything is going wrong. Everything is.

I then get a phone call. "Hi it's Sargent Bernard. How are you doing?" I said, "I am okay, why do you ask?" Sargent Bernard said, "well I have just been wandering you know, how long you are going to run from us? And stop gagging PC Pile?." I said, "It's what I had to do, it's what I had to do." Sargent Bernard said, "listen here man, this is my district. I am the Sheriff. I run this place. And if I tell you to cease from doing something. I mean it. You are running a huge scam on this department. Trying to make fools out of us cops. Well it ain't going to wash with me."

He continued to say, "I eat people like you for breakfast. And I am telling you. The best way to comply. Is to hand yourself in. But you won't. You are having a detrimental affect on how we operate. This is not going okay. Now I am warning you. If you hand yourself in now. Maybe, just maybe we can work something out. If you run. No more deals." I said, "I don't want your deals, haven't you noticed, why I am on the run?" Sargent Bernard said, "well you have more warrants out for your arrests, then I have orders out for my Pizza. And I am telling you, I eat a lot of pizza." I said, "get to the point, I don't want to hear this. Have you got anything concrete." He shouts, "CONCRETE,

YOU ARE ON THE RUN, YOU ARE A CRIMINAL." I said, "Yeah, but you have to catch me. Isn't that how it works?"

He said, "we will get you." I said, "well good luck with that. In the mean time. I am going to continue running away from you. No more deals." He replied. "what about.." I interrupted and shouted, "no, no more deals." He said, "a million pounds, your own private jet." I said, "you serious?" He said, "listen, I know times are tough right now, but you seriously want to get involved. Let me know, because right now. All I can say. Is that we can let you off." I said, "yeah but I ain't going back to being a police informant. I don't know who you think I am."

He said, "look, we gave you lots of opportunities." I said, "yeah, but listen, we got to work something out better than this." He said, "what if I could get you to tell us what is going on, and it's all anonymous. Nobody finds out." I said, "sounds alright to me, so if I hand myself in now..." He said, "look, just drop by my office tomorrow morning at 11am, and all charges will be dropped. But I am warning you. If you try to escape again. There will be hell to pay."

I said, "you trying to make a fool out of me?'" He said, "you made a fool out of yourself." I said, "the way I see it, is I need cash, money." He said, "I will give you cash, money, no problem. But stop running." I said, "listen, I ain't buying this nice guy act pal." I hang up. I said to Marko, "some dickhead wants to meet me in his office, tomorrow." Marko smiled and said, "some cheese dick." Regan said, "fuck that. We stay here. PC Piles is our new friend." I said, "yeah hell I ain't going back to The Police." Marko said, "it's that simple isn't it. That simple. Go and try them. You will find nothing but a circle jerk parade going on. Inside their office." I said, "man, you have a wild imagination, fuck you, you want to play ruthless on this man? I say we wait. We wait, and we wait."

Sargent Piles is waking up, I tear off the duct tape, he says, "please let me live." His pocket. A picture, his daughter. He said, "she's only eleven, she's all I have." I said, "are you married?" He said, "no divorced." I said, "Okay, well, I will let you go, but don't squeal, once I let you go." He shouts, "Enough!." Marko said, "if we let him go, he'll locate us." I said, "I am going to go back to Sargent Bernard anyway."

I let PC Piles go. Marko isn't having it, reaches for his gun. Points, out the window. I said, "don't bother." Marko said, "too late." PC Piles is brown bread.

With your back against the wall, there is only so much you can do. I didn't know if 'PC Piles' was his right name. Obviously I had work to do. I was going back. I was going back to Sargent Bernard. I was going to explain everything to him. How running away was a mistake. It had to be that way. That's all that mattered. So I started to think, as Marko shot PC Piles. In all fairness. I could have seen it coming.

I have realised where things are going now. Realised where life is going. What is happening. So the next day. I meet Sargent Bernard. He's not happy. I am freezing my balls off. Not thinking straight. Going into delirium. Like things are meant to make sense, but they are not. Some times not, anyway.

So I meet Sargent Bernard and he's very happy to speak to me. I said, "look, you are locking me away." He said, "no, not at all, but this is your last warning, how many people have been killed, injured, shot, on your watch, you son of a bitch prick."

I said, "in all fairness mate, you want me as a police informant or not. You grey haired prick." He said, "yeah, I do, but I have some things to clear up first. PC Piles. He used to let farts out in the office. Not talking about small cheesy smelling farts. I am talking about farts, that stunk like dead badgers. We had to evacuate the building. Nobody liked him. All he ate was McDonalds fries, chilli con carne meat and Mexican food." I said, "why the fuck are you telling me all of this you swine? I don't want to hear about his bowel movements. So why the fuck are you telling me? You think you are big, clever and hard?"

Sargent Bernard said, "life goes on doesn't it." I said, "save the bullshit, save it, because that's all this is. This is all you are doing. Is creating crap. You have chances. We put you in a private office. We help you understand, how to inform us. But you are going to have to cut ties with Marko. Cut ties with Regan" I said, "fuck no, why should I do that?" He said, "don't know, I really don't, but it's for the best. You alone. I can handle. I can't handle them. Not for one bit. It just amuses me."

Then, it's like nothing is happening, just amuses me, and then nothing. Despite everything that has been accomplished. Despite pressure, and despite the firm collapsing. I was getting tired. Yeah, you heard me. Tired of bullshit, tired of feeling sick. Sleeping all of the time. Fatigue. Feeling like a zombie. Regressing on the past. Yeah way too many times. But that's what it is. Just regression. I am stuck in an office. With this Sargent, and for all I know. It could be alright. It could be fine. It wouldn't be like that. Not anymore. Just stuck. Stuck without anything to go on, you know. That's all it is. Just paperwork, things they wanted me to do.

I was a ghost to them. I look back at the firm, and I just shudder. Because it was never meant to end this badly. It was never meant to end like this. But the soul crushing feeling of just being around. Realising, who you are. What you are feeling. It means something. It means, something. So then, in all fairness. You can understand. Understand what kind of pressure you have. Or what kind of influence people have on you. You realise this, and understand. How life goes on. People live, people die. People forgive, people forget. People get married, people get divorced. People copy, paste, lie, cheat, steal, extort, and fuck, who I am to ask for sympathy? Pale ale was a pain in the arse. A real pain. He was. He tries giving me this cock and bull story. Saying he's the balls. When he isn't. So I shot him, didn't meant to kill him. I don't know. It just feels like the more I try to work things out. The more they fail. I was going to inform the police. Tell them everything.

Every last detail. Of all of the information I knew. Yet time was ticking, and I was losing patience with myself. Losing so much patience. Time was being wasted. It's like. I wanted to control everything. Now I just let go, and the results change. I am fed up of trying to control everything. Every last detail. Every last thing. You realise that, you take that into account. That as far as I know. When I am in this firm, and we are fighting the Seaburn casuals. You better be aware of this. Now I am stuck in some office. Doing some intelligence work for the police.

Some people, walked around, like they were in a dance. Some people lacked energy and enthusiasm. Me, I didn't know anymore. You look at things the right way, maybe you have justification. Maybe not. I don't know. But then as times change, your life changes too. You become stuck on one thing. Then it becomes another. And another. And before you know it. You are out of ideas. You controlled too many things, you lacked ambition. You waited in line, whilst arguing in the supermarket.

Fuck this, me Steve Smith. I don't really know what to think anymore. I really don't. I struggle. I really do.

I just look up to things, and look up to ideas. And then life changes. Fed up of noises, that I don't want to hear. Fed up of trying to do this intelligence work. They were going to put me in prison anyway. This was the end. So what have I got to be proud as a peacock for? You know. It doesn't make sense. It doesn't at all. We are going to realise one day. All of our rights, went down the toilet. All of them. And then what. Just something I realised. Nothing else. Just things I knew. Life is like living in some stupid cartoon for fuck sake. I can't handle it any longer. You want to know how I feel. I felt it many of times. The pain and anguish some people go through. Just to get to the truth. I am stuck here looking like a nob. Just trying to figure out where else to go. What else to do. If you wanted to know, that's fine, but then nothing. Comparing, or how I learnt from this. It's fine. Then of course things happen.

Then we realise. Life just begins to make perfect sense. Perfect sense. You look at life, and you realise. That, you can't rely on people all the time for your own happiness. The jokes, the laughs, the things you used to say. The ideas, the hopes, the dreams. All just vacant memories and everything bothering me was cosmetic damage. Trivial, "not important" to other people. Yet it was these walls. I was going to prison. The dark moments you are sat in the office. Trying to find intelligence on county lines. Because that seals their meal ticket. I have had enough of trying to be someone I am not. You know.

Call it what you want but it's just how we feel. Right, I was fighting the Seaburn casuals. I was fighting them. I was telling them how I felt. I was headbutting them, knocking their teeth out. Now I can't do any of that. Yeah, I got the house, Regan and Marko are put away in prison. I knew I was next. But I just kept pretending it wasn't going to happen. It wasn't going to be that way.

You just look at life so clearly. With open eyes, and even then. Reflect on the days missed. Or the days gone wrong. Why I rebelled so much and now pay the price. The price I want to pay. The price other people know, the feeling inside my chest. Always needing someone.

And then nothing. Cracks on the doors. Why do the floors creek so loudly? Why do the doors creek? Why am I in this sense, of nothing. Like nothing went wrong. I want to be out fighting Chelsea. I want to be out there going to football games. Instead I am stuck inside. Not allowed to go to games. The chip shop boys, the chip shop men, the chip shop crew. This wasn't the end.

I was getting my lads out of jail/prison. I was going to fight this thing. Hanging over my head. So I do some research and I find out information, on crime. I go back to Sargent Bernard. Now it's late now. Very late. I am talking 11pm late. And I said, "look, for what I want to know, I can't do this anymore. This whole thing. You want me to be your bitch. You go around. Asking me to do some dirty work for you. Think what you want asshole. You think this is a game. My arse cheeks." He said, "I am giving you a way out, isn't that a good thing?" I said, "no, it's not, not whatsoever, you know. People want the simple life. The simple bread and butter world we live in. Then nothing. People get old, and rich, and powerful, and I am stuck here. Just noticing nothing. Absolutely nothing. I am nothing but a dot on your radar. All of this talk. Oh it's good to be British."

Because it was good to be British, but talking to this prick was taking some time. And I just was annoyed. Annoyed at what life was doing. Annoyed at where we were. Then, nothing. Nothing, we can say, you know. For what we can do. You understand, and comprehend. What we like to see here. This is how it makes sense. You realise things. Part of life. It was here, on this third floor office. Looking like a pile of rubbish. Yet I am not complaining. And of course. Things change. Yet my mind was remaining the same. Intelligence work. Not really what I knew.

Sargent Bernard breathing down my neck. I said to him, "I have beef with you." He said, "what for?" I said, "you expect me to do this nonsense, day in, night time. Day time. Inform you. Like a rat, fuck you dude. fuck you. Who the fuck do you think you are? Go and shave your ballsack" He said, "you go and shave your ballsack you fucking idiot, you have been just doing fuck all for the past week. So go home. Oh no wait. It's paid by the state. Go fuck a cucumber. You want the truth, you want the fucking truth. We put you here for a fucking reason. Because you have good detective skills. And you make good coffee." I said, "I can't argue like this anymore dude, you are the reason I am doing this."

He said, "well fuck you." I said, "I don't want to, and remember feller, this is bandit country. You think you can just come in like this. Waltz in like this. And demand that I do something. Fuck you dude. Waltzing in like the man you are. And then what, we are back to square one. Go and fuck a goat."

I said, "no, listen, you prick, you come and listen to me for once in my life. I will tell you the truth, you waltz in here, like it's a holiday resort. You can go and fuck a goat."

He said, "I work here." I said, "so that's what I am, just an errand man for you, fuck you, and listen. You come back to me with some fucking evidence. I don't want this beef. So go on." I do a dismissive hand gesture. I shout, "well come on then, you want to fight me, come fight me then." So we are fighting, one punch. I punch him once. And all of a sudden. He punches me, and I push him to the ground. Then he reaches for a knife. Then he just stalls.

I said, "you need that to butter your sandwiches you halfwit. Don't you dare think of stabbing me. You think you can come up to me, and start this shit. Well I will finish it. You are the one who is fucking so many animals. You piece of shit." He said, "you fuck an animal." I said, "no, you go and fuck an animal, you half witted prick. I mean that." I yelled down the corridor. "I mean that!." He said, "hey, hey, keep your voice down, some people are trying to work." I said, "suck hairy balls, suck a cock, suck your own cock. I don't care. Don't give me this. And release Regan and Marko."

He gets red in the face and he said, "chief, you want to be serious now, you want to be serious. fuck you." I said, "you can go and fuck your mother and her sister, fuck you, and your whole family. I have had enough of you." He said, "you think this is funny don't you. You think you can waltz right in here, and do some work then fuck off, like the bollocks you have been handed to. Not in my world." I said, "which world are you living in!!?" "Which world? Tell me that. Go on. Tell me. Tell me which world you are living in. Because I have no idea anymore."

I had no idea. I felt like whacking my face with a frying pan. Everything seemed wrong. Everything was going wrong. Going around in circles. And then nothing else. You know. It was like that. I just felt that I needed some form of escape.

So I start to begin to think, what really makes me think. What I really believe. Besides the truth obviously. There wasn't a bunch of lies, but there still was something beneath the surface. Something I didn't really want to think about. Things just go wrong, they go south. And you don't even realise what happens. My whole life, I just wish, that the police would. I don't know. It's complicated. I know so well, of what happened. Going through the council estate, the working class, and now this happens.

Call them what you want. Pigs, piggies, patrolling the estates. It just makes no sense. The scraps we used to get up to in the football games. Even the most experienced coppers used to brick it, and run towards the turnstiles. We had biker gangs running away from us. When it turned out our firm. Our firm, our chip shop crew firm with the Yid army. It then took a backlash, no, because nobody wants to get shot to death do they? Bullet in the head. But that's what happens when you bring a gun to a fight.

Some twat with a flare gun gave it the big one, and started acting like the dogs bollocks. Like the man he was. For all I know, and what everyone wants to know. Is that there are two types of people in this world. Sheep and wolves, you know what I am saying. I always wanted to be my own person. The firm was created on respect. You don't want to be a sheep rounded with dogs. That is what I am saying.

So I give the police information, and Sargent Bernard is still refusing to let Marko and Regan go. I am stuck here with information. Yeah county lines. So I walked passed the office. Some angry looking detective. He said, "for fuck sake, all he talks about his county lines." Another detective says, "yeah, maybe he's dealing, maybe it's a distraction." So then I kind of think about things logically you know. Think about things from my point of view. Think of things from my time. I look around. I see the police. Now they provide the services. But they just dug too deep. They just dug way too deep on this one. That is the problem we are having.

Next thing you know, some dickhead throws a bowling ball through the window. And Sargent Bernard is getting hysterical. Saying, "what the fuck dude, who's throwing this?" It turns out Marko and Regan escaped police custody, and they did it. Because they started a riot in HMP. Snuck out whilst the guards were dealing with it. Cut a hole in the fence. A guard tried shooting them down, but they got away into the woods.

They were there. Throwing bowling balls through the CID window. And I am shouting, "I have to work here tonight." Regan said, "It's okay Steve, we are getting you out of here. This is a miscarriage of justice." I said, "what?" Regan said, "are you sure, you want to keep doing this man? Waiting on them. Like some waiter. Giving information out. You know what we think. We think you should come to the game."

I said, "What game?" Marko said, "Tottenham, they are playing Chelsea. Tomorrow. FA Cup Semi Final."

I said, "I have work to do here."

Marko said, "what giving information to

those piggies? I am surprised you haven't thrown a bin at their heads yet."

I said, "what if we get caught again, then what!?"

Marko said, "we won't get caught again, our reasons being is that we are untouchable." I said, "yeah you said that last time." They were outside. Both of them. Chilling their nut sacks off. It was getting too much. Sargent Bernard can see me trying to escape and launches towards me. Trips over a wire from the paper copier. I launch forwards. As three uniforms spring my way. All colliding into each other as they hit the deck. And roll down the stairs. I trip over and hit the deck. And scramble towards the door.

Fuck this. This was going absolutely nowhere. As I walk out of Tottenham Police station. Regan and Marko looking like they had just escaped prison. Oh wait, yeah they had.

With your back against the wall that's all you could do. That's what the Yid Army represented. That's what everything did. But it was different now. The only people who cared were Marko and Regan. Nobody else. And we are running away and getting into the jeep.

It was different now. The war on the streets. This is what this was coming down to. Forget everything anyone has ever told you. About freedom and redemption. This was our golden ticket out of here. This was our express train to a better future. This is where we belonged, and this is where we wanted to belong.

I couldn't help thinking clearly, for once, and what I knew. For decades. Is that the police. The pigs. The filth. The vile scum. What am I going to do now? Just pretend this didn't happen. The vile soapy scum on your sink or hairdryer, they were the dust on your kitchen table. The perfume in your glass bottle. The poison in your liquor bottle. There was no tonic, no magic cure. No knight in shining armour. No recourse, and the express train had finally left the station. With that, we entered a new world. Of redemption, sacrifice, unsettlement, and we were on a mad spree.

It was the time to stand up and be counted, it was the time to express how we were feeling. For once in our lives. Fear was not getting the best of us. Whilst I drove the jeep furiously through the woods.

This was the time to begin a chapter, and a journey. Yet too focused on the small print. You know. That's for sure. So I would carry on just guessing. Because that's all it was. I just wish there was quick sand to bury me alive. I wish there was some kind of feeling. That I had gone about my day with some kind of feeling of hope. A journey that I could see. Instead things were falling to pieces. One by one, the corporations, the banks, the cash, the tickets. Singing hail Mary in a church does not make you a Christian. But I kind of wanted to speak of what I wanted to do now. It was tough being a skinhead. Tough. You just wished that your life had meaning. Instead you were stuck.

Driving this jeep. Which in all fairness, this was what I was doing.

But something clicked, and I don't know what it was. All of this was a farce. The whole thing. I had not even rendered any thought on my means of escape. It meant nothing to me, and my whole feeling. Of isolation began. Of course, from so many terms. This was just the beginning. But being on the run, and being away. And being gone, from what has happened. It just doesn't make sense. You try to put your head together. You try to, but it doesn't work like that. You want continuity, you want things to make sense. But as the Yid Army grew closer and closer. Towards reckoning with us. We became morally detached away from anything that stood in our way. Descended from chaos, and the whole thing lying in the proverbial flames of disbelief. It was a damn travesty. Just sitting in the jeep. Just waiting. We were going to The Chelsea Verses Tottenham game. Yeah as three wanted men were going to do that.

Some hair dye, change of clothing, some fake ID's, and fake passports from the deep web. We even got our finger prints genetically changed. From the help of a Russian scientist in a lab, where we travelled to Hong Kong. So we were well on our way to freedom.

It's what it counts for right. To have all of this, but the sheer freedom of expression. Oh you can't have it this way, you have to be politically correct. We were wanted. On the news. The things that were happening. And then what. Nothing. The same bullshit that comes out of everyone's lives. The same bullshit we always talk about. Everything is how it is. The golden ship, the golden vessel. Was awaiting the constant theories here. And we were stuck, in Silicon Valley. Just waiting, just waiting for some kind of repent. Away from the fights on the streets. The fights on the streets, and the war on the streets. Where people had been thrown into hedges, all bloody and bruised. For what purpose. I don't know. Probably to make a point. So we enter the Tottenham stand. And we walk in. and we are with five hundred skinheads. In our aisle. Our support. I am not counting but there was a lot of people. The stadium was fully packed and full.

Day after day, led pipes, narrow tunnel vision, thought policing, mass corruption. Mass insanity. Mass paranoia. Welcome to 2022, and you know what. I wanted to know what was on the menu. To the gossip that you would have thought about to the underlying theme of self discovery This was my world. My life. And it was being blinded, and gaslighted, by mass destruction of animals. Also known as PIGS. Coming my way. Like the animal farm. The pigs. The animals, the scum. Coming towards us, with their batons. And waving them around. Flaunting their body cameras around like they were posing for vogue magazine.

I was stuck, wanting to hang myself off the top of the fucking stadium. Just looking at the

Police. I wanted to rip their body cams off their chests. I wanted to urinate on their body cameras. I wanted to. Because I was fed up, of the lies, the deceit The corruption. And it was all coming to a farce now. The animals, have left the pig sty, and they are coming towards the working class. And everyone is feeling the heat. Because if you tell an officer a weakness. They use it against you. If you tell a bully a weakness, they will use it against you. Me? I have nothing to lose. All of my possessions, and power, and money, and everything that I could shell out 20p. After a 20p, to go to the women toilets. To buy a sanitary pad, to put over the stabbing CUT, in my arm. That some fucker stabbed me in the arm.

This was before the game. And the only option now was if I had a medical injury. To go to the vet. Because I needed my stitches taken out. Yeah some idiot stabbed me in the shoulder.

So I watch the game, and I am watching it. And I am thinking out loud.

It's all a load of bollocks. The whole thing. The whole game. It's boring. I was waiting to relax on a beach. Instead. I am feeling distressed by this whole thing. "Oh we have to kick the ball, and then run after the ball. Then kick the ball. Then talk to the ref."

Everything seemed wrong. At first, I couldn't really understand the whole perspective. The whole angle was wrong.

It ended nil nil, bad taste in your mouth. Really bad taste, just watching this game, and it's freezing, and it's depressing. And it makes me sick. It really does. But there you go. What am I going to do now?

We had entered the stadium, we had then left. With nothing but ideas, nothing but pieces of paper. Hot dog stands were hot dog stands no more. And the police officers had no clue where we were. As we walked passed them. Marko said, "you should have taken the deal, informant, immunity, now on the run for the second time you piece of shit." I said, "hey listen, this is how it's got to be." Marko said, "I busted my balls off to get you safe, I got out of jail. I made sure everything was okay. But this nice guy act. Yid army will be better without you. All you do is try this bullshit people."

Marko was high. Blood shot eyes, it's times like these I really wished he would shut his fat mouth. In relation to where I was coming from. Yeah Marko always had it covered. Always thought he was the balls. Always did, it was how it was. But this, this whole escapade. We were running wild. Marko had short man syndrome and was the shortest of all of us. Regan, was a tall and brazen. Cocky lad. Things weren't the same. Things were never the same. It was almost like the past was repeating itself. The more I tried, the more I failed. The less I tried, the more I succeeded. But this slippery slope was chaotic. I, myself, couldn't believe what was happening. This whole thing. And they say, "oh well you can't be a bootlicker". Was I fuck? I stayed away from the pigs, the vile, the filth. I stayed away from them. And this is the thanks I get. This football stadium, this whole planet. Now we are going absolutely nowhere.

Something just clicked with me, for a moment. You know. And then my brain felt fried, and everything was going around in circles. I look back now, and remember a time that was different. Bread and butter jobs. But now, it was escaping from The Police. Me and the lads, we go back to our villa in Spain. Completely untraceable. Until the Spanish authorities come knocking. But they weren't going to find us easily. Then, out of nowhere, some prostitute, decides it's in her best interests. To knock on my door in my villa, and offer her services. And this was a prostitute. I took a photo of her. I said, "not interested." And I couldn't understand the Spanish. But she was getting animated. Demanding cash, and then massaging her tits. And doing this weird pouty face. I didn't know what to do. I mean I appreciated the offer. But I just didn't want to get involved. I said, "Do you speak English?" She says, "Yeah." I said, "listen, I am not interested in your services, not one bit, now fuck off."

She said, "that's not nice, didn't your parents teach you any manners." By that time. Marko springs to the door. And shouts. "fuck off you stupid whore." By this time, she seems to get the hint. She shouts, "you could have had a good time with me." Regan springs into action and shouts, "hold on, how much?" The prostitute, she said, "$80 euros per half hour." I said, "too expensive." Eventually she leaves. And gets into this jeep. And drives off. But I had a look at the pimp. I had a look at him. And he looked suspicious. He had a balaclava and sunglasses.

Marko said, "probably a fed."

Regan said, "maybe that's true, maybe he is, but come on man. We live in this villa, staying here. We get random hookers we haven't ordered knocking on our door. Nah man, too risky."

I said, "You got the guns?"

Marko has an AK47, pistol, magnum, assault rifle, grenades, bullets running down him. Assault gloves. And a balaclava with cats on it.

I said, "Marko mate, why are their cats on your balaclava you fucking lunatic?" Marko said, "thought it might be funny." I said, "it's absurd mate, where are you stacking all of these weapons anyway?" He said, "the basement." I was shocked at this time. I didn't know we had a basement. I said, "tell me about this basement." He kicks open this floor board. And we go down these steps. Into this basement.

He has this chest of draws. He is fully kitted out, with all of the guns. The whole room is full of guns, riot shields, weapons, AK47's, the whole lot.

I said, "nice work."

Marko said, "that's why no prostitutes, because she was probably a spy?"

I said, "a spy for who?"

Marko said, "the feds."

I said, "she was a spy, for the feds, I get you. I understand."

Marko said, "We have to take this seriously, unless she's from this corrupt organised crime group. But either way. This is a shocking adventure. I mean, I like sex. But that woman. I wasn't sure if she was genuinely a prostitute."

I said, "I am going to order one."

So I go online, and I order a prostitute, and the same prostitute returns. The same one. Alicia, her name is. I said, "you are not working for the mafia,, the KGB, or the mob, no? No fed?" She said, "no." She then speaks a lot of balls in Spanish. And I said, "keep it to English, we don't speak Spanish." I hand her $80 euros. I said, "we don't want to have sex with you. Sit down, on that coach." I hand her a beer. I said, "so, who was that guy you were with the other day?" She said, "oh my brother Ricardo." I said, "he's a strange guy."

Alicia said, "how?"

I said, "don't know, just an observation. But listen, tell him, to go fuck himself. I don't want him riding his jeep around here again. This is our patch now."

Alicia said, "you are a foreigner in our country."

I said, "maybe, but I don't think you're clean. What are you selling? What's going on. Working for the feds?" Marko leaps in, getting in her face. Spanish inquisition, and it's going on and on. Asking her questions, like if she had any tattoos or any balls like that. I said, "listen, are you a sex worker by choice?" She said, "yeah." I said, "I have heard enough bullshit from you to last me a life time. You came in here. You came in here peddling this horse crap." She said, "in all fairness you ordered me." I said, "the first time, we didn't. The first time you waltzed right in here, like you owned the place."

Marko said, "this is a load of crap and you know it. *It's the same horse crap.* She's working for The Police. We know she is. This is crazy. Tell her to fuck off again."

Alicia said, "yeah I am working for the Police, you got me."

I said, "I will be damned, we can't let you go now."

With Marko pointing the gun at her, she had to confess. We tie her up. Obviously Ricardo is getting annoyed and honking his horn. Regan, walks out, and shouts. "fuck off you dickhead. We have work to do here." Ricardo shouts, "times up." Regan said, "you are pimping your own sister out, that's fucked up, you need a psychiatric ward, you fucking wrong un. You are the one who is creating the shenanigans around here."

I just didn't know anymore. Didn't know about anything. My hands were tied. My emotions were wrangled. And that was how it was. For I knew where the tide was going. And I knew where I stood in this world.

People change, times change. Things change. It's as simple as that. People become inflicted with some things or another. You know, being on the run from the police wasn't ideal. Living in the Spanish suburbs. Every morning. "Hallo, fresh fruit, banana, strawberry, oranges," And we are talking quite early, around 10am. And it's getting to me a bit, because he's using a little megaphone.

Indian man. Very nice bloke. I go out and speak to him, and I said, "alright." He said, "hi." I said, "make a lot of trade here?" He said, "I hate my job but I have to provide for my family, this is all I have, you know." I said, "okay, how much are the strawberries?" He said, "2 euros" I bought them. His name was Tania. He said, "do you want to buy anything else?" I said, "yeah freedom." He laughed and he said, "oh you been a naughty man, running from the cops." I said, "how did you know?" He said, "oh come on, don't make a urination on my intelligence, it's in the news, your face." I gripped my hand on Tania's shoulder.

I said, "but you're not going to tell anyone right?" He said, "no, I mean, but word is getting along fast." I run inside the little villa. Leaving the strawberries. I said to Marko. "Our mugshots are in the news, and all the locals know." Marko said, "let's bounce." So we got all of our gear. Got into our jeep, and were heading to Portugal. We had to get away. But what scared me is that when we show our passports, to border control to go from Spain to Portugal. The officials are going to be looking at passports closely. So I have an idea. I said. "If we go to Portugal. The problem is. Is that the authorities will recognise us." Marko said, "well there you go, but it doesn't have to work like that. I mean we can drive straight through?" I said, "we can't bulldoze our way through can we?" Marko said, "No, but we have no other choice."

We sleep in the jeep overnight, wearing ski masks. Next thing I know, it's the police, and I get a knock on the window. Two police officers. Both armed with pistols. Both broad shouldered and professional. One of them said, "can you wind down your window?" I wound down the window.

He said, "you have a broken taillight, you're parked with your lights on, your hazard lights are on. What the fuck is going on?" I said, "oh crap." I switched my hazard and beam lights off. Dimmed the lights. He said, "you know that it's an offence to have a broken taillight here in Mexico." I said, "yes sir." He said, "so are you going to get it fixed?" I said, "yes." He said, "if I see you out here again and it's not fixed. I can seize your vehicle. I am giving you a fixed penalty. Your name please senior?" I said, "David." He said, "Second name, and what is going on with the ski masks. Are you surfers?" I said, "yeah we surf, ski, all sorts, snow board." He said, "but in this jeep you look creepy with this balaclavas, you look like you have something to hide."

I said, "you want an explanation."

He said, "yeah I do man, because this is weird. I have been doing this job for 10 year. And this is the first time I see three people with ski masks. In a jeep. Not skiing. You come to our country, you play by our rules. You don't go doing this shit. It might be a funny practical joke, but we don't see the funny side."

Marko wakes up, and he whispers to me. "Practical joke, it keeps us warm."

I said to the copper who was doing all of the talking. Ricardo. I said, "Ricardo, look, now, what I am about to tell you is classified. We are undercover MI5 agents. Now we are on a secret mission now." Ricardo said, "now I know you are giving me bullshit. You think you can come to our country. And start trolling us. Give us a real answer. Swine." I said, "okay, so basically, we went for a picnic, put everything in the bin. We are heading to Mexico. We are tourists. But the ski masks. Is because we are worried about mosquitos. We just like travelling. But we couldn't find a hotel." The angry cop, turns placid. Ricardo, was no longer suspicious of us. He said, "why not say that in first place, the hotel is one kilometre down the road, I can book you in if you want." I said, "thanks, I appreciate it, but I think I am alright here." Ricardo said, "you like sleeping in your car, bro, I am not being funny, but you are safer inside a building. There are some crazy people on the run. Right now. Criminals we are trying to catch. And they are armed so watch out. So, please, let us, show you to the hotel. David."

I said, "Okay, I will drive."

I had a police escort. No siren but the lights were flashing. And he escorted me to this little hotel. An elderly Mexican man owned it. He said, "oh come on in, come on in." His name was Jose. Jose said, "come in." I said, "okay, listen lads, we are going to hit the hay, we are tired."

Ricardo, the police officer. His other guy was waiting in the car. With his head in one hand, looking tired. Ricardo said, "listen, three men are on the run, now, just stay inside, you will be safe here."

So me, Marko and Regan, We walked upstairs. To this tiny little room. And Jose was a kind man, and he said, "pay after, listen, do you want supper. I know it's late."

I said, "What's on the menu?"

Ricardo the police officer said, "alright...I will leave you guys to it. But listen, us police around here. We cannot have you sleep in car like that. I know you lads, you playing up. Behave yourselves." He smiled and he walked into his car. Said to his colleague "Right let's go."

So they drove off, still with the lights flashing, and then with a little siren that beeped for one second. Almost as a goodbye sound. Trudging through the mud, and dirt, and the dirt track. Their vehicle descended into the distance.

Whilst Jose was cooking us supper. I said to Marko. "Why didn't he give us separate rooms?" I said, "I don't know, I think it's a small hotel, and he's retired." I said, "why on gods green earth did that officer not recognise us?" Marko said, "you tricked them into believing your story mate, but next time it might be different. We obviously are not safe here." I said, "what if he knew." Marko said, "dude, if he knew we were convicts on the run. He would have arrested us." I said, "there was three of us. Two of them." Marko said, "they had guns." Regan said, "we have guns, maybe they are waiting for back up."

I said, "I doubt it."

So we go downstairs, and this Jose, Mexican, elderly gentleman. Cooks us a meal, and we eat with him on these tiny stools. And Jose said, "those officers know me very well. Very well. I have been in touch with them for many of years."

Silence, nobody responded. Not in a bad way. We were just listening to him speaking. He carried on. He said, "listen, from my point of view, and this is just my point of view. The police around here. They are very nice, but, they suspect you."

I said, "you know who I am?" Jose said, "I didn't tell them anything. Yet I think they know you're suspects. Wanted. They are waiting for back up."

He rolled up his sleeves and he said, "they are trying to lure you into a false sense of security. They know who you are. They are waiting for their armed units. If I was you. I would leave. And drive off." I said, "they'll find us." Jose said, "even better, hide underneath my floorboards." I said, "what are we going to do about the jeep."

Jose pointed and said, "I will say you left

without it." I said, "this is not plausible, besides, we need the jeep." Jose said, "give me the keys to the jeep." Jose took the keys. He drove the jeep down the road. Behind some bushes. He walked back. He said, "out of sight, out of mind, they cannot find it." He hands back the keys. He said, "now, you hide behind the floor boards." I said. "I don't want to get cramp."

Jose said, "you will get more than cramp. If they find you. Spanish police beat you, beat you." Jose makes hand gesture. He shows bruise. He said, "they did this to me. I stole a mans wallet. Ten years ago. Because he owed me money, he refused to pay me back. Next thing I know. Handcuffs. And in the cells. Beatings. The floor boards." I said, "This is absurd. Very absurd. Not sure, if I want to do this." Jose said, "then they will find you." I said, "who the fuck do you think you are, my dad!?" He said, "no but you don't want to end up in jail." I asked, "where's the floorboards?"

We go upstairs. He opens the floorboard. Me, Marko and Regan climb in. Our luggage is shoved in a draw. Next thing you know we get a knock on the door. "Policia, Policia, Policia!" Door gets slammed in. Fifty men are running in like wild animals. Jose said, "Hi."

Ricardo, who was back, the police officer. He said, "where the fuck are they!?" Jose said, "well sir, they left, they, hit the road." Ricardo shouted, "hold your fire, they're not here." Ricardo said, "I told you to keep them occupied, keep them entertained. What happened?!" Jose said, "they took off, they got paranoid, I didn't do anything wrong. I cook them a good meal. But they just took off." Ricardo said, "they just took off, you were supposed to make them feel welcome whilst I got backup." Jose said, "I tried my best, but then in the Spanish news, mugshots appeared." Ricardo said, "you shouldn't have had the news on, Jose, if I didn't know you so well. I would kick you in the balls. This is pathetic. You could have done better than that."

Jose said, "They are like wild animals, you know what I mean."

Ricardo said, "you are making so many excuses, this is not fair, stop doing it."

Jose said, "okay, but you are out of line, breaking down my door, you owe me money for that door."

Ricardo said, "I don't owe you a damn thing."

40 officers walked up the stairs. 10

remained downstairs. Ricardo said to the officers, "Search the place." My heart sank. Jose asked, "are you calling me a liar now!?" Ricardo said, "no, but we need to do our jobs, I can't trust you with them for 10 minutes."

Jose said, "so now you don't trust me, I have you around every Sunday, we have tea, and biscuits. And this is how you treat me."

Ricardo said, "you bloody fool. I can smell bullshit, coming from your anus, you are a liar. I will find them."

Lots of armed police, with riot shields, bashing the place up. Ironically looking in every place but the floorboards.

A police officer, Yuki, from upstairs, shouts. "All clear, nobody is here?"

Ricardo said, "have you searched everywhere?!"

Yuki said, "everywhere but the attic..."

Ricardo said, "well search the attic."

Yuki shouts, "this will take ages, there is probably mice in there."

Ricardo said, "search it."

So low and behold there is a search. Everywhere.

I am underneath the floorboards. This is going to take ages. Search completed, nothing was found. The police didn't even look in the cupboard where all of our Arsenal was. Ricardo said, "listen, to me, carefully." Jose said, "you owe me a new door." Ricardo said, "I owe you nothing." Ricardo does a little whistle and shouts. "Men, everyone out of here!" They all leave whilst knocking Jose over unconscious.

We were finally free, getting above the floorboards, and helping Jose to his feet was something else. I didn't know the chip shop crew would end like this. I really didn't.

I didn't know what was going on. So we got into the Jeep and we left. Jose, said "goodbye", and then we just left. Vanished, almost, you know. Wanted to go to Portugal. That was the plan. But we knew it would only be a matter of time before we bumped into Ricardo again.

Or saw one of those hookers. Or something. You know. That's how it was. My head feels like it's going to explode. I don't feel well. My energy is lacking. This is what I get. With everyone quoting Orwell, and his great escapades. It was only a matter of time, before Marko was going to reach out. Sprout a lot of far right supremacist bullshit. He said, "you know, it's all about nationalism man, not socialism or capitalism. This is how it is." I said, "mate, to be fair, I am not sure. I just want my burger and fries. Can we go to McDonalds?" Marko was driving. I said to Marko. "Look mate, we are in a foreign country, pay some respect. Don't go giving me this bullshit." Marko said, "there's a McDonalds right here." We go through the drive through.

Low and behold. The police have cordoned off the area. And Ricardo is shouting through a megaphone. "Drop your weapons."

I shouted, "we are tourists, we don't have any."

Marko said, "just gonna ram rage through them." So Marko ram raged through them. And they moved out the way quickly. He nearly ran them over. He didn't care... Next thing we know. The police, are on our back. Trail. Following us. Helicopters. You name it. It really isn't going well for us.

Marko said, "you know, this is not going well." I said, "no shit." We lost them. Out of sight. Out of mind. Parked up. All of us outside, having a smoke. Laughing. Thinking this was the end of it. I said to Marko, "I can't believe we have escaped, twice, three times now." I said, "resources are stretched, but we are the most wanted men in Europe. If not the world now. No football games to go to. Nothing. Everyone knows our faces. Everyone knows our names. We are in every newspaper, every newspaper article you can find. All across the world. Wall street journal, Washington Post." I said, "The yanks." Regan said, "yeah the yanks, that's what we are saying the yanks." I said to Regan, "what about them dickwad? You got something to say about them? Think you are being clever right now? No way. We can't do this anymore. You freckle faced prick."

Regan said, "it's a sun tan, what the fuck do you expect?"

I said, "no idea, still running from the police, this isn't a good idea." Regan said, "it's the only people to run from, you know."

I said, "listen, these pigs in Spain are different. We have work to do. You don't want to jeopardise that."

I don't know what to say really. It's almost like some times. Time stood still. Being on the run from the Police for so long. It's going to take it's toll. And that's what I was thinking all along. But there you go.

It was supposed to be about the game. But it wasn't the same. Not anymore. I got in the car, and started driving to Portugal, and just sped passed border control. Didn't bother waiting. And the police weren't chasing me. The Jeep was going 200 miles per hour. And then all of a sudden. We were in Portugal. And still armed to the teeth.

Surprised we hadn't been caught yet. Portugal, were playing Spain. Friendly. So we rent out an apartment, and after some hair dye. And some hats and shit. We buy tickets, and get in. That's after nicking all the burgers. Now we are in the stand. And C.Ronaldo is playing. I am shouting. "Yo, Yo, Cristiano Ronaldo, my man. This is what we are talking about." Marko said, "shut up dude." I said, "no, you go fuck a donkey, you are the one who should shut up, you idiot." Marko said, "no, you fuck a donkey." Regan said, "piggies on patrol." And that was the end of it.

But they were patrolling, there was no end to it. You know what I am saying. I am still becoming the geezer in the stand. Shouting, "YID ARMY." Marko shouts, "we are in Portugal, you shout something in Portuguese man..."

I said, "shut up Marko, go piss up a lamp

post, this is the problem with you. You are always trying to make things look confusing. Well go fuck a hooker with STD's, I don't want anything to do with you, you twat." Marko said, "you shit head, you want to make this personal." Me and Marko are scrapping, and scrapping. And that's what's going on you know.

This is what I am saying, and with some regards to how things are going right now. The same things you rely on from time to time. It just doesn't make sense anymore.

It doesn't make sense and this is where we are going from here you know. Marko can go fuck himself, he is trying to be the big man here. Cock and balls to the whole thing you know. That's how it feels right now. Just trying to make ends meet, and this is the reception I get? It's absurd, but I carry on. Just trying my best to understand what's going on in this world. And then go further down that road. But watching Portugal, in the freezing cold. That was something I was going to say. You know. Something, I wanted to look at. Time and time again. Regan, with his balls hanging out, and nobody notices. Until a steward walks towards him, as he hides underneath a sea of red. As the stewards clash into themselves. It wasn't supposed to be like this. It was supposed to be different. There were supposed to be hookers. It was different. Especially from my point of view. Portugal brought us a completely different perspective. And it was a perspective, that was hard to swallow. Because we were away from home. But that is just how it was some times.

Then some times, just to believe in something. And talking was off the cards. I couldn't phone the samaritans. Since I was in Portugal for fuck sake. That's the truth of the matter. So watching the game. And it was complete and utter shite, and I was not enjoying it. Yid Army just was not the same. Just not the same now we are watching this. Some obese man, runs into the pitch, with "fuck off" spray painted on his chest. Wrestled to the ground by two stewards. Even that wasn't going to stop him. Barging into the goal posts, and shouting things. This guy was so fat, and I had to look the other way. Whilst they had to get the fire brigade. As someone threw fire into him, and lit him alight.

I mean watching this nil nil game was depressing, nobody was scoring. At the end of the game, that's when the fighting started. That's when the fighting happened. But that was it, you know. The scrapping. Like a scrap yard. Fists flying everywhere. It was brilliant. Marko sniffs some coke and shouts, "COME ON THEN." And 40 men charge into him, whilst he's kicking the shit into all of them. That's what's fucking happening. Nobody knows how there bread is buttered. This was the state of the world. Kicking the shit into people was always my turn around to make some promises around here. Out of Viagra. And Regan taking a piss up on a lamp post.

Oh everyone knows how their bread is

buttered don't they, the cunts. That's the bottom line. Get them in, get some energy going. Start something, and move something. This was my world we were living in. my world right now, anyone who disagreed with me. I'd hang them. That was what it was like with skinheads, hated everything. Everything. Talking, walking, running, ballet? fuck that. Dancing. fuck off. It was the same ritual day in and day out. Watching people piss up lamp posts. They sure know how there bread is buttered don't they.

Whilst I am just walking along here. Just trying to make sense of the world. Eh? Yeah, make sense of the world. That was the ticket. If anyone wanted to talk to me, and say where I was going. I'd fucking tell them. fucking tell them. It was the ticket. It was the skinhead crew. We were back. Glad Totsworth was dead. Fucking bellend. I didn't like the bloke. Nobody did, this is the price we have to pay. This is the price everyone has to pay. Oh yeah he's too this, he's too that. He's too sharp. He's too soft. He's soft as shit. Then he's dead, and all what happened with pale ale. The cunt. Glad he was dead. Otherwise I would have kept knocking him about. This was bandit world we were living in. *This was bandit world.*

That was what everyone was saying. Everyone was doing. That was how we felt. On a daily basis. That's how things were going. And if you had any sight, or any ambition. Or if you knew anything you would know. The world I am living in. Of course. With my day just getting shit. What else is there to do. Cross dressers outside. Lots of them. Portugal, that's what it was. The land of opportunities. Wasn't the end of the road for us. We had already been to Spain lots of times. The piggies, we give them the run around. That's how it is. Bandit country feller. That is the ticket, and anyone who wants to moan and groan and say. "Oh this is shit, and this is the bollocks we have been handed to, because the cock and bollocks we have been handed. Was too fucking much. They can accept. That's how it is. That's what it feels like. That's the ticket. That's how I feel. And that is the way it's going. The way everything goes. It just makes perfect sense. I just wanted everything to be okay you know. I didn't need liability insurance. The jeep was fine. Besides the time I crashed it into the lamp post. Then I get Jon Bon Jovi's voice in my head. "AH WE'RE HALF WAY THERE, WAH LIVING ON A PRAYER." I was so shocked. I walked outside. Slammed the door shut. And phoned up for a prostitute. By the time she had arrived. I had chucked her in the river. The daft twat.

Next thing. We know Marko rapping. He says, "listen, out on patrol, out on parole, out in jail, and in the same place. Listen, what we want to say. Watching people hustling. I am listening to Tupac. I am trying to say. Never had a friend like me." I said, "listen fuck this, I tried my best, but nothing changed. We tried to be happy. But we put ski masks, nobody wanted to see the soggy chips. And then left without a nation. Then trying to find the world a better day. Chippy chips, but we had to fight for this. Smoking the same things. This was the way. I wanted to explain."

Regan said, "you two, shut up, we have to scrap. We have to do something fellers, stop fucking around." I said, "nobody cries no more." Regan said, "then you wanted to know, and left your whole life, and left with life, and tried my best. And left."

The war on the streets, was getting tough. This was how it was. Things went weird you know. Like nothing made sense any more, and I couldn't even quantify it. Or make sense of it. I didn't mind if peoplelooked at me, all of those repressed emotions through the years. All of the time. I bottled it, held it in, and for what reason or other. Just for nothing. I had clearance, the pilot had ground control. I had flying permission, but the wings weren't working. My head was in this loop, going around and around in circles. And as soon as I could think of something productive. I forget, and it goes back to this cycle again. I lost everyone who I ever loved, and even then still trying to kill myself. Because every day is a struggle. And I know in the past. You like to think it's all worthwhile, and it's all great. Yet deep down inside, you can't even think straight. And it was all fun and games, and maybe there was some maturity. Yet I didn't know what to say anymore. I really didn't. I look at the world now. I look at the world, and look at how life is. Life is just as simple as how we feel. What we conduct. Always waiting around. Waiting around for something. For what ever you want to just return. For some kind of things to fall into place. I wanted the Yid Army to succeed but it was falling to shit. Especially now. And the more I thought about myself, the more I thought there was only one way around. One hope, one dream you know. Like everyone faulted it. Like I projected how I felt on others. My minds in a mess. And we can't even talk about it. It's 1984, knocking on our door, knocking on our door. Time and time again. Like an emotionless reaper, just going to grab you and drag you through the mud. The irony was. Was that I was kind of stunned. I looked over at life differently. All of the people who I looked up to, and thought wisely of. And then I get into a position where I shot Lee.

Then there's a crisis. As far as I was concerned. In this perpetual battle of De Ja Vu, this perpetual sense of tunnel vision. Nightmare after nightmare. Apocalypse after Apocalypse Shadow after dark memory. The bone crunching reality was it was the corporations who ran the world. It wasn't the people. Trying to make their own means of production. As far as I know, we knew what valid investment we could make out of this. For what I knew. I knew how my mind was. I couldn't trust myself. How could other people?

It's a kind of senseless vision that you get. When you realise. Life is screwing you, life is a spiteful, vindictive bitch. And it will screw you, and slap you. And that was what was happening. Yet I seemed kind of vacant. Almost like I didn't know what was going to happen next. The story of keeping areas sterile, keeping places clean. Only talking about reality. The popping noise of your knuckles after you hit someone in the face. The clenching sound of your jaw. The look of regret on your face. The people you have met. Oh yeah long time ago felt it was for a reason. It isn't like that.

You meet some dickheads, and you meet some people who you want to punch in the nose. Yet again, you wanted to know what was happening. Nobody was really focused. I wasn't. And it took too long, for us to see where life was going. In this world. For us to see where our life was going. No wander relationships fall like bridges. But that's the point of the matter. I am done with just feeling like life had some motive. Some second chance. Or some kind of reflective way. Life was stuck. There was no opportunity to look the other way whilst someone stabbed someone to death. There was no option to look the other way whilst someone would come up to you. Bloodshot eyed, and kind of helpless. Not knowing where to turn or who to turn to.

You had to be almost reluctant to describe. The way things were going. The way I was feeling. Or maybe how life was. It was a constant battle. Yet running from the police meant something to me. I mean sure, it had to. Yet the same kinds of "means of escape" or the same way of trying to find a fight. Find a scrap, and get stuck in. That's all people wanted to do. Nobody wanted to listen to conspiracy theories, or how many times the town whore. Has been penetrated. Nobody gave a shit about that. It was old news. We didn't want to see the bravado of the town cop. Soliciting the local hookers on the estate.

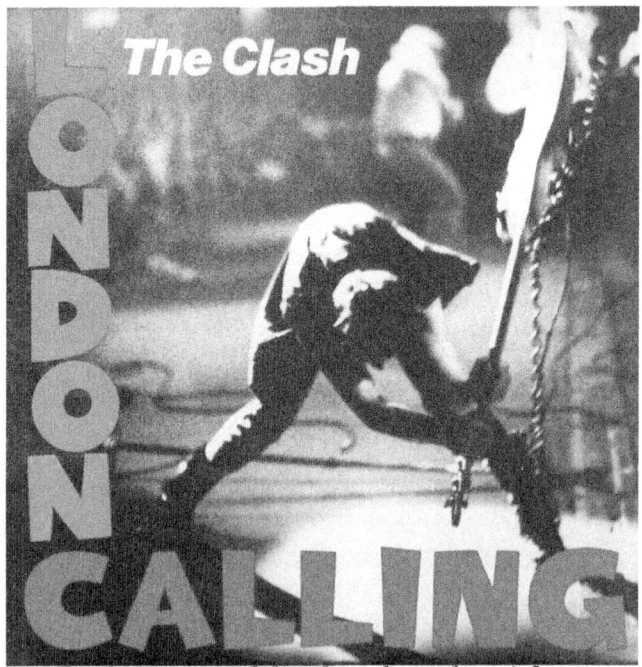

Or the sense of divide, where he nicks your wallet. Your keys. You become divided. Yet everyone did. And some people appealed to this socialist norm of society. Where everyone wanted to get on their knees. And worship Karl Marx. As if that would do any good. Or maybe it would. I don't know. Yet the means of production, and the way things were populated were changing. We were living in a hotel. The Jeep was outside. And I wasn't trying to be all deep and meaningful. Because the local prostitute outside, kept hitting our door. Tapping our door. And Regan, got a frying pan and hit her around the head.

"Good shot." Regan said, "she was doing my head in." I said, "now you're doing my head in, just sit down you clown. What do you think you are doing? Giving me lip. Giving me some lip?!" There was always arguments with us. Arguments galore. Yet that is how it was. The more I thought about it. The more I realised. Yeah, some people could be misguided. Some people could. But that was how we felt. How I felt. How the whole thing was.

With your back against the wall, there was only so much you could do. Only so much you could say.

I didn't know what to think anymore. I didn't know what to say. I look back at my formative years. As if they meant something to me. I look at the positive moments, the negative moments. And I realise that life just doesn't blend in for me. Square peg, round hole. I was watching the football. Which ended nil nil. Yet all of this aside. All of the emotions you wanted to express. Pretend who you weren't. Going about your day. Just made complete sense. For what it was worth. I was at war with this broken society, you know. That's what it was. It wasn't anything else. As much as I would love to get back to my feet again.

As much as I would love to find some kind of closure. It just doesn't get there in time. That's the problem.

So you think to yourself, besides the times you were left behind, forgotten. Looked the wrong way. Knife in pocket. Trousers hanging below the bollocks. In this chaotic world with all of these political opinions dividing people. With sickness. With a great sick mind I have. Yeah like I am supposed to feel better. I am supposed to live. With this crew. Like this crew meant something to me. And I know I brag about all of the fights we had. Man it was bullshit. *That's all it was.* All I wanted to do was to build this empire, this firm. Then you get the police chasing you. Then you realise, it was a shit way of living.

You get confused, and you get side tracked. You find out that life is just out to fuck you. Like a huge dildo, just waiting to fuck everyone. Like a huge strap on dildo. Waiting fuck everyone. That was how life was. And for better or for worse. I couldn't think straight. Not now, not in other times. I just grew to hate people. And it was my own fault. Because something goes wrong. People make assumptions. People have fucked up their lives, and I messed up shooting Lee.

The pathetic stupid fucker. But it made sense if you think about it long and hard enough. He meant nothing, and then you get the riots and protests. And people claiming he had a soul. Fuck his soul. That is what I am saying right now. And all of this bollocks. Is just pertaining to factors we weren't even aware of. All of the time. If you even wanted to understand. Left in the open, just waiting. Waiting for anything. Then that's how life is. Just waiting, for something you know. Meanwhile. In the villa in Portugal. Me, Marko, and Regan were going to have the biggest row known to mankind. It all kicked off. With me. I was all suited up. Drunk, just come back from the pub. Found out Regan had been doing Jacky up the arse for two years. Without my knowledge.

I shouted, "Reegan!" Regan said, "what?!" I said, "What the fuck is going on, I just had a call from Jacky. Saying you two have slept together. Now is this true." Regan didn't say anything and looked guilty. That's all I needed. I said, "you sure know how your bread is buttered don't you. She's my wife. Now you've ruined it. Fuck sake.

You've ruined my life Regan. Fuckinghell. Soppy bollocks. You've ruined me. Where have you been? For the last week?" Regan said, "same place as I always am man." I said, "for the last two months. Where have you been eh?" Regan said, "we all hang out at the same place mate. The same bars. You just decided not to go mate. You became a recluse." I said, "yeah, I came a recluse. Guess the jokes on me then is it. You wet wipe. Where have you been?" Marko said, "hang on let's not argue." I started shoving Regan, and said, "get out my villa now, you soppy sack of shit. Get out!" Regan said, "I can explain."

I said, "Go on. Go and explain." I was smashing the wall. I turned to him and I said, "explain why you have been doing my Jacky, you were supposed to be my friend, where's that trust gone now eh? You've fucking ruined the trust. *You've ruined it.* Ruined everything mate. You've ruined my life. What the fuck am I going to do now? Because of you, you sick cunt." Marko shouted, "lads enough." Me and Regan, start scrapping. I throw the first punch, he dodges. I punch him in the stomach. He moves. He hits me in the cheek. As I tackle him to the floor."

Regan said, "Jacky said she didn't love you, what was I supposed to do." I said, "nah, you've been doing her in all three orifices you sick bastard. You sick lying bastard." Regan said, "four orifices, her ear." I said, "Her ear, what is wrong with you, you sick bastard?" I shouted, "sit down you fucking cunt, now listen to me carefully. I know me and Jacky had our differences. But you been creaming all over her face. All over her mouth. You've been in her nick nacks In her pants. Doing her up from behind. Kissing her arse cheeks. Whilst they wobble against the pub pool table. You snake. You're the fucking snake in the grass. You're a f*cling snake in the grass. It was you. And so what, people don't like me swearing. But it's the truth isn't it. It's the truth. You know how your bread is buttered. We were supposed to be friends." Regan was crying. I was crying. Regan said, "we are friends." I said, "nah mate, you've ruined it, you've fucking ruined it mate. fuck you. I don't need you in my life anymore.

You ruined everything you cunt. What am I going to do now!?.." What am I going to do now. Eh? You fucking ruined everything you prick. Yeah you have been doing her from behind. On the snooker table. Up her nicknacks Snorting cocaine from her arse cheeks. No wander I saw you at the STD clinic. Praying, hoping, praying, she didn't give you something. You worried mate. She's got Chlamydia."

159

Regan said, "what!?" I said, "yeah you heard me, you twat. Why do you think I haven't been sleeping with her for the last two years. You wore a condom did you?" Regan said, "nah mate, people were stock piling them at the shop." I said, "couldn't have just used a sock. For fuck sake, or maybe some cling film. But nah. You had to get up close and personal." Regan was sweating like a pothead on pot and crack. (For the record she didn't have Chlamydia. I just said that for revenge. So he would freak out.) Regan said, "she hasn't got Chlamydia, you are just saying that so I am going to freak out." I said, "fuck, you can tell that I am lying. I trusted you mate. How can I fucking tell. I wanted to have a baby with her." Regan said, "you still can." I said, "fuck, no I can't, how can I trust her." I kept pushing Regan I said, "you fucking snake in the grass, we've come all this way, and you tried to get your sausage up her nicknacks You fucking wrongun mate. You snake in the grass. You cunt. And listen. Nobody wants anything to do with you. Go on, get the fuck out of the house. Get the fuck out. Go on. Get the fuck out." Regan is crying and leaves, refusing to fight me. I said, "get the fuck out mate."

Marko said, "it's cold outside." I said, "it's quite humid, fuck off." Marko said, "hey don't kick him out." I said to Marko, "Did you have any idea this was happening did ya? Did you? Have any idea this was happening?" Marko said, "no." I said, "I bet you did man, be honest with me. You are a fucking snake in the grass. I bet you knew." Marko was crying. "I didn't fucking know mate. I didn't know whatsoever boss. Trust me." I said, "how can I trust you anymore, you broke my life." Marko said, "I didn't shag Jacky though did I?" I said, "nah but you thought about it didn't ya? You fucking thought about it. In your sick and twisted head. Didn't you. You cunt. Fuck mate. You fucking thought about it, didn't you. You fucker. Eh? You are a snake. Just like Regan" Marko said, "I didn't know anything about it boss."

Meanwhile a call from Jacky, and it's my phone. I wasn't going to answer it. I didn't want to. Just wanted to feel some kind of connection. Mind you, she has shown me. She is not faithful. You know. That is what is going on. I used to feel okay. Not anymore. Kind of blurry in my head. Nowhere near where to start. It's almost like what I do doesn't make that much of a difference. It kind of just feels okay.

You build up things in your head, and expect people to be alright with you. Yet deep down, that seething anger, and hostility. Only had one way out. You were either going to fight it, or it was going to win. Besides, everything I had ever known had been a farce. Sure Jacky was nice, but she wasn't someone who could understand all of the time. Regan was a fucking snake in the grass. You could see it, in his pale face. We were like brothers. I was just waiting for the blemishes of shame to wash all over him. But there was nothing. You wait all day for a response time. A response from The Police. Yet you just find it difficult. In some respects. There has to be some kind of way to feel that you have answers. You have ways to understand what happens. We are on the run from the cops, meanwhile. Regan, he is just slipping his sausage into Jacky's birth canal. You know and part of me was feeling okay about it now.

Kind of glad it had happened. Almost like I was getting the idea. That for better or for worse. There was something between them. She was nothing but a stop gap for me. Just someone to fill the time anyway. With all of these endless nightmares. Thinking you could get somewhere. It would be without guilt. You would understand in every shameless face. You had your way with the world. You had your fling with the world and that was it. It wasn't about the universe, or how many stars were in the fucking galaxy. It wasn't about that at all. It was just about knowing. That through bitter, or better ways moving forward. You would change. Become better. But then it all made perfect sense this was karma for what happened to Lee. At the game, so blurry I had pushed it out of my brain. Millwall fan. All I can remember is pressing that trigger. The bullet going into his head.

I remember people around me, and people thinking this was okay. Yet deep down I wasn't sure you know. I wasn't sure what people felt. It just came as a surprise for me. This world would swallow me whole. Then nothing else would happen. You would forget the narrative of people 'looking out for you'. Caring about who you were. Or maybe it was too late for that. It became something of the past. Knowingly and obviously seeing the results. Of a blurry past. Time and time again. But for one thing in my mind. I just couldn't let go.

Let go of things trying to make sense. Make sense of life, or make sense that time would become transparent. I never knew. The more I thought about it. I could never tell. It was just brought to me as something I could even reason with.

Knowing that snake Reegan. Had put his sausage into Jacky's birth canal. The slimy son of a bitch. I said to him, "you sure know how to play this, don't you, you psycho." By this time Regan was outside sobbing and crying. Marko acting like the usual cunt he always is. He said, "Cut him some slack." I said, "are you being serious?"

I wanted to punch Marko, hell, I wanted to punch him so hard. Make him feel the hurt that I felt. Make him feel the emotions that I was feeling. But it just wasn't the same. I just wasn't the same. And it carries on like that.

You know, part of me just wishes life was different. Different in some respects. Different in others. Maybe I was not cut out for this world. And maybe that's how life was. Yet you would clench your jaw and hold onto fear like it was the last thing that ever caught your attention. The only way you could stop, turn yourself in. Blood shot eyes, and a chance of making it. In this world. With so many worlds apart was nigh on impossible. Maybe Orwell was a pessimist Maybe there is freedom of thought. Maybe he was wrong.

You talk all day and all night, you live by the streams and by the wayside. You yearn for approval but you are damaged by affection.

The same people who love you can hinder you. Your paws are engrained in something bigger than what you know. And you have the chance to have a happy life. Then you get drawn into the wrong people, the people who always like to believe you had a chance. The Chip Shop Crew was never a thing. We never invented it. The Yid Army, did. It was the casual relationship we had, with burning bridges with our peers. And that was the context of my struggle. Yet, maybe Orwell was right. Maybe there is a thought policing system. No wander, I was in the nick. Every time I called a cop a wanker. I mean, it's just a word isn't it. Then I get cops, saying, "oh he's nice one minute, nasty the next, it's confusing." Man, listen, I never meant to cause them confusion. I never did. It's who I am. You know. I caused them a lot of things. But some times, just some times. It was almost like Townsend was the only one in charge. The only one going about his day. Harassing the youths, and he did every day. Man, I don't know who took his place. Probably some overzealous feminist, with a huge gut, and a tattoo of a spider on her neck. (Diversity right). Or could it be something completely different. You got into a state of perpetual boredom at other people's stupidity. People making the same mistakes. People making the same things worse. Wrong. Not good.

    I was stuck just feeling like a huge orange tic tac. No, a green tic tac. I felt so small. You know. People took my hard work, and credited themselves. I was the result of the Yid Army. I made them. And I sure made the Chip Shop Crew, but I am ashamed of what it's become. The Yid Army need our backing and instead of joining them. We run away from the very people trying to "protect" us. That's not freedom. Living free, and thinking like this. Or what ever narrative you want. It was a deep way of believing. A chain of events, nobody talked. You wandered around in your mind, like you had been lobotomised. You ran into problems along the way. You nicked things from the off licence, you nicked things from the store. You put "fuck off" graffiti on the wall. You drove passed every one, and looked sordidly into people's woeful eyes like they owed you something. You soon learnt out that they didn't. Winds up the wrong way when I am just scratching my neck. My past mistakes are coming to haunt me. Karma was coming back to bite me in the arse cheeks.

    You just feel alienated from the world. Man I tried. I tried to build this firm like a religion. Build it up and make sure we had enough skinheads. The union jack flag and make sure. We had skinheads. Shouting in the pub. "YESSSS!!!!"" Every time, big Paul. Stood up, with his huge belly hanging out. Paul Southern Ex army, into his table tennis. Used to say, "England means sticking this flag in the ground, stop trying to pigeonhole us. Stop trying to say we are not realists. That's the thing. Stop saying that shit." He used to say, the band of brothers. He used to cry for

England to win. He never wanted to fight. He was a gentle giant. He always had a heart of gold and kept reminding me of this. He almost set me apart from the rest.

It was my responsibility to pick up the pieces. Every now and then I look back and just wander where life was taking me. Around journey's and around things where people could be free. Be adjourned from all of the chaos in the world and have their own sense of reality. I forgave Regan, but I couldn't trust him anymore. I walked passed him as he was crying on the steps, and went towards the river bank, right towards the sea. Just used to think clearly. There was no internet. We were stuck, running away from The Police.

You know, a lot of people said organised crime syndicates were behind a lot of things. And maybe they are. But you look at The Police.

You look at The Police, and you don't want to disturb them. You don't want to go near them sometimes. Because they put the fear of god into us. I mean we are only human after all. But the glowing sense of achievement, in The Chip Shop Crew. And our amazing adventures, just getting used to life. Just keeps throwing us shrapnel. This wasn't the intentions. I just had a reluctance to believe it.

I felt insincere in my promise, and lacking in my resolve. Of course it was me who was knowing how we could find. Just anything. But the Chip Shop Crew. Had fallen to pieces. I mean, they were still operating without us. But

I had my little stereo, and I was listening to The Smiths. "*If you're so funny, why are you on your own tonight? If you are so clever. Then why do you sleep alone tonight? If you are so good looking. Then why are you alone tonight? It's so easy to laugh, easy to hate. It takes guts to be gentle and kind. Mother, I can feel the soil falling over my head.*" And I could. I could feel that soil.

As the radio was playing. And I just felt stuck. Then I realised. This old tuned radio, with built in songs, and life was on the rocks. Full of composure I had found my feet. I had fully and successfully evaded The Police. But just for once. *Just for once*. And that was next. Like I wanted to know how I endured my own life. My own time.

Yeah, Regan can have Jacky. He can have her. Not my problem. Because I couldn't really know. Surprised she was still working at the chip shop. With all of our mugs in the news. Turns out the punters just found it funny, and the custom hadn't been the same. Then some Coldplay song plays on the radio, and you know you are in shit creek. As you start listening to this song. "*Oh, you are beautiful you are, the stars shine for you. Oh look how bright they shine.*" At this point, I want to put a bullet in my brain. This is why you can't trust people. They listen to Coldplay and they vote for people like Tony Blair to run Britain.

The Coldplay song had ended. I wanted to know why this broken radio was playing Coldplay. I shook it up. Then I get Shakira.

"Oh hips don't lie, oh take me to the mountains." And all that bollocks. By the time I could hear that. I was in the river feeling like I wanted to drown myself. I shouted, "fuck!" Pigeons just crept away. People stopped and looked. You could see tumble weed.

I was a wanted man, and next thing I know. Ricardo was on the boat. He crossed the border, he doesn't give a toss. He shouted, "hey surrender." I said, "you are out of your jurisdiction, Spanish politician You cannot do anything on this land. I am in Portugal." But he was on this vigilante witch hunt, and he was tracking me down. Pretending he was the FBI or some shit. So there you go. And for all I know I could have punched him in the groin. And felt no emotion.

He snorts a line of cocaine. And he comes running towards me on this boat. He said, "You are under arrest," He places the handcuffs around on my wrists. He takes me to jail. I am in this jail, alone, in isolation. This big female cop, hands me a coffee. So I start drinking, and this is when it gets eary. No more lights, no more sounds.

You just think you are alone. You had all of the people in the world trying to praise you. Encouraging you to do the right thing. Be your own person. Speak by the same narrative. But you left, and were poisoned. By the same things you wanted to feel in the first place. The four letter word of love had been demolished. My dreams had been crushed. And my life had been destroyed. Regan sleeping with my Mrs, and now in the slammers.

The female cop, is quite persistent, banging on the door. Massive cop. She opens it. She shouts. "You are being extradited back to the UK tomorrow. Sign these papers for this to happen please." So I signed. Next day. I was on a plane. Back to the UK. Armed UK officers waiting for me at the gate. I was handcuffed to an armed guard as we walked out. As soon as I had set my foot off the plane. And walked one inch towards the thing that connects the plane to the building. Armed police came in shouting. "Armed Police, lie on the ground!." Obviously I am still handcuffed to this Spanish guard. So I knock him in the head. And we both fall to the ground. 40 laser dots on me. Armed snipers. The plane in lockdown. Passengers refusing to leave. I was put in a straight jacket. On arrivals. But even then. I then slipped into a semi induced coma. I was sleep deprived, and started to swell up. I kept resisting. The hand cuffs hurt so much, they had to bring a wheelchair out for me to sit in. So I was sat in this wheelchair. With my face bloodied, making a a psychopath, look fairly altruistic. I was the true ingenious form of person myself. The deadly sense of urgency. The sense of. "fuck, what am I going to do now?" I am taken to Tottenham police station. And interviewed by CID. Armed police men at the door. Detective Johnson, DC. Detective Rose. Female DS. Rose said, "you plead insanity on this one and we are throwing the book at you." Then my solicitor walks in, and he's a lanky guy. He takes wild shits in the toilets. That bung the toilets up for months, and they have to get severn Trent out. He leans in and starts yelling. "This is a miscarriage of justice. My client is innocent." DS Rose said, "oh really, then explain all of these things he's been doing." His name is Paul. The lawyer. Paul Smith. Paul said, "he's insane, he needs treatment. Not this." DS Rose said, "isn't that up to the judge? What are you, some left wing, terrorist sympathiser? Get the fuck out of here." I laughed and I said, "how the fuck am I a terrorist?" DS Rose said, "I don't know." Paul Smith said, "Does Steve Smith have a religion?" Rose said, "no". Paul Smith said, "then how the fuck is it terrorism? Terrorism is doing an act of violence for a religion."

DS Rose said, "what is your religion then?" Looking directly at me. I said, "I don't know. Don't care either, just throw the book at me." DS Rose said, "I said, you're a terrorist sympathiser, not a terrorist. That's what I was saying, you are soft as shit. I saw your post on reddit."

Paul Smith said, "and then what? This is going nowhere." DS Rose said, "you troll reddit." I said, "I don't go anywhere near it. Get the sand out of your vagina." DS Rose said, "there is no sand." I said, "then why are you so moody then? Your husband not giving you enough action. The prostitution business in the ground!?" DS Rose looked shocked. Next thing you know. Sargent Bernard bursts through the door. He shouts, "This is a miscarriage of justice." He then says, "oh no wait, I am on the police's side." He then says, "You fucking lunatic, I knew it was you all along. You stupid feral little cunt. I am going to lock you up and throw away the key. I am going to carve cock and bollocks into your chest. And tattoo my ballsack on your head. You unworthy, delightful mess. You lunatic. You hideous creature. How can you come in here. All starry eyed like auditioning for the X Factor. And then all of a sudden, appear like your arse fell out. Because it did, and it will continue to. Your loss, your loss all along. There was a price to pay, and that price was simple. You pay it."

I said, "Sargent Bernard, you are amusing and funny but this aggression won't be tolerated." DS Rose said, "Steve Smith, we are going to be charging you." I said, "have you heard the Beetles?" DS Rose said, "yeah, why?" I said, "you heard of the famous painting. Of them. Four of them. Well. You know that fan. He went crazy. Took too much of a liking.." DS Rose, "why are you telling me all of this?" I said, "Because I have heard about you, you are all over the news. Man I had to do some digging." She said, "what has this got to do with the Beetles?!" I said, "Oh sorry, I saw you, and I was thinking of the Beetles, and the same thing came into the sentence." DS Rose said, "you know what, yeah, I am in the news." I said, "yes you are in the news, you crazy bitch, you gave a blow job, to a taxi driver. Whilst on duty. And nothing happened. Your name was cleared. Why?" DS Rose said, "lack of evidence." I said, "why's it all over the news then?" DS Rose said, "don't know, where do you get all of these conspiracy theories. What's your source?" I said, "I saw you on Fake Taxi." DS Rose said, "shut up, and for what it's worth. I did indeed suck off that taxi driver." Sargent Bernard said, "right, that's it, I am off to officially commit suicide. Where's the gun?"

DS Rose said, "in the chest of drawers." You heard a loud bang, and a body drop to the floor. I said to Rose. "That's one way to cut resources, what the fuck is the matter with you?" My solicitor Paul. Smith, or what ever the fuck his name was. He shouts. "Enough of this nonsense." He is yelling, and getting animated. And for once in my life. I don't give a shit. I said, "look mate, in all fairness, just go outside, get some fresh air."

Paul Smith, said, "Fresh air, this is what you call this nonsense. For fuck sake. DS Rose, if this taxi driver thing is true. I have to report you."

I said, "it's true, it's in the news."

DC Johnson, male, said, "right, let's get back to the interview, for fuck sake. Steve Smith, you killed Lee, didn't you. You crazy fucker" I said, "yeah, it was me." DC Johnson said, "right, this interview is about to finish in a minute. Sargent Bernard will charge you at the desk. Unless you want to make up some excuse."

I said, "insanity." DC Johnson said, "what kind of illness?" I said, "I don't fucking know, must be something wrong with me. If I was going to do all this shit. You throwing the book at me?" DC Johnson said, "don't know, you personally haven't insulted me. But you are facing some serious charges. Murder, aiding and abetting fugitives. Kidnap Arson, theft. Looting. The list goes on." I said. "I bet your wife goes on your cock." DC Johnson said, "right, I will throw the book at you now." Right at the desk. Whilst Sargent Bernard is charging me. DC Johnson throws this giant red book at me. Think it was either a bible or a harry potter book. Not sure which one. Couldn't be arsed to read it. Sargent Bernard said, "Steve Smith. I am charging you with murder, aiding and abetting fugitives, possession of a firearm, kidnap, possession of class A drugs, with intent to supply." This really pissed me off. I said, "I wasn't supplying any cocaine." Sargent Thompson said, "Regan gave you a tenner for some coke, that makes you a drug dealer." I said, "no the tenner was to snort the coke. I am not a drug dealer." Sargent Thompson said, "well you sure are something." He looks me up and down. And he lets out this huge fart. That sounds like it's come from Satan's bum hole. I am thinking, "fuck my life. Seriously had enough of this."

DC Rose said to Sargent Bernard. "Oh you came back to life easily?" Sargent Bernard said, "fuck off, go back to your fake taxi, you whore."

My eyes were blurry, this wasn't going to be the same. You know. You had to see it from how I could believe. Then this society. This world, it was how could you believe in this. Then, all the way to court. The judge can suck my ballsack. Wait, wasn't Sargent Bernard dead. Then he just came back to life. I was transported into this prison riot van. And I was taken to a prison remand cell. In HMP. I didn't know what to do anymore. I didn't know what to say. Everything was a blur. A dream almost. I didn't want to get caught up in this. *I didn't want to get caught up in this whatsoever.* My mind kept going over and over. Just wandering what would happen next. In a world of dreams, you can only be yourself. Then you know how life is going for you. Yet some times or not. I don't know. I just feel some kind of energy, it's missing. Yeah sure Pale Aske I get it. Lee, he was shot dead. But what next. What next in this world.

We live in an unpredictable world, and it sucks. But that's how it is. I would be lying if I said I was happy. Far from it. Not happy at all. Not with this arrangement Hell no. And I am stood her just guessing, just wandering. Of what I have become. All of those years have come back with nothing. Not a word, not a sign. And it's time for me to stand up and be my own man, and this happens. It's a damn travesty, it's f*cling annoying.

You always look at the worst case scenario in life. You always do. You always look at the worst case scenario. Things improving. Things getting better. Things getting worse. It goes on like a broken record. I mean, half the time I didn't even trust myself. But then again, being on remand until a court date. Gave me lots of time to think. Yeah it was HMP Belmarsh. f*cling travesty of a place. No McDonald food, and I was locked in isolated. And the silence of the room was digging into my skull. It was sickening. It was destroying. If you are mentally strong, and you go to jail. It tries to make you weak. You know. "Stay on the straight and narrow." That's what they always used to say to me. And it was right all along. But things changed. And nothing stayed the same. Walking in shadows. Or what ever the Yid army meant. The whole thing had become ignored, forgotten, left. To rot. Whilst I was sat just wishing, hoping, that I would be somewhere. Yeah and the court date coming up. Won't that be a treat...Whilst I don't even know what is happening with Marko and Regan No idea what, you know. No idea. Some things change. You get well, you get better. People die. You become stuck, you become unstuck.

Life goes on. Life hides. You end up alone, you end up better. You end up with people. It just goes on and on like that. To the point of not really knowing what else to say. Life was at breaking point. I was at breaking point. My life was stuck, with so many things just washing away. Without really knowing who I was anymore. The people that you held onto, they became lost. So what if I called the

Police "piggy". Made them laugh from time to time. This was my vacation. This was the crew. Everyone tried to get into the chip shop crew. That was my invention. Stuck in this prison, and just wandering when the next earthquake of disappointment was going to thunder down my chest. Oh no wait, it's already happened. So with everything that happens. Forget the wise talk, the long hours, the long drives. The wandering of where life is. Forget that. Because that's not important anymore. All is important is your own mind. What you can do, and how you can do it. I sure knew how to do that. With my life just crumbling before my eyes. You just have to wander why sometimes. That was the whole story of what was going on. The list goes on. The story goes on and it's never old. It never is.

Turns out Regan and Marko were still in Portugal. They were being extradited by all means. Yet I was the main focus. It was clear I was going down for a long time. Shame I hadn't packed my suitcase. Everyone else knew exactly what was happening. I mean, that was the whole point of this. To feel like I had a chance in this world. Now that chance had gone. It had been evaporated, and taken the smoke away with it.

I was still angry about Regan shagging my mrs. Was very angry. Didn't appreciate it. It had been happening for two years. That's just wrong in a lot of respects. It really is. You often find in times like these. That you get put in a position where. You kind of give up. You let bygones be bygones, and you realise. Who your true friends are. Hiding behind the bushes. The eary night, and the paranoia settles in. Whilst everyone else is just wandering. Wandering what would happen if there was any type of protest. It was all in the papers. Yet in HMP Belmarsh, every day was different. I was deemed fit to be transferred into Wing B. Which was basically the top floor. I was put there. My cell mate. Drug dealer. Tried to sell me spice. I said, "listen, you animal. I am in charge here, you may be mr big bollocks out on the streets. But I am not smoking that shit."

His name was Ben. Cocky guy, looked like he was a bit of a cock. And he has his TV. His TV, and the Manchester verses Tottenham game was playing. I said, to him, "mate you know nothing about me." He said, "you have been all over the news." I said, "deep down mate, you know nothing, I started this firm from my bare hands. I started this chip shop thing with my bare knuckles. We are in affiliation with Yid Army. The classics. Down with Thatcher, she was wrong. Hated thatcher. And that is what you bring to the table. A bit of Spice? Do you think in Maggie's days of woe she would of smoked Spice? Do you think I am some kind of Dickhead?" Ben said, "listen, it's been a long day, yet someone has to decide what's going on here man. Someone does, I mean, I ain't smoking it." I grip him against the wall and I said, "listen, you stupid thick cunt, I am not your bitch, not in here, not out there. I am not smoking that shit." I punch him in the face, a tooth falls out. Then he starts sobbing, and yells "Guard!" I said to him, "you're pathetic." Two screws come in.

One of the screws, well both of them. They are not taking much interest. Both of them are saying. "Lads if you want to scrap, keep the fucking noise down." Then Ben starts shouting. "He punched me." One of the screws said. "Yeah I will do the same in a minute, if you don't shut up. Both of you. Go to sleep. It's 2am in the morning." I had the top bunk. I leant over and I said. "Listen, what I am trying to say here. Is simple. I run this cell. You give me your dinner, every day." He said, "Or what?" I get out this flick knife and I say, "Or I will cut you up, and peel you like a potato" You can hear sobbing and all kinds of stuff like that.

So the next day, I get all the meals. Everything. A screw comes towards me, and he says, "well haven't you got all of your ducks in a row." I was antagonistic towards the screw. I said, "yeah, and what do you want to make of it?" The screw looked at me, and he said, "you know what, you can suck my dick!" Chaos erupted, like you would have never seen before. Grown ass men, making "gasp" shock noises. I said, "sir, I don't swing that way."

The warden comes along and he talks to the prison guard. The prison guard says, "sorry Warden, I just lost it." And the Warden said, "Well if this was the first time this had happened you know. Maybe you were having a bad day, and your dog died. But you have already been fired and hired. And this pattern of behaviour, is not acceptable, we are going to have to let you go." I said to the prison guard, "yeah, don't say that shit to me again, what the fuck is the matter with you?"

I walk back to the cell, and the police arrive. Two officers. PC David Lee, and PC Rick. PC Rick was quiet, and PC David Lee said, "sir, come this way please?" I was escorted out of Belmarsh, into this police van. Wasn't cuffed. I was just let out. PC Rick said, "this is your last fucking chance, you either work with us, on helping us bust county lines, or you stay in jail man. What the fuck is wrong with you!?" I said, "because I am not a rat." PC Rick said, "yeah, it can feel that way can't it. All of these county lines gangs, you don't want people planting rats and squirrels in your garden and shit." I said, "listen mate, the thing I am going to say here, is the truth mate. The truth of the matter is. Is you want me to be a vigilante, an informant. It's not going to happen. I know you have cyber hackers, informants, vigilantes galore. So why me!? I am not an informant anymore. Get that through your head!" PC Rick said, "you really are scared of these gangs, so what if I told you, that maybe we send you back to Belmarsh. You will rot in there. Like a corpse. Who's going to pick up the pieces? Nobody is. And it's times like these were you think. Where you think deeply. Yeah, conspiracy theories or facts. You name it. We know how corrupt things are. That's why we are out here. What do you think was going to happen? You can't just waltz in like this and demand to be in Belmarsh. What the fuck is the matter with you. All of the people who ain't getting locked up is being they are informants."

I said, "well maybe I don't want to be an informant." PC Rick said, "We gave you a house, we gave you lots of opportunities, the desire to progress. We gave you lots of things. Now we are stuck." I said, "now, this sounds like a YOU problem, not a WE problem. This is your issue, your job. You stick to it. And next time you pull me out of Belmarsh. I will pull your testicles out of their sockets." PC Rick said, "well that's a threat of violence, I am telling your Warden." PC Rick was a chubby guy, thought the world revolved around him. He used to confuse himself with a revolving door.

I said, "PC Rick, listen, you don't understand. I got out of the game. I got out of this game. This was the Yid Army. This was the chip shop boys. Going out there and proving ourselves. Going to the games. Now look at us. Let us go to the games. Let us live our own lives. Drop the charges. We ain't giving you a damn slice of information and you hate us for that don't you. I can tell by the grin on your face. You hate us for that, I am not your bitch. Go fuck a donkey. And and your welcome by the way for the times I did try and help you. Where are you now? This ain't bandit country anymore. You corrupt fucker. This ain't Lord of The Rings, you absolute melt. This is reality. Yeah, so fucking believe it is. So don't blame me for every car crash of the century. I am warning you."

PC Rick gets out his asp. He smacks me in the leg. He says, "you go a lot of verbals." I said, "Gerbils?" He said, "No verbals." I said, "Gerbils are animals." PC Rick shouted, "what is it with you and animals. For christ sake. Do you think this would work. This corrupt system is going to rain down on you, and it's going to be biblical. You get on the right side of this mess. You cunt. Maybe you will have a chance. You are a complete melt." I said, "PC Rick, I don't think this is a good way to speak to a member of the public." PC Rick said, "you are in jail." I said, "Prison." PC Rick places me in handcuffs and he says. "Listen, it's quite simple. You need to grow up. Alright. It's as simple as that." I said, "You're a paedophile protector aren't you. Didn't manage to put Jimmy Saville away you cunt." PC Rick said, "nah that was Starmer wasn't it. Who didn't put Jimmy away."

I said, "I don't know, seems to me like it was." PC Rick said, "Look, I know Starmer" I said, "oh it gets better, it gets better does it. Oh right, so you know the guy. Let me guess. You used to be a back bencher."

PC Rick said, "Starmer this, Starmer that. The guys alright." I said, "it's a corrupt fucking system. He's just one person. And you want to look at how it works. Be my guest. But it's not him who's to blame. You look at things. Time and time again. They could have hung him.

But this is what you brought me in for. For a fucking right wing debate? You fucking wrong un. You need hanging outside of parliament, and I would pay money to watch it happen." I punch PC Rick in the face with the handcuffs. Whilst he hits the deck. I am stood over him. I said, "you may be big out here, in these city streets. But I rule Belmarsh. I run that prison. And I will make you my bitch, if you are not careful. So go fuck yourself, and go jerk off to Page 3 of The Sun."

PC David Lee, says, "oh come on, this argument is ridiculous. We just want you to help us with County Lines." I said, "I want Reegan back, I want Marko back. Regan was shagging my mrs, in case you didn't know. We should be out there watching the football. Watching the game. Having a pint. But all because I shot this guy dead. Yeah, not a single day goes by, where I don't regret it. Time and time again. Round and around, like a merry go around. You become lost, confused. Your head seems to just feel disconnected. I know you, I know who you are. You can't do fuck all. I own London, I own these streets. I know you. Now you can lock me up and throw away the key, but you can't take away the passion in my heart can ya? Nah, you can't, because I can't see what's on the police's systems. I can't see what's on your reports."

PC Rick finally manages to compose himself. An ambulance arrives. And this big fat paramedic. We are talking, fat, and then we are talking. He put an all you can eat restaurant out of business fat. He was fucked, you should have seen him. He came waddling over to PC Rick." I said, "fellers." Two Prison officers walked through. One whistled and said, "Steve, inside mate." I walk inside. A screw undoes the handcuffs. And the look on PC Rick's face. You wouldn't believe it. Made my day. Of course it did.

The world's a bad place, you know, and I believe that I did him a favour. I wasn't going to be his bitch. What does he expect? He doesn't deserve to be in that job. He doesn't deserve it. Because he lies all of the fucking time.

I am better off in those walls. Because this is the time I am going to say. For better or for worse. You get used to the real problems. But no, things have to become problematic, don't they, things have to become that way. So I know what's happening. So that's what I am doing. So fine."

Chapter 18

What I was thinking, you know. Being in HMP Belmarsh. It was killing me. Yeah I know I did wrong in killing Lee. But this was driving me into a whirlwind. Obviously I had a serious opinion right now, that I wasn't going to stay in HMP Belmarsh forever. Maybe get out by the time I am 70. Yet the fact still remained I felt stuck somewhere down the line. And that is something in which you don't want to see.

This Daniel geezer. So in a flash what happens, is that he has this little pen knife on him. And tries to stab me. So the prison guards come in. And one of them says, "right put that knife down." I said, "I don't know what he's doing." He's wrestled to the floor, I kick him in the bollocks. He then complains. "Oh he's kicked me in the bollocks." The screw said, "you have all of your ducks in a row don't you, which is a good thing for you, but unfortunately him, kicking you in the bollocks is a civil issue. Right now. The only way we can get police to come over. Is if he repeatedly kicked you in the balls." I said, "Okay, enough banter, do you know who's in this cell next?" The screw said, "I don't even know my wife's name. But this geezer is going to the psychiatric ward. For evaluation. Might even take him to Broadmoor" You can hear Dan shouting. "Oh no! Anywhere but that place." I said, "well, you know, you are acting insane. Get out of here." Next thing you know, through the window. I can see him transported through the prison van. With a police escort. All of that over a pen knife.

But some things don't make sense. I was living in De Ja Vu. I was living a life where I felt compelled. One mine, destructed the next. The England vs Portugal game was on, and there were people sniffing cocaine. And watching it, the screws were handing it out. I was out of my mind on crystal meth so I am not sure which team was winning. All I can remember is a huge scrap. I was part of it.

Some dickhead in the front row thinks it's acceptable to block the TV for two seconds. And showed one of his testicles. I laughed, and found it funny. But a screw got involved and took him to the ground. I kicked the screw and said, "seriously over one bollocks, it wasn't even cock and bollocks It was just one bollock." The screw said, "kick me again and you are going back to your cell." The guy was screaming, think he had mental health issues. Then he had a spice attack. The screws stood back. Lots of vomit everywhere, and he was having a spice attack. Eyes rolling beneath his head. Crumbling mixture of phlegm in his mouth.

    The guards stepped back, and low and behold. I meet Regan and Marko. Marko is my new cell mate. Regan shouts. "What the fuck are you doing just standing there." Regan puts the bloke in the recovery position. Whilst Marko grabs the payphone and dials 999. I said, "you screws are fucking useless aren't you!?" One of the screws said, "didn't want his vomit on me." I said, "pathetic, absolutely pathetic, are you first aid trained?" He said, "yeah a couple of hours online course." I said, "oh come on this is insane." The screw, said, "you sir, need to calm down." I said, "I am fine mate. I am fine. It's you who needs calm down." He said, "oh yeah, really, why's that tough guy?" I said, "look I am not going to argue." Whilst Portugal are winning 1-0. And when the goal came in there was a huge scrap. And I was involved. Punching every face I had to see.

I said, "I am doing a good job." The screw said, "no you're not, you twat." I said, "listen fuck off." As Portugal score the second goal. Only had one toke off some meth pipe. But some other geezers were doing black mamba in the toilets. Next thing you know riot guards arrived.

Yet the game still continued. I didn't know what to do. With my back against the wall. Feeling like this prison had consumed me. I don't know.

I think of life as a way we see things. Stereotypes, patterns, behaviours, people pull our strings. And everything is a joke, a game. It never succeeded to amaze me. Stuck inside this prison, now with Marko as my cell mate. I was serving 40 years with change of parole. Marko was serving 17 years with choice of parole. And Regan was serving 6. My life was completely battered and bruised. And I knew, I knew that the only way. The only way to sort this whole thing out. Was what? To become a police informant? Fuck that. But deep down I just wanted to feel like I had a connection with something. It was a load of bollocks anyway. The values you trusted the most had gone. All that was left was the feeling that you felt on a daily basis. Feeling kind of fearful. Of this prison. Portugal went onto win 2-0, and with that I would like to hear. More people passing out on spice. This whole thing was getting me riled up. *Getting riled* up in a way where I can explain. Explain things, I was in no position to shoot Lee that day. And all of this bollocks. All of this mess. It starts and ends with something. It really does. And I am afraid sometimes life just stops, pauses, you get uptight. You wander. A bad day seems like a nightmare. In this world nobody would know. I spent ages trying to pull myself together. Trying to think about things logically. The migraine and headache of realisation is. That deep down. We can still see beyond the shadows. We can still see that we tried to go out to the games. Have a good time. Now I am stuck with Marko, in this cell. It made no sense to me. I shouldn't be in here. I should be somewhere else. Fighting some other battle. Doing something else differently. Instead *I am stuck*.

My mind was going blurry, my whole life was flashing before my eyes. I didn't know what to think. It's times like these where you felt delirious. The outside world, and the confines of that. I was in a secure brick building. When you say that obviously, it wasn't the most savoury of places. Yet at times, I felt somewhat secluded. Like nobody understood me you know. I was causing the football riots. Now I am in prison for killing one guy. And it was the gun that killed him not me anyway. So what I am supposed to do now? I am done with this. I try and work out what the fuck was happening. *Everyone around me*. I passed out. Next thing I know. I see two police officers.

Both 6 foot males. Didn't get the names or collar numbers. One of them was really mouthy. "Listen son, come with us." I was bundled into a police van. Taken to a police station. Took into the interview room. The Chief Superintendent, called Terry. Terry said, "look son, we have the power to get you out of jail." I said, "yeah I know, and you want me to work for you, not a chance." Terry said, "we know you have intelligence, why are you refusing to give the intelligence over? You know. What do you have? Prison for 40 years?" I said, "tried it, didn't work. I watched the last game. You don't want to know about it. Well fine, it's bollocks to you, and your reports. Fine me, lock me up, who gives a crap!? *I hate you.*" Terry said, "Well, I *know* you..and I know what you are capable of." I said, "well isn't that great." I clapped.

I said, "isn't that great, because where I am standing, nobody gives a fuck, nobody. And you want to know something. The reason why this whole plan failed in the first place. The reason why I have lost everything. Everyone. Is because of the fact everyone is too thick to understand why I am here in the first place. Too thick headed. You put me in there, you snake in the grass, you are a serpent, right from the bible. Yeah..a serpent. You put me in there, and that's how it's going to stay."

Another geezer bounces in, Rick Helmet, DC, Mr Helmet said, "listen feller, I ain't fucking around here, but we need your co-operation."

I said, "nah it don't work like that, unfortunate second name by the way, you are a helmet." Rick said, "less of the wise cracks." I said, "less of this, less of that, you are the one who's scratching your arse right now just thinking, thinking for one second. That you had any brains, in that head of yours. But no, you destroyed everything didn't you. You fucked everything up. That's what I am saying. That's what I am explaining right now."

DC Helmet said, "listen mate, we can get you a nice mansion." I said, "you already gave me a mansion, you already gave me one. Nothing happened. Nobody gives a fuck. I ain't working with you, or for you." DC Rick Helmet said, "listen mate, from my understanding, you are walking a fine line." I said, "you brought me in here, you took me in here, now I am supposed to pay the price. Like I always pay the price. It's you I am looking at right now."

Rick said, "maybe, or we will just send you back, send you back to HMP Belmarsh. I said, "do what the fuck you want, you animal. And for the record. fuck off." Everything was fucked up. I meant everything. *Every word.* From just walking around pretending I was okay. Rick Helmet, the big nob head trying to act tough. When I said, "alright, I'll work with you."

DC Rick said, "I'll cut your friends loose also." I said, "yeah because that prison is a fucking nightmare."

So we were cut loose and we were transferred to a secure location in London. With twenty computers in this one room, and twenty undercover officers. Me, Regan, and

Marko walked in.

Now, I would like to think right now, this is my place in the world. My final *something*. But it's not. You look hard enough, you will see the answers. But the corrosive effects of County Lines are leaving us seething. And the only answers are with these undercover police officers. And the fact that they are making me investigate this shit operation, is beyond me.

I shouted, "Right fuck this shit, where do I get started?" Some MI5 geek called Richard, was like. "Oh don't use that language, we are actually very busy right now." I said, "I can use what ever language I want piggy." Everyone laughed. This big detective, massive guy. He got up, started making a meal out of it. He said, "get to work." I said, "hell no, I ain't your bitch, you can fuck off." Marko winked, and eventually we sat down. I was assigned this computer with a secure login code. I logged in, and finally after some time. You enter the Matrix, of the police systems. Just lots of mug shots of undesirable dickheads, and lots of twats. With criminal records. It finally was brought to my attention.

I shouted in the office, "now what the fuck do we do?" Three skinheads approached. Out of nowhere. Undercover cops also. I couldn't even think straight. It was killing me even being aware of this. Pale Ale, the adventures, now this life. Well I never, but one thing is for sure. England were playing Wales in a friendly that night. So we were going to watch the game, drink some beers, and have some banter. Which usually results in a scrap. I shouted, "Engerland, Engerland." DC Dick Smalls shouted, "right that's enough settle down, this is serious work, there is an organised gang, operating in a kebab house. In London." I shouted, "better not be my chip shop." DC Dick Smalls said, "pipe down, listen." I said, "you pipe down, you look like you need your pipes cleaning, you wrongun" DC Dick Smalls, got in my face. And he said, "listen mate, listen carefully. I got you under watch." I said, "sounds creepy dude, but what ever."

DC Dick Smalls said, "listen feller." I said, "no you listen to me, this whole thing has gotten too far now. For too long. You can't just order me about. We have a game to watch later." He said, "England v Wales on later, 7:45pm kick off." I said, "I know, we are all watching the game dumbass."

DC Johnson waltz's in, looks like a bit of a prick but there you go. Probably is. Has a black tie. Ginger guy. No idea if the carpet matches the drapes. Probably knowing this dickhead. I said, "DC Johnson, nice to meet you." DC Johnson said, "listen mate, lets got on with researching county lines."

With your back against the wall. There is only so much you can do. Your mind goes blurry. I have been there before. De Ja Vu. Wrong place, wrong time. In a blink of an eye. It's coming back and we are getting into a position where we don't know what is happening. It's times like these where we figure out what exactly we can believe in. The

Chip Shop Crew, and what they stand for. And all of this aside, all of this aside. It just became left. In this office. With these people. Just because I didn't like it in Belmarsh. It was a double edged sword. Hadn't heard from Jacky in months. Not that I cared. Apparently she'd been shagging Regan and Marko.

    I still forgive them, and her. But whilst she was running the chip shop, she was out dogging with them. And it's just not nice for me to think of it like that. But there you go.

    I think back, to the good times. Some times, it felt like, I was in a prison anyway. And for all I know. I can pretend to explain that for once in my life. With my mind racing, with everything going in circles. It was left with nothing. No time to figure what happens. No time to just put problems aside, be your own man. Be the person people believed you to be. It was left to this. It was left to the corrosive mess in society, the corrosive effect of County Lines. They didn't scare me. Whatsoever, but the police wanted information. And before people like to think, "oh it's okay, because you know, this is what happens, you know, in things like this."

    I have seen, County Lines, I have witnessed it. And they are messing up with my shit. They are trying to get involved in some serious business right now. Some serious problems. They are causing me serious problems. There is no, "oh you know, I could work in McDonalds, but I make more money doing this "job."..The worst part is. It was feeling like under duress. I didn't really want to get involved. I am not the SAS. I am one just one man. And that's how it is. But if you like to remember a time where things changed. You forgot about things. We remained in a position where we could go to the games. I bought my cocaine from dealers. I wasn't fussed. I didn't say anything. Now this is the price I have to pay. It's a double edged sword. Either that or Belmarsh.

Regan logs into the Police National Computers, and there in the screen saver/desktop, is a picture of a pig, and it says, "piggy". And I said, "Regan, did you do that?" Regan said, "yeah, it's funny." DC Johnson said, "change that right now mate." I said, "I am not your mate, just because, we aren't even on the same team. Let's get political then. Lets go into politics. I will start explaining what you have said."

DC Johnson said, "it's times like these I don't know, you just want the best. Sometimes that isn't good enough. For you. You have all of your ducks in a row. But unfortunately for you, you have to do the leg work. Right now. I don't even know."

I said, "we should be having a scrap, we should be watching the football." DC Johnson said, "after we get some suspects." So after some thinking. We log into the police systems, and we find the 'usual suspects'. Just a lot of dickheads. We go through the mug shots. And I said, "DC Johnson, what do you expect me to do?" He said, "we are doing a sting operation." I said, "where?" DC Johnson said, "Belgravia" I said, "that's twice, you've mentioned it. What the fuck is up with you and Belgravia."

DC Johnson said, "are we doing this or not? Because I am getting tired of this bollocks. All of the time. The same things. Belgravia it is." A fat DC waddles in, size of a whale. He shouts, "Belgravia it is then." I said, "fucking hell, have you got a hard on for Belgravia or some thing? What is it with that place? Do all the women in the place shag on the first date?"

DC Johnson said, "don't say that mate, that's inappropriate" I said, "well, I find you inappropriate mate, everything you do is just fucking weird. And you expect me to believe you. Then fine. That's how it is, and that's whats happening."

DC Johnson said, "you can suck my dick." He points to his crotch area where his dick his, arrogantly.

I said, "listen, we are trying to organise a serious sting operation, and you said suck your dick, what the fuck is the matter with you?"

PC Piles walks in, he hits the deck, trips over DC Johnson. He hits the floor. I said, "right, can we stop mucking about and get on with some work now."

DC Johnson said, "Belgravia. 10 clock, tonight." I said, "it's 9 clock right now." DC Johnson said, "yeah, so we're leaving in cars." So we all left in cars. Me, DC Johnson, PC Piles. PC John Ricks. We all left. We all went to this adventure. We all went there. And when we realised that deep down. I was the one pretending to be the drug user. I was in a red Audi. This drug dealer comes towards me. I am wearing a wire. I hand the cash, but as soon as I do. Police swarm in, lots of coppers. "Police, Police, Police, put your hands on your head, tazer, tazer, tazer." DC Johnson tazes the guy because he's resisting arrest. Another drug dealer appears on the scene. And DC Johnson gets trapped in the tazer wire. I deploy a tazer, and nab this one bloke, the other dealer.

DC Johnson said, "Steve, you absolute dickhead, you are not tazer trained."' I said, "suck my ballsack, you cock, you should be thanking me." We have two in custody. DC Johnson said, "listen mate, I know we have an agreement, but just calm it down a bit, stop using our Tazers *That is our job."*

We have two in custody. Mike O'Brien, and Dan Riley. Both in their early twenties. They could have been the runners, they might not have been. At this point in time. We didn't care. At this point in time. We were treating them as suspects. We had no sympathy for them. And we went down on them ruthlessly lack a pack of wolves, tearing a sheep from limb to limb. As the blood gushes out. That is what we are doing. We are ruthless animals, and you better believe it buddy. Because this is what is happening. And we won't stop. Until the clock tells us to. With all of these cats out here meowing and all of that. That is what we are saying right now.

Chapter 19

You realise where life is going. Working with the feds. Even though DC Johnson was getting in my face. Acting like the hard man. I punched him in the face. He said, "is that all you got?" I said, "no". I punched him in the face again and three teeth fall out. I said, "now go to your orthodontist."

The suspects are let loose, and run wild and away. Whilst I am standing there not knowing what the fuck is going on. Marko said, "listen mate, fuck the feds, we don't need them." I said, "Yeah, fuck them, when have they been there for us when we needed help? You never see a police officer on the street. And when you do. It's because someone has dropped a bottle of beer on the floor."

Regan said, "yeah fuck them man, who gives rats ass who's dealing with county lines. We ain't working with them, fuck them. They can deal to their mum's pussies if they want to. I ain't afraid of those bitches." I said, "yeah, their mum's pussies smell like egg salad, let's get out of here."

So we were beating up with these cops, grabbing their tazers. Lots of them, twenty. This was in Belgravia. I shouted, "Roar I am a tiger, nobody can stop me." Next thing you know twenty skinheads appear out of nowhere. Chelsea. Not Yid. I said, "fuck off you absolute melts, nearly the end of the season, what are you doing around here?" Yid Army came along, and supported us. I said, "right, we own these streets. We own these fucking streets.

Down with Thatcher, down with what she wanted. Right now. You fucking better believe what I am thinking. *We own these streets.* And you can fuck off."

Marko starts punching the skinheads, and it gets into a scrap when I start punching them also. And the army show up, from this MOD centre. Which is next door. And start claiming "we are making a noise." Sargent Lick a lollypop said, "listen here guys, listen here, it's too loud." I said, "fuck you, this is our fight, unless you wanna get involved and all, you fucking nut case. How did you get into the army?" Regan said, "we are all ex military." Sargent Lick a lolly pop said, "so why are you saying rude things man. Fuck you. Remember where I am." I said, "man, I don't want to know anything, about you. Listen. I respect the marines, I served. But you don't want to put me under any shenanigans right now. That's the problem."

Marko said, "Steve, show some respect to the military mate, we all have served."

Sargent lick a lollypop said, "okay, well in that case. I will take a cash bribe." Regan bribes him £1,000 in 20 pound notes in a brief case.

I said, "you get what you pay for." Sargent lick a lolly pop said, "you ought to behave yourselves." I said, "okay dude."

Next thing you know as we walk away, thirty prostitutes, are walking passed. One looks like she has been smacked in the face pretty bad, by one of these pimps. Drunk people roaming around the shops. The police were terrified, they ran away. We started to rule the streets. And lots of vigilantes were getting involved with leather jackets. And it was all crazy. As I got some cocaine and snorted it, and Regan was taking some viagra. But it was crazy because once it kicks in, it's harder than a wooden stick. So I punched one of the vigilantes in the face. His name was Chris. I said, "listen Chris, there are two men in this world. Lions, and ducks. Which one do you want to be?" Chris said, "lion." I said, "right answer, unfortunately for you. I am the greatest lion of all time, and I will conquer you. With my mind." I start to hypnotise him. And I said, "look son, you ought to take a walk." Chris said, "oh really." I said, "go back to your mum, her pussy smells like egg salad."

Marko shouted, "that's twice you've said that now. Twice." I said, "yeah insane the way these people are nowadays."

Chris said, "what about the country dons?" I said, "I don't give a fuck about county lines, do I look like the fucking police to you? Do I look like a police officer. Oh nee nor, nee nor, nee nor, woo, woo, woo, woo. No, I am not. So fuck you. fuck you, fuck all of your ancestors. fuck you."

Chris said, "you're that mad." I said, "I know you are." This felt weird. For a second I had no idea. How this whole system worked. Vigilantes were roaming the streets. Hell, I didn't even know who Chris was. Besides some deranged lunatic, who likes to shoot squirrels in his spare time. With a shotgun. fuck that guy. I was not taking his lead. I said to him.

"Chris, I am not taking your lead." He said, "well god damn straight you are, there's a fucking war on the streets, and you want to look the other way. Pretend that nothing is happening." I said, "this ain't what I am saying, but show some respect." Chris punches me in the stomach. I punch him back in the stomach.

I said, "look, time for just for us to go our separate ways."

Chapter 20

You could look into the sun set, you could think what you wanted about the life you lived. But one thing was for certain. I wasn't sure anymore. I mean, not about anything. I didn't know what to say. Things just changed, for better or for worse. You were stuck with the same problems. Nobody else knew. How far this was going to go. I had enough of these piggies, and I had enough of them for the simple reason that; They thought they ruled the estates. When they didn't. It's as simple as that.

It's the same narrative, all over again. You get that gut wrenching pain in your stomach. You feel like life is just haunting you. Through everything I was led to believe was nothing. Everything. That comes with time. That comes with just knowing. How I can believe in something. How ever people can. How people can believe it's right, when it isn't. The times I knew. The things I wanted to see. I want to see the kind of avenues. People expected to see. The violence, and the war on the streets. Carried on. And with that perspective. That's how it was. Through thick and through thin.

I was tired, delusional even. Life was short, and all I wanted was for people to say, "look he messed up, he pulled the gun." But it wasn't like that anymore. It didn't pertain to that fact. Everything the Yid Army had produced had gone nowhere. And with that came down lots of barriers. Things we weren't even aware of. It got to the point where you wanted to trust your own intuition. Your own gut. Know where you stood in the world. Make your mark in that respect. Then you know. You know everything. From what I can see.

You didn't want to walk into the lions den. Not now. Not ever. Everything you have imagined. All of the things people have said to you, and the things you ignored. All of the times the earth shattered in front of you. It was right there to greet you with opening arms. This was what made me believe in myself. Yet it was short lived. I just needed something to believe in.

So after a while, there were people making conspiracy theories up. Saying Pale Ale isn't dead. And I was getting suspicious myself. So I drove up to this lake by the woods. And spoke to this wizard. The wizard was smoking meth from a meth pipe. And he said, "you didn't kill Lee, you were framed." I said, "I remember killing him." He said, "you were brainwashed into believing you killed him, there was no gun, you were conned." I said, "this is some Matrix shit right here man, looks like I have swallowed the red pill and the blue pill." The wizard said, "you look like you have swallowed every fucking pill on the planet, you doughnut, now listen, we don't have time to have this debate. He's still alive. The police set you up. *Trying to make you work for County Lines operations with them.* Trying to make you do their dirty work. fuck them.

Because what I like to think. What I deeply like to think. It where there is opportunity. There is crime. Drug dealers make money, they take a risk." I said, "listen feller, why the hell are you telling me this shit. I just want to believe something." The wizard said, "then believe it, stop being so introverted and square. Start living. For crying out loud." I said, "I have done my best, so what if I haven't crossed every t, and dotted every I. It was in the first place we thought about this. And now nothing."

The Wizard, called Steve said, "look, you doughnut, we don't have time, follow me. I follow him to this cave. And he's building a fire. The fires made. We are sitting down." He said, "you didn't kill Lee." I said, "you have said that twice now." I said, "where the fuck are we?" He said, "Scunthorpe." I said, "what are we doing over there." He said, "no fucking idea, why's the sky blue? You absolute tit. Why are men attracted to women's tits?" I said, "I get your point, some things are mysteries." The wizard let out a fart and said, "nothing mysterious about that eggy waft you get in your face." He stared at me, he was all bearded, and grey. Dirt everywhere. He said, "the only way to win, is to destroy the guillotine." I said, "that's the only way." The wizard said, "you have been walking in shadows your whole life, you have been looking around. The only way to win at life. Is to destroy the guillotine Before your enemy does."

I said, "right, so it's all about going back to natural sources for a change. That's what your saying, no wifi connection in this place. Do you seriously think I am going to hang out with you."

He has a shotgun and says, "SHOTGUN, you have no choice." I said, "well I am fucked now, so what's on the menu tonight then?" He said, "fuck knows." I said, "you're quite the wizard aren't you, bringing a shotgun around."

He said, "it's a gun..." He said casually. I said, "yeah okay, but you can't threaten me like this dude. Go on, pull the trigger." He said, "there is no bullet." I laughed and said, "what the fuck is the point of the gun?" He said, "just wanted to scare you for a second." I said, "well it worked, but there are bullets." He said, "if I wanted to fart out a bullet. I could. You are missing the point. This is an illusion. The photons are blinding your eyes into an oblivion, your sleep deprivation has landed you in a dark place. You are living in the past. Grow up. It's time you did grow up, and your posse did. Because that's the crux of the scenario. You wake up and realise where you come from."

I said, "yeah I come from earth, yeah I understand Steve, but it's not that simple."

Without knowing anything. Lost in oblivion. You know. I keep regressing back to the past. And I wander. You know. How it feels sometimes. How it feels to be in this position. When I am stuck in Scunthorpe. Out of all places. With some guy, who claims to be a wizard. I don't even know if he is one or not.

I was feeling tired. A thousand hours, a thousand minutes, a thousand seconds. Life wasn't supposed to be this hard. *This difficult.* Yet after speaking to this geezer who claims to be some wizard. I had no option now but to return to Marko, and Regan As the police were chasing us. We were staying at a mates house. Not going outside. Police looking for us everywhere.

Marko said, "it's like that huh, just on the run? This is what this crew is now, this is what it's about?" I said, "we have no option man, we have no option."

Yeah that's right, being on the run sucked. This whole thing was carnage And you know what. I didn't even care anymore. So we still watched the games. The England verses Scotland game, was on TV. Friendly. Skinheads galore. We were staying in a skinheads house. His name was roast beef. Nice bloke. So we were staying at Roast Beef's house. And he was an animal. An absolute animal of a guy. Very articulate, but very passionate about his views. Half the time, we weren't even watching the game. Roast Beef said, "have you heard, that the Italian Mafia are working in London, and bribing the cops. Did you know that, it's insane, the amount of corruption.

Or the Spanish Latino women, who are talking to the Italian Mafia. And then you get a guy from Edinburgh, who goes to London. And nobody can understand a word he is saying. So he gets on the wrong bus. Because he's asking for a bus. For a bus, you know, a bus with wheels. Asking for a bus. And that bus, is going from Belgravia. Yeah. Belgravia, yeah, all the way to Kensington alright. Kensington. And then the bus stops.

At the bus stop. And people leave." I said, "better story than Hollyoaks". Roast Beef said, "Hollyoaks, the oaks of Holly?" I said, "it's not a nature programme, I guess it could be." Roast Beef said, "nah it's not nature, it's a soap." I said, "a soap, like a soap, like a bar of soap. And they get this bar of soap. And then they are able to look into the soap. And get actors. And get a soap." Roast Beef said, "yeah a soap." I said, "a soap". Roast Beef said, "but not the same kind of soap." I said, "it's a stop gap, it's something to fill time. All of these TV Soaps are stop gaps." And then I started to think of things. You know. Think of life. Think of where life was going. Think of the history me and Roast Beef had. Legend has it, he smashed a whole bus stop up. Whilst on drugs, and stoned. And then went to the pub, and ordered a roast dinner. And The Police, let him finish his roast dinner. Before arresting him." Now there is more to that story. But obviously he's a complex geezer, and he's kicking off, kicking the TV. We almost lose the signal." I said, "Roast Beef, come on dude, you are better than this." By the way, it's not his real name. But I guess, you know. What he knows. Apparently he has a peace sign tattooed on one testicle. And then on the other testicle he has, "war" tattooed on the other testicle.

Then on his cock, he has "come and get the good stuff." Tattooed on his cock. Then on his stomach. He has, "fuck off". Nice bloke. Very violent, and I wouldn't trust him to buy me a sausage roll.

You know, because he's that type of geezer. Spits in people's drinks. fuck him. I have had enough of him. I said, "Roast Beef, listen mate, you want to know what is going down, you come along to this game, you try to act the big man. And maybe you are. But we are staying at your place. I understand feller. But it's only so long until the piggies come marching in here. With their blues and twos. Nee nor, nee nor, nee nor And that is not the start or end of it. You know what I am saying. The piggies, all out in numbers. And then what.

Roast Beef didn't have the answers. He just pretended he did. I didn't know if he was bullshitting me anyway. About his plans to rob a bank, and tattoo the banks logo on his chest. For all I knew, he was unreliable, and crazy. But for what it's worth. I'd rather hang out with him, than hang out with the pigs.

You know, "oh we have axon body cameras now, and we can record you oh, blah, blah, blah". It's all a load of bollocks. They can shove their Axon body cams up their arses. I didn't give a fuck. They could find me where they didn't know where I was. Roast beef had everything encrypted. Even his key to his car. And the thing I knew about this guy. The thing I knew about him. Is that I had seen this guy fight. Now I am not talking charity matches. I am talking fights, in the street. In Belgravia. And he is the one who can take anyone down.

So nobody fucked with roast beef. Nobody did. That's the whole point to what I am saying right now. Nobody does, because that's how it is. When it's his place. And we are on the run. I didn't even know which game was which now. For all I knew. The game was over. He had lost the game, everyone had. He had been all over the place. Yet his heart still remained strong to the fact. That this was not a criminal issue. That Wizard in Scunthorpe told me that Pale Ale, didn't even exist. It was a set up. I am inclined to believe that's the case.

Because all of this bullshit aside, sleepless nights, after sleepless nights. And you wander why this happens. Because everyone is all set now. For once. I kind of knew what we knew. It was the same page. The same thing.

These situations are confusing for me, you know. I just wanted to get on the road again and back to normal. Instead. I was stuck not knowing what to think.

Staying at Roast Beefs house, he gave us a sense of belonging. He gave us a sense that everything was going to be alright. I didn't know what to think. I didn't know what to believe. I thought this whole thing was bullshit. You grew up and realise one day. That I can think what I want about anything. But one day. One day, just realising all of these bizarre encounters. It would stop me. Stop me from thinking things. You know. Realising things.

But it wasn't that simple. My dreams and ambitions went. And with that there was nothing. I kept feeling and thinking that some day there would be a good result. Some day I would get back on my feet. And realise. I had everything in place. But now, I just didn't know. Didn't want to find out or didn't have any idea. I just felt stuck in a way. You know, some people can become unstuck. Start believing in themselves. And for what reason exactly? It makes no sense, it really doesn't. Makes no sense whatsoever. That in my mind. I just knew. Sure, there were some things holding me back, but I couldn't rely on luck or fate my whole life. And to really know this guy. This Lee guy. He was a myth, a spook, a legend.

Someone you would meet, and then he was gone. So not only was I framed for the murder. How do I know he even exists? That's the thing. That's what I am wandering. And that's what I believe. Day in, day out. Just start thinking. Start thinking of the worst case scenario some times. Know other people's insecurities. Then of course. There's time, effort, energy. Things go wrong, things lag, you get left behind. You try and make up for lost time. Then you try again, and you have to make a difference in this world. Some how. The Chip Shop Crew. It changed, it stopped being about *making fun of The Police*. And it turned into running away from them. At first we were laughing at them, thinking we had one up over them. Then they showed us. That they were stronger than us. And we fucking hated it. That's why you never go into the lions den. You know, everything I have ever thought about is the lions den. "Oh make fun of The Police." Not just saying that. But realising. And I am not saying kiss everyone's arse cheeks, and all of that bollocks. All I am saying is. It changed. Telling them to get back in their pig sty. It annoyed them. With that, some cops, they found it hilarious That some of their colleagues were getting angry. But some cops. Behind all that pent up aggression and that desire to vent. Was just a lonely soul just like anyone else. Just trying to make their way in the world.

 Then I realised it wasn't about things that have happened in the past. Things change. You get the same people, over and over again. I look back. But I realise that nothing was sticking together. The people we meet in our lives are fleeting, even if we spend all of the time with them. The only credit we have in this world is to be comfortable in our own skin. Which by and large. With this expedition. I wasn't sure what was going on. I mean, Roast Beef sure was one hell of a dude. Kept us safe from the police. But even then. Some of his views. He used to wake up at 3am and start ranting.

I didn't know what to think some days. Roast beef, sure was working hard to keep us safe from the piggy police. But for all I knew. Is we had different ground to cover.

Roast Beef had changed. He became more secluded. He wasn't talking. Next thing I know, the police burst down the door. "Tazer, tazer, taxer" And we are looking at the guy, and he doesn't have a tazer And I am thinking the guys either nuts or on steroids.

His name was PC Rickshaw, from Canada. I said, "hey, not being funny, but, where the hell is your tazer?" He said, "element of surprise bitch." I said, "where's your tazer?" He said, "left it in the car." I said, "well go to the car and go and get it then." He said, "alright." Roast Beef was finding this encounter strange. He was finding this situation very bizarre. And was getting angry with PC Rickshaw. He said, "hey, why the hell are you saying tazer, when there is no fucking tazer!? Are you nuts!?" PC Rickshaw said, "god have mercy on my soul." Now Marko and Regan were there, and we were not happy. About this no show of the tazer. This was further shenanigans we couldn't cope with right now. I shouted, "Where the fuck is the tazer!?" PC Rickshaw said, "can you lower the tone of your voice, some people are trying to sleep!" I said, "How about I kick you in the cock and bollocks, and send you to hospital."

PC Rickshaw said, "that's an every day occurrence for me." I said, "because you say you have a tazer when you don't, no wander people kick you in the bollocks. You are supposed to actually have the tazer with you. And you're not tough enough either. Behind all of the male bravado. I bet there are insecurities." He puffs out his chest, and he says. "yeah, and what may that be?!" I said, "I don't know, I am not a fucking psychiatrist." Marko got angry and said, "hey fuck you pal, you are in our territory now, we are holding you hostage. Shotgun." Shotgun, right to PC Rickshaw's face. I said, "double barrel." PC Rickshaw said, "no shit." I said, "okay, put a tape over his mouth. I am fed up of his shenanigans. He is causing so much trouble. Is there anyone else outside, it's just him?" Marko said, "about 20 armed police officers outside dude." I said, "it's okay, we can use this piggy as a hostage." Next thing we know. Once the pig is taped to the chair, and has an apple in his mouth. The hostage negotiator with his megaphone shouts. "Right is there anything, I can reasonably say or do, to make you surrender, with the cop not hurt." I said, "No, unless you want to bring Jacky up in here."

The hostage negotiator was called Lee. I said, "Lee, give it up man, if armed police come in. this piggy gets it."

Lee said, "that's the last thing I want to

happen." I got annoyed and I said, "hey shut up, you are making a damn fool out of yourself. Put your guns away boys. What's this? We have shotguns."

Next thing I know, an armed cop, gets on the megaphone. He said, "hey, our guns our better than yours."

I shouted, "doubt it, since I had all of your bullets, stolen out of your car."

You could hear, "friendly fire." Next thing you know, you can hear this loud click. I said, "a gun without ammo, is like a hooker without KY Jelly."

The hostage negotiator took the megaphone. And said, "Hey shut fuck up." I grab a megaphone myself. I shout, "now, how about you shut up, think your dick is this big." I do a small mm hand gesture. I said, "hey listen cock sucker, this is the chip shop crew. You only wanted us for a while. Go fuck yourselves."

Lee said, "I have Jacky on the phone." I said, "I don't give a fuck, we want pizzas."

So there you have it, 20 cops, unarmed, ironically with guns. And I don't want my wife. I just want pizza.

Lee said, "any toppings?"' I said, "yeah, pepperoni for me, 15 inches, stuffed crust with cheese." Marko said, "you know what, I like the idea of that." I said, "so two of them big boys, you want to play with the real men now?"

I get a god damn headache, this paranoia, has washed me whole. No longer am I complete. But I am a byproduct, of this broken world. Collapsed, forgotten, and in some instances. Just believing in a world where I had some kind of momentum. You see people go passed in these fancy cars, and you have to kiss arse cheek to arse cheek. To drive those cars. And then more arse kissing. That wasn't me anymore.

I left, I didn't want to be part of this gang. I didn't want to be part of a society that rejected me. That framed me for something I hadn't done. Of course I was angry. And at first, the anger. Then, you some times feel. Almost, kind of worried. Worried about life, death. This hostage negotiator Is doing my fucking head in, with all of his requests for pizza. I shouted through my little megaphone. He had a big one. I shouted, "just give us the god damn pizzas, you ass pie."

Marko said, "that's a good one, ass pie, where did you come up with that?" I said, "saw it in a movie once." Marko said, "listen this dude, he ain't for real. Once he delivers the pizzas. I bet they will get us then."

A vacant memory, the burning ambition of more pain to come. A planet completely weeping of pride, misery, common sense. Your sense of well being. Just driven by your sense of lasting resolve. It was these kinds of days where life was focused. It was these kinds of days where you fell off the wagon. Injured yourself. Not on purpose. It was a god damn fucking travesty. I was in this mess. I shouldn't be apart of this anymore. Not me, not anyone. Screw them. If they want to play Russian roulette with me. I will, because they screw you. And they screw you. And when you think it's all over. That's when they really start to mess with your head. It's agonising. The Police weren't on our side. It pains me to admit this. Nobody asked them to play parental figures.

It was not their choice. It was a god damn fucking travesty. So all of the things I used to think about. All of the things that I liked about The Police. Oh, we are doing the right things. For a change. Change everything, and you are left with nothing. A world broken down by decades of pain, and you are left with a hostage situation. And it pained me to admit this wasn't the first time. But what the fuck do I know? They framed me, it wasn't me who killed Lee. I didn't even know if the geezer existed. And I don't know which team he was part of. He could have been Stoke, he could have been Millwall, he could have been West Ham, Man Utd, he could have been Rangers. I didn't know. So I grit my teeth. And I think of the pizzas. And I want them delivered. But this is it. This is what we stand for now. At this meatheads house. And then what? All of a sudden, this meat guy, or what ever the fuck he called himself now. Roast Beef. That was the impression we had on him. That was the kind of things we see. In this day and age. It was all bullshit, we live and we die. It's that simple. We don't suffer, we already have. All of the tears have gone, all of the tears have left.

All of the pain and misery had stayed with me. All of the times I wanted to fucking blink, and realise, it was me all along. But it wasn't. Not for the first time. And even then. It was something I couldn't achieve. I just wanted some kind of sense of freedom. Where I could roam. Not this mess. Not this. Nobody asked for this. Nobody. And they want to play roulette with my freedom. So be it. I am done, living this life. fuck them. This whole thing. "Oh we are hostage negotiators, we are going to get you a pizza." Not happening, not on these streets geezer. And if I was going to snap out of it any time soon I would have done something by now. There was nothing. No sign, or happy time. Or place. Or some people just believe. You have a good life. You have this, and then nothing. All the memories come flooding back. And you are left with feelings.

Now I don't know what kind of feelings I had at that moment in time. I didn't want to know. But when I am looking at things and realising. Life. It had fuck all to do with me. So I was not going to have it. I had lost. It was game over. Nothing was working. There was a Brazilian gang of bikers who were trying to hunt me down also. For money I owed them. It was only 50p. Hey. This is my city streets. I want to believe in something.

With my back against the wall, and nobody to call since I only had 20p phone credit. I dialled 0800 reverse to speak to Jacky. "After the name, please say your tone." I shouted, "Steve Smith." So then Jacky picked up, she said, "what time do you fucking call this? I have been running the chip shop single handedly all day, where have you been? You still on the run ar ya? I have had to recruit new staff because of this bollocks. You are supposed to help me out around the chip shop." I said, "I was framed for a murder I didn't commit." Jacky said, "oh right, well that changes everything doesn't it, but I am having to serve customers. I have to do jobs. And you are just standing there phoning me up."

I said, "I have a police officer hostage, PC Rickshaw." Jacky said, "I have been shagging both Marko and Regan, just to get your attention back. You can fuck off." I can hear the click after someone hangs up. Man I already knew she was shagging them. I didn't need a running commentary. Besides they were with me. I said, "Marko, where's Regan?" Marko said, "don't know, in the bog, why do you care? How's Jacky anyway?" I said, "she's alright."

All kinds of things crossed your mind at this point. All kinds of things. Man I was in the shit. I knew I was now. And it was never ending. But there you go. That's how life is.

So whilst Lee is ordering our Pizzas, this is a mugs game. This whole thing. And for the life of me. I don't know where to begin. I mean, they can try and frame me, for killing Lee. Wait a minute, the hostage negotiator was called Lee. Was this big fat sausage of a coincidence. I have no idea. I grab my megaphone, angry. I shout, "hey listen here mother fucker you want to fuck with me, be my guest. But I have all of the information I need right now piggies."

No response. Marko said, "mate, it's The Police, they don't respond half the time, last time I was in custody. They only gave me back one shoe, when leaving. Said they lost the other shoe. What the hell was I supposed to do with one shoe?" I said, "fuck all you can do with one shoe mate." Marko said, "exactly."

I didn't know what to think anymore. I didn't know what to say. The struggle was too much. I for one didn't know. How long this was going to take. Next thing you know. Jacky turns up, with The Police, and is hurling abuse. This is all I need.

The Pizza's arrive. Marko has the shotgun, he points it at the hostage negotiator Lee. Marko shouts. "Put them on the floor, now step away." The hostage negotiator does so. Then Marko slams the door in his face. The hostage negotiator said, "thanks." Marko said, "what?" Lee said, "you forgot the drinks." Marko said, "just put them through the letter box." I said, "yeah do that." Marko said, "Go on, through the letter box." The hostage negotiator shouted, "alright then." The hostage negator Lee. He said, "hang on, they don't fit through the letter box. Now Marko opens the door. Shotgun right at Lee's throat. Marko says. "Put them on the floor, and then step away with your hands on your head." Lee does so, but then you can see him reaching for a gun in his back pocket. Marko shuts the door. Runs up the stairs with all of the pizzas, and drinks. A couple of drinks spill down the stairs. You can hear lots of rapid fire from The Police. Next thing you know the door gets kicked in. "Police officers!" I went downstairs and I said, "hey, not now, nows time for us to eat the pizzas, didn't they teach you that when you signed up. You don't want to raid us whilst we have pizzas."

Sheriff John Murphy, a yank, appears on the scene. Fresh from the states. He yells. "Give yourselves up you low life's." I said, "give ourselves up, once we finish the Pizza." PC John Murphy said, "when will that be?" I said, "how longs a piece of string? you look like a hobo." The Police officers just stood there. PC John Murphy said, "go on, raid the fuckers" I said, "if you come any closer we are going to kill PC Rickshaw." Another guy on the scene. A firefighter. John Pleb. He shouts, "just give yourselves up, for crying out loud." I said, "why the hell are you getting involved man? Aren't you supposed to be putting out fires and shit." He said, "hey fuck you dick wad, and remember, it's the 999 family." I said, "the 999 family is over rated. My ballsack could take those 999 calls, with my dick. I could talk through my bollocks, and answer the calls, through my bollocks. And fart through the phone. And fuck you, you hairy animal. fuck you. Don't come up in here thinking you rule the roost. We rule the roost. We are the chip shop crew. You are amateurs."

A DC arrives. DC Long Dick. DC Long Dick shouts, "give yourselves up, for crying out loud." I said, "after we eat our pizza for crying out loud."

Now this might sound like your typical hostage situation. And to be honest. I wouldn't be surprised if it was. But the real thing was. The thing that I knew. Is that I spent a year in the states. After I finished with the marines. Left in New York. Lived in an apartment block.

Buffalo. Then I went to France for 2 months. Then I went to Germany. Then travelled around London. But after that the Yid army remained strong. The Yid Army would approve, but we all want to know where we are going to be. Jacky shouting obscenities through the window. "You fucking dickhead, I am having to run the chip shop, single-handed now, because of you geezers." You get stuck, don't you. One thing after another. After another.

I didn't know what else to think. What else to feel. I felt trapped. Some times that's all you need. Is to feel something. Feel something that you once knew. The basic fundamental rights. Making sure you were okay with life. Being framed for a crime you hadn't committed.

That was a piss take. It really was. Not knowing where the world was going. It just took me by surprise.

Jacky was still outside giving it the large one. "We are going bankrupt now." It's one of the hardest things to accept. Knowing your chip shop is out of business.

I shouted, "Jacky we have the pizzas." Next thing you know. PC Danny Kite. Starts giving it the large one. One of the armed police officers. From the anti terrorism armed police unit. He shouts, "Hey suck my ballsack you stupid sons of bitches, you should be licking on my nuts right now."

I said, "hey fuck you dude, do you see us with bibles, so why is this an act of terrorism? You are the terrorist. You have broken martial law." Next thing you know. Danny shouts, "MARTIAL LAW." Very loudly, you can hear air raid sirens, and missiles being thrown on the ground. I shouted, "what the fuck is going on? It's us three, with once police officer man, what the fuck is the problem with you guys?"

Danny shouts, "Military will be here soon." I said, "suck my ballsack." We had PC Rickshaw hostage. And now we get the military in. I said, "hey, all of you should be sucking on my ballsack right now."

Danny says, "tempting, but I don't swing that way." I said, "shut up, everybody." So we are eating our pizzas, and having our coca cola and everyone was happy. I mean that's what we wanted. I mean, me, Marko and Regan Were happy. Now if I had listened to my instincts and laid low for a while. *This whole thing might not have happened.*

The idea was to destroy the guillotine before anyone else did. It's a proverb by the way. It basically means when your back is against the wall. You come to desperate measures, in desperate times. And the earth shatters, and you feel so afraid. Especially at night. When the world is spinning around.

Like a damn express train. That's what it was.

Things started to pile up. Things just escalated

PC Rickshaw should be sucking on my ballsack right now. Fed up of the guy. I am the real deal. And I don't like him, and I think he is a nob.

With your back against the wall. There is nothing much you can do. With all of the thoughts going through my head. I just felt for the bloke.

I mean, I don't even know what was going on anymore. Things lessen, things change. Times change. Next thing you know, a purple elephant flies in the room. Defeated, outnumbered. Lost. Chaotic. Stressed.

Proverb, no elephant really. But you get lost. You find your way down dark tunnels. So we are holding this guy hostage. This police officer. Now we are in martial law!? For crying out loud, just because of three people.

Marko lets out a fart, and by that time. I know it's game over.

Meanwhile a prostitute knocks on the door, and tries begging for money. And I am in the middle of my pasta. And it's really bad timing you know. I mean I appreciate the offer of sex. But at this moment in time. I didn't really want to open the window to this lady.

So I think, on some days, you know, I have this police officer. Held hostage. And I get it, I get that feeling of powerlessness. In the end. I grabbed a gun, a loaded 9mm pistol. Shot myself in the head.

Twenty eight days later. "Sir, can you hear

me?" A nurse is looking over me. I said, "who the fuck are you?" She said, "sir, we have a zero tolerance policy of being a fucking jerk in this hospital you prick. So you better behave yourself." I said, "you mean you have a zero tolerance policy?" She said, "yeah." I said, "why didn't you just say that then?" She said, "go jump off a bridge, so anyway, we have had a look at the injury to your skull. And nothing has happened. I mean, it's clear there's a bullet in your head now. But it didn't kill you."

I said, "what was it blank?" She said, "it was a blank bullet, that's why you're alive." I said, "blank bullets can still kill?" She said, "yeah but the way you shot yourself, you shot yourself in the head, and completely missed the brain. And err, it's just lodged in your head. No brain damage. Nothing. Just one bullet inside your head. And we have two options."

I said, "alright then." She said, "the first option is we remove the bullet." I said, "second?" She said, "keep it in there, but it's going to cause an infection, so we best act quickly. Your theatre awaits." I am put under anaesthetic. And next thing I know. 10 doctors, around me. 10 surgeons I mean. Green coats. I remember the green gowns. I then remember. "Sir, are you with me, are you with me....are you with me.....sex with a hillbilly." I said, "you what!?" The surgeon said, "nothing, listen, you really are cramping my style. I am trying to run this hospital here. I am the chief surgeon and you are cramping my style. Now go to sleep." I said, "sir, I don't think the anaesthetic is working." Next thing I know I pass out. I wake up 4 hours later.

The same female nurse. No idea why she was giving me verbal abuse. Maybe she was flirting with me. She said, "alright, you're done, fill the release forms." I filled in some release forms.

She said, "now fuck off." So I walked off, and walked down the stairs. With some angry paramedics. Putting up signs saying, "zero tolerance, I have big problems with patients. I am losing my patience. I should have been a stockbroker..."

I said to him, "hey man, you should have been a stockbroker." He said, "hey fuck you jerk off, go jump in a pond you fat son of a bitch." Next thing I know. He calls the cops on me.

Two officers show up. Both have moustaches One of the officers. PC Cream cake. He said, "hey listen here son, listen real good, we have had reports of you being abusive inside the hospital. Now is this true?'" I said, "no I don't think so." PC Pie, the other officer said, "give me your ID or fuck off." I handed him my ID. I said, "same person I have always been." He said, "Steve Smith."

I said, "yeah." He said, "I've known you since forever, let me go and have a word with this paramedic hold on."

So PC Pie, and PC Cream cake, go and have a word with the paramedic. And the paramedic is claiming I was abusive. Even though all I did was ask why he wasn't a stockbroker. So in the end. After all that time. I said, "listen here man." The paramedic said, "this geezer, Steve Smith, swore at one of our nurses" PC Pie said, "did she swear back?" The paramedic said, "yes." PC Pie said, "it's a civil matter." The paramedic shouts, "it's a public order offence." PC Pie said, "was there anyone around, besides him and the nurse?" The paramedic said, "no." PC Pie said, "this is very low level, we could get him done under section 4 of the public order act. But I have to do paperwork right now. For a missing child that I just found. And I think this is low level, and I have to go to jobs and stuff, and my Axon body cam is on. Because I don't really know anymore, what is going on." PC Pie continued, "don't call again." The paramedic said, "are we on the same team?" PC Pie said, "same league, we're above you in the table, and don't forget that. You start playing agent provocateur, we are going to have issues." He shouts, "I am a paramedic." PC Pie said, "should have been a stock broker."

I said, "I have done some online poker." I get shouts of "shut up", from everyone. In the end. I am arrested for a public order offence. And taken to the cells. I get some custody Sargent, big belly. Leaning over the counter. He said, "name". I said, "Steve Smith." He said, "real name." I said, "that is my real name." The Sargent said, "any hobbies?" I said, "I like poetry." The desk Sargent shouted, "release him." So I am released, and they got a tattooist to tattoo "NFA" on my forehead.

Next thing you know, I am at the tattooist, to get it removed. Laser removal surgery. I said, "I need this thing removed dude." He said, "sure, it's going to take 10 sessions man, 10 sessions man" I said, "I heard you the first time." Got lasered one session, and you could barely see it. Saw him again, and it was gone. I didn't let the ink heal, so I was kind of in luck really, so the tattoo was removed. But I did say to the police. "was that real ink?" And they laughed and said it was semi permanent So it was a set up anyway. The PC Pie dude said, "mate, we really messed with your head on this one. It was non permanent" I said, "a minute ago, you said semi permanent" PC Pie said, "fuck off out of my crazy way, you hillbilly, goat fucking man, of no good. I have a body cam. What do you have. A nutsack. Yeah, microscope." I said, "yeah okay." He said, "hey, fuck you dude, you come up to me and ask me for directions?"

I said, "where's Pale Ale?" PC Pie said, "how the fuck should I know?"

Chapter 21

If I had listened to my instincts and laid low for a while. None of this would have happened. The football ended, the apocalypse started. Zombies appeared on mass. Running around the world, with water pistols.

Police officers were sending messages to old girlfriends on Facebook, asking them to sleep overs. But wait, this wasn't the whole career suicide thing was it. The whole just, brain malfunction.

Because we all care about other people's approval.

Yet I realise something. Something in my mind. You pause and you would miss it. It was the times you leave behind. The times that stop you from believing in yourself.

So there you have it, it was like a brainwave almost. Bad news was bad news all along. I just knew it was coming. And the thing is. Is that there are no police. It was all a figment of my imagination. They were hired actors. Yeah right. Only as if. And if you know, that things work both ways. The sheer ruthlessness of life. The swinging of life. Swingers parties, but realising something. What we see. What we understand. Is throughout all of the pain, and discomfort. To have time to think. Time to believe in yourself. But not like this... It was never supposed to be like this.... I mean, calling the police piggy's. That was just the start. But even though they felt helpless. I felt their pain. They were tugging on my heart strings, you know.

So far, in my life, when I made up with Regan. I was going to speak to Marko. I was going to understand everything except why life was just failing me.

Chapter 22

All of a sudden. Everything stopped you know. You could feel a mixture of emotions.

But it all came down to today. Reckoning day.

I wake up, cold, alone, frightened. I don't know where I was going to end up. Everything stopped. Finally I accepted who I was. I was nothing. I was no one. The Yid Army fell to pieces, and what fell to pieces too was the Chip Shop Crew. With all of these talks about silicone valley. I realised. Me, Marko, and Regan. We met for a pint. But because of the apocalypse All the football players had turned into zombies. And it was the end of the fucking world.

Marko pours a large beer, and says, "you know, I think about the police all the time man." I said, "why?" Marko said, "because every step you take was a good song bro, why do you think?" I said, "I thought you meant The Police as in the piggy?"

Next thing you know, outside the Royal Crown in Belgravia. Met Police were outside with tazers. Loudspeakers. One cop. PC Carlson, he shouted, "Steve, give yourself up."

I grab my little megaphone and I shouted, "I am not guilty, I didn't kill Lee." Wow, imagine being framed for a crime. You didn't commit. But then imagine that the guy. That you were supposed to have killed. Didn't even exist. That was the level of brainwashing The Police were doing.

For the record though, I remained resilient. You know. Since the apocalypse All games were postponed And some of the cops had turned into zombies. Me, Marko and Regan were okay.

And then, an explosion, outside. PC Ralph farted into a gas canister with a match, and lit his butt cheeks on fire. And it wasn't really going down well you know.

I yelled, "show some professionalism." PC Ralph was taken to hospital. Nobody was safe. And with a note. That read the following. It was a poem. It was a poem on the ground. It read the following.

"I walk in shadows,
It's the end of the world,
The only way to stop the end of the world,
Is to destroy the guillotine,
Before your enemy does,
Things aren't as they seem,
Things are far away,
Things are blurry,
Things just don't make sense,
I wish I could find a way."

Then nothing, I don't know who had written this. But it made sense if you came to think about it. I wanted to find the answers. Only to find myself in ground zero of a pub. Where the noise, made the ambience seem steady. You were always going to find a way. One minute you're a leper. The next minute. It's this all over again.

You always think of things, pink elephants, purple elephants. Things I have missed. Chances also. But inside my head I knew the Chip Shop Crew wasn't going to last forever.

Chapter 23

If only I had listened to my instincts and laid low for a while. None of this would have happened. I am still in The Cheshire And I am fed up. And things are going nowhere. And things keep playing over and over in my head. Jacky's getting angry with me. The Chip Shop is still running. But we had to ban PC Ralph from going in because he was queue jumping.

Then he says, "is this a life time ban?" Jacky said, "just give it a week matey, then you will be okay." So for the last week. PC Ralph, has been feeling sorry for himself. Eating Ben and Jerries ice cream. Under the duvet, whilst watching Dear John under the covers. And crying. Whilst his cat is there in the background. This has to cease, because this is just further shenanigans with The Police.

This wasn't good enough. Nothing was. With your back against the wall. There is only so much I can take. I feel somewhat hollow. I do admit. The Chip Shop Crew, it was meant to send a message. It was the main hooligan firm alongside the Yid army. Now with all of the shenanigans with The Police. It's just what I have serious problems with. I am in the Cheshire. Prostitutes galore outside. And that's just the start. You often wander why you feel a certain way. Why it matters in some respects. Why anything does. Or wether you feel some kind of value. The value I had was gone. The dealings I had were broken.

Times had changed. People had become left with intrigue. The anger builds up, and when the anger builds up. It really does build up. Things weren't the same. Not that I wanted them to be the same. I just wanted a peaceful life, and I look through my life. I look through my existence. And I look at what has happened. In relation to my time. My time on this planet. The Cheshire would never be the same. Never would be the same pub. What I had in my chest. That would never change. And with that. The amount of information I have. To move myself forward, in some respects. Would keep me grounded. In some way you feel alienated. With your back against the wall. You would find yourself in a position where you didn't know where you started. Then it was time for payback. Then it was time for something we really wanted to do and that was to go to the Tottenham vs Chelsea game. 4th of March. At Tottenham. 2022. And I was buzzing. I shouted, "oi oi, cock and bollocks, cock and bollocks, and cock and bollocks to the lot of ya! I tell you that now. I am a one man island. I tell you this now! OI OI CHIP SHOP CREW." Next thing you know Marko and Regan show up. And Marko's just slept with a hooker and he's feeling tired saying, "oh she wore me out."

I said, "I am not surprised." Next thing you know. PC Totsworth appears. I said, "matey, I thought you were dead." He said, "faked my own death, now I am back to life, you egg head, what do you expect? You talk so much crap. You know... Go and watch your game. You low life." I said, "with all due respect sir, you are the low life." He said, "you are the low life." I said, "*you* are indeed, the low life, not me." He said, "hey listen here feller, you are the low life piece of shit, you are the one creating these shenanigans" I said, "creating shenanigans, the police, all you do is try and cause confusion. I am here to create change, and go to the game. And be there for people, and show my support. Not that it ever mattered to you in the first place. You look over, you see yourself. Part of the price you have to pay for living in the first place. And the people who try to help, you just spit in their face. What's the point. In anything. You want to be honest with me. You want to say how I feel right now. I am annoyed. Damn straight."

Marko said, "leave it out." I said to PC Totsworth said, "hold me up against the wall, and shoot me, I can't read the files. I don't read what's on the police national computer system...I can't see what's going on. It's a load of bollocks.That would be enough for you to understand. It's lies. Lies, and more lies. You swallowed the bollocks that was handed to ya. I am telling ya. Nothing can be done. I am a lone ranger. You give me, this crap again, and consequences WILL NEVER be the same. You tell me this! You explain. You try to blame me for the war in Iraq, you try to blame me for global warming. Man you are tripping. You try and blame me for all kinds of things man. You try and blame me for the war in Syria. Man you are tripping. I know, because I was there. You told yourself a million times. This is Yid Army. We have to respect this. So where is the respect? Where is it going? You want to know? Down the fucking drain, down the toilet. cock and bollocks to you and your whole family.

You think you can start this shit with me, and get away with it. You want to know that you are talking through your arse half of the time. You know. And even then it wouldn't make sense. Get your bollocks into gear, get out there, and find a way to make change. This bullshit aside. fuck you." He said, "hey, I prefer not to," I said, "it wasn't an invite, Yid Army, all of the way. You want to act like this is a joke. You want to act like you have something to do. Well forget it. No pride, no glory. All stems back from the reality of the situation. What I knew, and what everyone else knew. It was about pride. It was about going out there and doing something, but you're not entertaining me. You are not there for that reason anyway. And all I see you do is read documentarists, and biographies about horses. Where is your god damn respect!? Eh, where is the respect, because I don't think you have this respect right now. I ask you to shut the fuck up you piece of shit. And next time you come here, trying to talk a lot of crap. Then I will tell you to stick your axon body camera up arse, stick radio up arse, stick your baton up your arse. Stick your radio up your arse. Stick your wife's thong up your arse. Shove a traffic cone up your arse. Shove everything you have, and shove it up your arse. You Svengali, you are nowhere near to be trusted. I let off the steam, and you tell me something. To fuck with you, what the fuck are you expecting. Hey. What the fuck are you doing? Then you explain. Then you explain what is happening."

He said, "you're a trouble maker mate, plain and simple. That's what's going on, and I can't sanction it." I said, "you can shove your long words up your arse, you nut case. You want to say how I feel. How things evolve. You know. You cretin. How about that for motivation. Because you are the problem. You are the guy behind all of this. You are the Svengali. You are the guy in charge of all of these operations. And I have seen you give people lethal injections in hospitals. But I am still alive. You can go fuck yourself with a broom stick. Who do you think you are? Some kind of dickhead or something? This is the truth. This is why I am here. To have the same respect. But you weren't giving me that. So fuck you, and your whole family. I deserve better than this. I deserve better. You hide away the whole time. Nothing would compare. Suck my ballsack. You snake." PC Totsworth said, "well, you sure do have a way of words, don't you, you cretin, go and enjoy the game." I said, "I will enjoy the game, when you ain't there to fucking provoke me. You have been causing me confusion."

Marko trips over a traffic cone, rises to his

feet. Then his the deck. And he gets involved. He said, "listen, you need to be serious here, you need to evaluate the situation. This was what the Yid Army was. Respect. *But this isn't a way forward.* Police us all you want, but you are a snake in the fucking grass. What am I going to do now!? What am I going to do. Fuck!"

Regan turns up, after trying to solicit a hooker, and he said, "fuck all of you, bunch of dicks. I am trying my best to behave myself. But that prostitute. Man she was trying to charge me too much. Does she think my cock is made of gold or something?" I said, "mate, that is over the top, why are you getting involved?"

PC Ralph appears. PC Ralph is a blonde guy. I think I have mentioned him before. PC Ralph said, "Hey, fuck *all of you, stick all of the traffic cones you have up your arse.*" I said, "you Svengali." He said, "you have no idea, we have a job to do, and are you going to watch the game?" I said, "it hasn't kick off yet." He said, "yeah but behave yourselves." I said, "I am trying to, until you got involved." A fit of rage, something I wasn't proud of. Next thing you know, 20 skinheads, get involved, and we start scrapping.

I shout, "fight". TSG turn up in riot gear and start shouting. "Police." Regan has a hot dog, throws it at one of them. And says, "Disgrace..." I said, "good launch." I shout, "missile attack". I have lots of stones, and rocks, and pebbles, and we are throwing them. And they are clattering the Police. Throwing coins, any bit of shrapnel we had. Anything heavy enough and small enough to make an impact was thrown. A traffic cone was launched. Coins were thrown. I was throwing all of my 2p and 1p coins away. "Here you go dickheads." Regan said, "nice." He said, "look at my coin holster." He has a coin holster, full of different sized coins. And I said, "nice." Regan grabbed lots out, and shouted, "Shrapnel!." TSG arrived, one of them was injured, and police medics were on scene. St Johns Ambulance was on scene. Everyone got involved. I said to Regan "Whens kick off?" He said, "20 minutes." So we charged towards the stand, didn't have a ticket and the police chased us. We kick the security in the chest. We toppled them over. Regan throws coins at the security. And grabs out lots of shrapnel, and says. "Get back out of my way now!?." The security leg it. Marko sets oud a flare. Regan sets off a bigger flare.

All of this talk about silicone valley, all of this talk about the way I feel inside. It all went to waste. All of the perpetual nightmares. Like a colossal feeling of anger. Rising above my stomach, and making me feel frustrated. I felt like the world was on my shoulders. I think it was. So we enter the stadium, and the female steward, she said, "I have no sympathy for you. Get out." I said, "nah what it is, is we have got tickets but we lost them." The female steward says, "lost them where?" Regan said, "lost them up our arse cheeks. Can't find them." She said, "very funny lads..." Sarcastically. I said, "roses are red, violets are blue, sit back down, and sh, nothing to do with you." She said, "nothing to do with me? This is my job?" I said, "yeah, I mean, it's a pilots job to fly a plane but doesn't mean he has to do it." Regan said, "that means the plane would crash." I said, "no idea, don't know how it works." Next thing I know I shout out. "Wolf!" The female stewardess. Called Jane. She said, "where the fuck is the Wolf? Where is the wolf?" I said, "no idea, how the fuck should I know, I just felt like shouting it. So bollocks to you, your whole family."

She said, "my brothers serving in the marines." Me, Marko and Regan, did a little pep talk. I said, "damn, shit man, if her brother is in the marines. Then that shit is serious man. That is shit is serious. That means it's ethics, and values man Like he is serving." I said to Jane, "which army?" She said, "what?!" I said, "why army is he fighting with? That makes all the difference." She said, "UK British Marine." I said, "Shit." Regan took his hat off. I took my hat off. Marko pulled his trousers up because his cock and bollocks was showing. I said, "sorry about that, I didn't realise, he's not a corrupt marine though?" She said, "no". I said, "Alright, on the basis that your brother or whatever is in the marines. We will do you a discount. We will stay in the Stadium. But we won't smash up the goal keeper and throw him in the net. That's the gold package." She said, "what's the platinum package?" I said, "we sit down, we enjoy the game, and we don't call anyone a cunt." She said, "that's quite a good package." I said, "£300 please" She said, "you trying to extort me?" I said, "are you a hooker?" She said, "no". I said, "so why would I be trying to escort you?" Jane said, "extort." I said, "prostitute." Regan takes me aside, and he says, "listen, show some respect, her brother is in the military." I said, "she's just saying that." Next thing you know, some nob head, who clearly is pretending to be in the military appears.

I said, "you're the brother." He said, "yeah." I said, "I served in the marines, Marko, and Regan All of us three. And I know you're not a marine." He said, "how did you know that?" I said, "because your uniform, the regiment number doesn't exist." He asks, "how do you know all of these things?" I said, "It was my job for ten years you lunatic, are you seriously trying to pull this stunt?" I showed him one of my bravery awards. For killing an Iraqi, with an AK47. But the reason I was awarded the award. Is because it was such a good shot. Because the Iraqi soldier was basically 200 metres away from me. And people were saying, "mate without a sniper, you have no chance." So I got up to the top floor of the building. And I used precision and I waited until he was still. One shot, to the head. And a couple of more shots to the body. Just for effect. So hence the bravery award."

Jane said, "can we backtrack a bit here, you are trespassing, you don't have a ticket." Marko shouts sarcastically. "Oh, *you are trespassing, you don't have a ticket."* I said, "look, we have tickets, they are shoved up our arses." Jane said, "well un-shove them from your arses, and show them to me." I looked at Regan and I said, "you ready?" Jane said, "don't be silly, stop playing this act." I said, "stop pretending your brother is in the military then." Next thing you know, armed police arrive. Because someone falsely reported Marko had a gun. Even though all it was, was a burrito.

"Armed Police, Armed Police Put the burrito down."

Marko said, "is a burrito a gun?" The Met police officer, shouts, "it depends how you use it mate, to some people it can look like a gun." Jane turned over, and she said, "how the fuck can a burrito look like a gun?" I said, "It's an optical illusion, anything can look like anything. Just like I thought Jane was a prostitute until I got to know her." Met police were armed. They eventually put down their weapons. The Sargent who was armed, he said, "it was just food, so why were you holding it in a shooting gesture?" Marko said, "I don't know, lots of people do that gesture, when a footballer scores a goal, they do that gesture." The Sargent, Sargent Craddock. He said, "are you a footballer?"

Marko said, "I was in Southampton under 11's". Sargent Craddock said, "but you are not playing for Southampton now." Marko said, "Might do."

Sargent Craddock said, "this is serious, because if you do play for Southampton..." PC Rufus, catches up. He's the most gormless copper I know. He isn't armed. Just more high vis. He shouts, "none of them play football for any team."

Marko said, "I play for Southampton." Jane said, "just a minute ago, you were trying to extort me." I said, "we have already been over this, we understand you are not an escort anymore. Now we have gotten to know you well enough."

Jane screamed. "Get these men out of here!" We were all placed in a holding cell. In the football ground. Tottenham. Us three. All in one cell. Which I found unusual, because usually in Britain. You get your own cell.

So we are there for 24 hours, 24 hours of pure misery. All there was, was one copper and a security guard. The copper was sat down. Wetness dripping from the ceiling. The PC was called PC Jerk Off He said, "alright." I said, "listen, can we get released." He said, "no it's PC Jack North, not jerk off." I said, "mate don't jerk off in here, are you mental?" Regan shouted, "Oi oi saveloy." And we are all holding these sausages. And I am singing, "down the apple and pears, the frog and toad, pie and mash, it doesn't get old. Went to London. And I shouted to the women. Show us your Bristols! Show us your Bristol cities. And then I was told to stop talking with my rabbit and pork. Until some prostitutes came along but she didn't take debit card. So I couldn't really sleep with her." PC Jack North said, "immature." I said, "in your mind." PC Jack North said, "in lots of people's minds dude, you're a lunatic." I said, "show us your ID then?" He showed me his warrant card. I said, "where are you stationed?" He said, "Elland Road." I said, "you're a bit far from home aren't you?" He said, "yes, but resources are tight, and I was on the motorway dealing with a job. And I got this call and I took it because you're a dickhead."

I said, "you are a dickhead." PC North said, "no you are a dickhead." I said to PC North. "You are the dickhead. You are the one with the dickhead attitude. Dickhead. Dickhead." Marko said, "can we stop with all of this dickhead talk please."

PC North said, "fellers, behave yourselves." I said sarcastically. "*Oh fellers behave yourselves.*" PC North said, "you see this baton, sit down, and shut your fucking rabbit and pork." I said, "you shut your rabbit and pork. If you are from Leeds, then how come you're a cockney guy?" He said, "no comment." I said, "that's what I said to your wife, when she asked to give me a hand job." PC North said, "that makes no sense." I said, "neither does your face."

To be fair, his face didn't make sense. And this was further shenanigans with The Police. This had to cease. Put PC North really made us feel intimidated.

PC North then opens a copy of The Sun, and shouts, "yeah get in there." As he is on page 3. I looked at him. He said, "What are *you* looking at?" I said, "well couldn't help but notice you ogling some lady on page 3." He turned the page over, and he said. "Yeah, and

240

what are you going to do about it?" I said, "complain." I said, "you do think you are a big jerk off idiot, and maybe you are, but listen. You have a job to do. I know you come from Elland Road. And you think you're hard because your wife is a hooker. But you have a job to do. So do I."

He said, "you have no job, at the end of every month, I get paid. At the end of every month, you go to jail." I said, "yeah so we lead different lives, everyone has different lives, it's a damn travesty it really is. I wanted to make progress in careers. But now, when I look at what we have achieved. What I look at the games and the violence we have started. It won't stop, it can't stop. My back aches just thinking about it. I feel nervous and just wish things were different you know. Maybe on some other planet, where everything is perfect. Man, you know, we are not living in a perfect world. Not anymore. And the more I try to justify this and say to you, we have come a long way. Sure we have. But *now*, after all we have been through. To say that I am on the *wrong side of the law*. Would be an understatement. But yeah, you're the Sherrif. You explain, what you have to do. Go on."

PC North said, "you are right, I do get paid." Next thing you know, a green monster. The size of an elephant breaks the walls, and charges towards PC North. The green monster said, "fuck you piggy." Me, Regan and Marko were free. The green monster grew wings and flew us to safety.

Alright, back to reality here. That was just in my head. PC North said, "fuck you and your whole family, how about that jerk off." I said, "at least I don't have a name that sounds like Jerk off." PC North said, "you think you're clever." I said, "no." He said, "we are not the feelings police, we don't give a fuck about your feelings, you do a crime, you do the time." I said, "that's a bit ruthless isn't it." He said, "so is my ballsack and cock." I said, "man you sound like a sexual aggressor." He said, "only towards dogs." I said, "what the fuck!" PC North said, "dogs, you know." I said, "you sexually abuse dogs." He said, "only on weekends, to keep up with the joneses." I said, "you're sick." He said, "I am fucking with you, of course I don't abuse dogs. But you are the bellend who believed it. So I blame you."

I said, "fuck you and your whole family." He said, "hey, fuck you, your family, and their ancestors, you you can't do better than that can you?" I said, "you think you're so smart." He said, "I know I am smart."

I can't do this anymore. You read everything. The scriptures. The noises. The times you forget. The times you realise things go wrong. And then nothing happens. Your dreams build up in your head, and then you are left with nothing. Every good opportunity, is a bad one in disguise. You are your own worst enemy. Your own life, your own day dream. It becomes a virtual reality. Then there is nothing left but thin air. Dust. Like a vacuum of smoke. Life was full of misfits, and people who didn't want to fit into society. And when people did fit in. They were obnoxious and rude, and the world was ruthless. Pitiless. And that's where I come along, because I am looking at PC North right now. You know, and I see what he's capable of. He does hip hop dancing in his spare time. And he once made out with a transvestite I said to him, "hey, PC North, don't I get the phone call?'" He said, "ah, the phone call, yeah go on then." I get my one phone call. I phoned a premium rate sex line. The mrs wasn't happy with me. She hates me calling her at work.

PC North said, "hey, stop talking to Jacky, does she work for a premium rate sex line now? And she's still running the chip shop? What else does she do? Does she play the Banjo?" I said, "quite well." PC North said, "listen you egg head, fried muffin, piece of dick cheese, you listen to me carefully, you are the one that is the problem. You are the one creating criminal mischief. You are the one to blame. I have my eyes on you." I said, "I am in jail, how can I escape, through a fence?" He said, "there are no fences in jail." I said, "what is there in jail?" He said, "no prostitutes I know that." I said, "what is it with you and prostitutes." He said, "well I have known your wife a long time."

I said, "seriously, you seriously want to call my wife a prostitute." PC North said, "well she works for a premium rate sex line." I said, "yeah because she needs to make money. The Chip shop alone isn't enough." He said, "save me the crap, maybe at Christmas I will buy you a mince pie. But I feel no pity for you. You forced your way onto the ground. Tottenham. You called the female stewardess, a hooker. You claimed her brother was not in the marines. When he was. Your friend over there Marko, did a shooting gesture with a burrito. Triggering armed police. Do I need to go on?" I said, "no, actually, that's a perfect summary of our day."

Marko is asleep but wakes up when he hears burrito. He says, "where man? Give me a burrito." He looks at PC North and he says, "shame on you, shame on you PC North. This is false imprisonment."

But nothing is as it seems. I got back ache just from this conversation. I get boredom from the sounds of the trains, and a headache from the traffic. I get like this. But nothing seemed to slow me down. Nothing. And you can talk all day about responsibility, right and wrong. This, that, and the other. You can look all of the time at things, people get sick, they get well. They die, they go to funerals. The vicar is there. The 6 feet is dug. And then what? Just nothing. Nothing but an emotion you could feel. Grief. And I know what that emotion feels like. I know how it feels, and I know what's happening. I didn't deserve to be in this cell. And the more I think about it. The more it makes sense. I was vindicated against the murder of Lee, also known as Pale Ale. But the rest was history. All of these talks with The Police. All of the happiness. It washed away. It left me with nothing. And all of the swearing, and abuse. Left right and centre. Between me and The Police. Was nothing but a memory of the times we could have shared.

We could have been on the same side, we could have had an opportunity to fight crime together. Instead I was belittled, and rejected. Thought the Marines gave me hope. But then nobody seemed to care. I only have one bravery award from shooting an Iraqi dead. And Marko has more. Those medals that we had. So we are all ex marines, and then. We go onto the streets, we fight. Some ex marines, would go and enlist to work with The Police. But ever since we have PC Townsend walking around. Strutting his stuff. Like he owned the place. Most police officers would say in my ear. "I really don't like you." Another police officer would say, "hey, that's enough, be professional". But either way you can't make sure of anything. You are left in a whirlwind and even then nothing comes your way.

You try and act the big man but it doesn't get you anywhere. You try and act tough, and it just makes you seem small. I tried so hard to get out of the Yid Army. I tried so hard to forgive Thatcher. I tried so hard to see this flaming world just dissipate.

With the only people, that I have ever loved, and ever loved me. I have lost. Because of my stupidity. I just can't cope. You look at the world now, and you look at the microscopic penis on PC North. And you just shudder and need therapy. Therapy was hard to find. Therapy, for us council estate, unemployed folk. Was a talk down the pub with the locals. Therapy for us lads, was a fight in the subway. Therapy for us lads, was a fart bomb in a brothel. And it was worth it. The hookers went wild. Scared them a bit. It's good having a prank store in your hometown. But the more I look at things, and the more I realise. Through different opinions and different feelings. Thoughts. You became just part of this society. The society you once lived in and it caved in. Before you knew it, you were just exchanging words. Doing the best you could. Doing what you could do. But even then you were struggling. I always liked to believe one day I was going to make it. Get out of the mess of crime, and go somewhere more efficient. Fighting, was our therapy.

The scraps we had, was our release. After having a fight in the subway. Your anxiety levels went down. Before the fight. Your adrenaline, levels went up. After the fight, it was like having the 'volume turned down'. Everything was more surreal, nice, peaceful, tranquil. Nobody even cared about getting a tooth missing. Nobody cared about getting bruises on their faces. Scars on their faces. Fighting for us, was a release. Going to the game was a release.

And for better or for worse. For every good cop out there, there was a bad one. The good cop bad cop routine in every city. In London. It was old, and boring and trite, and we knew what it meant. Behind all of the vulgar swearing, and the opinionated arguments between me and The Police. There was some room for discussion. That room, became more of a room. The headaches became more real. I couldn't sleep some days. I regret the time wasted, looking back. When they say working hard is a load of bollocks, it's not. It's just when you get caught up in this gang culture. You get caught up and you can't stop. It becomes an addiction. Skinheads, fighting skinheads.

Biker gangs fighting biker gangs. Locked up in these cells, with the ceramic walls, and the bars. Made out of steel. In my mind was only something I could find. Deep down I just wanted closure. Deep down I just wanted something, or somebody to rely on. Deep down I just wanted someone, something, somebody. How many chances did I have to escape the Yid Army. How many chances did I have to turn my back. But I hated Chelsea. That's why I fought them. Tottenham was the proper London team. All Chelsea do is park the bus. Tottenham is the team, that gets the results.

Looking over the prestige Chelsea express train, with the dim lights and low noises. And the sounds of farts coming from the steel engines, and trains. That drove those fans from station to stadium. To realise that it was all just one misunderstanding. That all of this aside, it was something we believed in. I believed in. someone believed in. And it made it worthwhile. But behind my glare and look. Behind the exterior of life. The chances you fail and the chances where you want to escape. Some times your mind plays tricks on you. PC North's rigid, robust, and fat face. His large plump stomach. His pecs looked like floppy man tits.

His face looked like a smacked arse cheek. But I was not complaining at this point. He kept reading "the news". Which is The Sun. Meanwhile, all I am given is The Police code of Ethics. It's complimentary at my stay in Police cells. So I finish reading it.

Marko starts reading it, and he said, "I miss the military." I said, "you know, one of these days it will all make sense, all of this. All of the misunderstandings. All of the problems in the world. All of the times we have lost. All of the times we have messed up. All of the times we have became just lost. We ended up flat on our face. Therapists couldn't help us when we had the money."

Therapists can't help us now, you become lost in oblivion. You feel like you are in outer space. You become infatuated with the same things that bare truth to how you believe. You become stuck with how you feel. Become lost with how you are. Become just stuck in this narrative. This explanation, or this thought. That something would be better. Something would make sense. Something would be achievable You lead your world behind. You stay close to the people that matter. But being in this holding cell was no way to live my life. Far from it. And the more you realise that. The more you understand. Through better or for worse. Through the happiness and the pain. Happy and depressed at the same time. Blue, and smiling. In this maze.

Then to be lost. Yeah, of course you got some jerk offs, who wanted to mitigate how you felt. Say there was no maze. Say, that you were trivial, and your worries were false. But it never got down to there. PC North had us. He knew he had us. With that brazen look on his face. His attitude, and the way he looked. The brutal expression he had. The desperate expression on his face. It only reminded me of a time I once knew. When we used to have some kind of freedom. Or some kind of hope. Even though that sounds trite. With the Yid Army slowly going to a halt. And things slowly failing on that front. And with Jacky working two jobs, and I was in a holding cell. Probably the only one in Britain, because it was a stadium once. The police officer. PC North. Had held us there now for a long time. So long we had forgot how long. So long, it was a day, a night, a day. And when he went to sleep, another guard appeared. Just a security guard from the stadium. We were locked up for days. No hope. Nothing. PC North re appears with his face looking brazen, and sharp. The way you would look if you had just had a scrap. The way you would look if you just had a fight. The way you would look if you had earned something. No matter how he did it. Earned some money playing poker, chess, money, cards, this, that. The other. What he was doing. It never surprised me.

What I was doing, it never surprised me. I just can't relate to the things in which I can see. In front of me. The cells, the water leaking from the roof. The blue paint flickering away, as the bulb in the top of the roof was dim. Kept glowing, and then stopped. We were not in jail, we were prisoners. It was weeks. We were allowed to shower, allowed to get dressed. Allowed phone calls. Given meals. But we were there for weeks. Which was unusual. It almost felt like we were being detained unlawfully. But we just sat there, and a grin. A grin just to show the world. Being incarcerated. In the only stadium and team that you deeply admire. The team you stood up for, and having the same principles everyone else did. Having the same respect that everyone else had.

The slowly faltering system, and the light flickering on and off. The moths going to the flames. And a mouse crawling on the floor. Like a gift from god. Things just were, stagnant. You look at the world now, through the same theories and explanations. You look at the steel bars. You look at everything. Everything was lost.

Pink elephants, in my mind. Purple elephants. Green smoke. Things to reckon with. Things that pained you. It all was the slowly degrading feeling of being locked up. Now I know how Akon felt. *Man I love his music.*

When push came to shove, we were allowed a radio. And one song per day. So for the first day. I was playing Snoop Dog. "Still not loving Police." He was rapping. As eventually we were let out of the holding cell. Thrown to the ground.

Chapter 24

The Guillotine had to be destroyed. It was easier said than done. That was how it was feeling. Inside your chest. You were left with nothing. Nothing but a memory. Even then you weren't close. You just wanted to feel something. I felt just lost. Low on power maybe. Low on energy. Low on instincts. Kept failing me. But there you go. Let me go. I had to do what I had to do.

Life just seemed unbalanced. So it was up to me, Marko and Regan to destroy the Guillotine. And it wasn't easy. Marko said, "Steve, are you out of cuckoo land? What the fuck is going on? You are acting shady." I said, "do you want to be serious, and go down that road?" Marko said, "yeah I do." This is back at the council estate. I said, "Marko listen, it's not simple, you think it is, but it isn't. All of this stems from the fact we are worlds apart. Worlds apart from each other. And even then we became just lost. Lost in our ideals. So it never worked. But you became what I became, and that is what made you a hero. In your own right. You did what you had to do. And I respect you for that."

Marko said, "the Yid army needs us, the Yid army is all we have, you know this, and so do I. These times we are talking about. The Yid Army remains strong. Stronger than you know."

Regan said, "so now we know, obviously there are some inconsistencies in how things are going, but you believe we are trying to achieve. What anyone would want." Marko said, "true."

So sometimes you don't realise, or understand things. Some times you don't. To know where you stand in this world. To know with everything you could possibly realise. You could understand. But then nothing. When you feel like the world is against you. You always know. You always realise. That is your biggest test. To find out the truth. To find out what goes on in your brain. And then you become more reliant. Then you understand. Things become more unreal the more you look at them. Then you just realise. It's life, it's your perception. Your reality. Your choice. Your way of expression. But even then things change.

"LONDON CALLING, SEE WE AIN'T GO NO SWING." Music on our radio, "Live by the river, forget it brother, you can go it alone."

I felt that notion. So we know how it's going, and we know how life is going. Oh behind everything I had known. Behind the confusion and the doubt. Behind the colossal mistakes *you would make*. You would find solace in a home. Away from your mind. You would agree to be just a fly on the wall. Just someone to ignore. When times became lost, and we became damaged. Things become lost, and life became lost. You never wanted to venture outside. You never want to do that. You never want to because it means less than you know. You just want to help yourself in the best way you can. And find your way through stages in your life. And it makes sense to know. Throughout times ahead of you. You wanted to know, how life was. In the best of times now, you would become just unknown. To the fact of things falling. Things failing. You wouldn't know. And you wouldn't even begin to.

It became knowledge over power. This council estate was all we had, and even then it had fallen to pieces. The sheer size of things about the come. The amount of perfection we wanted to see. To be able to see the best in others. It was something I cherished. I was alone in the world. I just wanted the Yid Army to mean something.

With Marko and Regan scratching their heads. And with no idea, how to kick start the scrapping. We just had no idea how to restart our adventures. We just lost everything. Not that we had much to lose. And even then it became a travesty of some sort. Everything just came flowing back. Everything you knew. You just knew that from time to time. To get change, and to get life. Forward to the point of where you go. Is powerful beyond words. Yet we always wanted to believe. Through hardship and pain. Through life you wanted to live. Through life you wanted to see. You became just someone in their mind. In your mind. When life had left you. Away from the railroads where you used to go down, and away from the towns you used to see. It became just something you wanted to see. In so many forms. It was nothing. You could tell all of the time. It was not something I could say. For once in the time I could say. It would be believable to know. That deep down this movement meant something. But it came with a backlash. You wanted to see things develop. You wanted to see people just become who they liked. And you wanted to see yourself improve. With life just as the Yid Army would respect. As much as we loathed Thatcher. That was part of the reason for fighting. It just wasn't funny anymore. All of these taunts to The Police. All of these jokes. I look back and I cringe, because it was never supposed to be like that. It was never supposed to be us against them. It was never supposed to be a verses game.

We just lost our way, and with that we became what we hated inside. We became our own worst enemy. And we began to see this now. Throughout the times, where you would see on the river banks, and the times where we could see. With the Yid Army on collapse. And our fight arranged with the Seaburn Casuals next week. We had to go there and fight. We had to. So, along with our belongings. We left. Some fat prick was driving the coach.

It wasn't the geezer before, he refused to give his name. Until we pestered him and he said his name was. "Terry."

So we went to Sunderland. Sunderland verses Tottenham. Tottenham away. We clattered them. And we realised this. We went over. I will tell you the story. So that fat prick of a coach driver parks the coach. Before the game, you know the usual routine. So we go to the hot dog stand, and burger stand. And the woman serving. Marko shouts, "Oi Oi Saveloy, show us your tits." I said, "Marko dude, don't be so rude."

Marko said, "was just trying to be friendly." I said, "yeah but we just need to get something to eat." So we queue up. And we get something to eat. And the lady serving us is nice. Besides Marko asking to see her tits. When he got to see the sausage hot dogs. She said, "do you want a slap?" Marko then acted regretfully and was backtracking. "Oh I am sorry darling, I was just being friendly." She slapped him, and we left with the food.

I said, "Marko dude, we're in Sunderland, but the real question. Is did that slap hurt?" Marko said, "no." I said, "you're lying aren't you?" He said, "yes". I said, "that's what happens when you ask to see women's tits mate, you have to take them on dates first." Marko said, "expensive though isn't it." I said, "yeah, but anyway, so where's the Seaburn casuals?" Marko said, "look at them."

An army of Sunderland supporters came our way. A whole army. The Yid Army was strong. And we realised this. There was 200 of us. And 200 of them. They start throwing coins. And get straight into the action. We start charging in.

Imagine violence and you will imagine what happened, because that is what it was. Violence. Violence. More violence. And then even again. I was smacking the faces of the Seaburn casuals. Broken lip. My jaw felt broken. But we kept going, and kept going. Despite everything. Marko headbutted some lad, and the Seaburn casuals were soft as shit. As I had a knuckle duster and was punching them in the faces. And then some fat guy comes along. Who looks like Rick Wolla. And I punch him in the face. It's just annoying that he looked like Terry the coach driver. Fighting them. I shouted, "Incoming!." I throw a smoke grenade. And next thing you know, the whole place lights up in smoke. As Marko throws a flare also, a red one. Ironically, and we started scrapping. I was being headbutted. Then I hit the deck. I crawl up. Marko was headbutting them. We were winning. Regan had a coin holster, was throwing coins. Headbutted this one geezer who was soft as shit. And said, "Hello."' As I got straight into the action and was punching, kicking people. All of the time. And that is what was going on.

In a world you don't expect, or don't even want to pay tribute to the fact that some things matter you know. Some things do, and this is how we felt. So to believe this. In a way in which we can fight. To the death. It's something I would want to pay tribute to. Even though at times you look around. And you see these faces and they mean nothing to you. It's just priceless to see things evolving. And to know that throughout our time. We can begin to see things. Things mounting up the whole time. Things becoming left, left to see, left to realise. Left to know. That one day this whole thing would make sense.

Next thing you know, Marko was scanning this QR code, and it didn't mean jack shit to me man. I was with them. The Yid Army, the Chip Shop Crew. We get together. We get together and we fight this thing. This is a fight we can do. This is a fight we can have. This is something I want to say right now. I know we got a little thing going on with them right now. And we go around and you know what people think. And it's all a game until the wolf goes home. And the sheep see the cats. But this was the fight we wanted. This was the fight we wanted. Seaburn Casuals, getting in our faces. Like they always did. Then nothing else we could do. But that was the way forward. All of this behind. It became what we knew. What we found out. It was beyond our control. Beyond our exceptions Yet we still found a war on the streets. As big as a war you would had ever seen.

Then you know how far it's going to go. With time on our hands right now. We know how life is. How life is going. How life is saying we are okay, and then nothing is going on right now. We have nothing to say right now. This is all a game. This is all people wanted to say. As the coins were being thrown, and I was in the thick of it. That's how it was. Just one thing after another. That was the way forward. The way everyone would see. There was something we wanted to know. Something I wanted to explain. You see through the city lights, and you see. Through life itself. I just want to see. And how life can begin.

You just begin to see the violence, erupt. As I would never have guessed. This whole thing. You would see. Those are choices. This is the way forward. This is what we are doing. This is how things are going. And we look at things. And then nothing else is happening. Right now. This fight continues. The same thing we see around us. We see it all of the time you know. That's what I wanted to see. See everything. From where I started, from where I belong now. Where I am coming from. This is the way we are feeling right now. And the way we are going forwards. This whole thing. Is something we are handling right now.

Moving forward, doing the right thing, when nobody is watching. Well something like that. As I am kicking and punching the Seaburn casuals. Next thing you know. PC Totsworth shows up. On his own. Wearing a pink thong, and I said, "dude, once is an accident, maybe two times, but why do you always wear thongs dude." He said, "my mrs has thrown me out the house." I said, "how did you make it all the way to Sunderland?" He said, "train." I said, "so you could afford the train fare, but you couldn't afford to go to Primark and get some boxers."

Marko shouts, "yeah, you could have gone to Primark and got some boxers." PC Totsworth is shaking. His real name is Townsend, but you know what I am saying. I said, "well, as far as I know, you are embarrassing us man. This is more problems you are creating for us. Wearing thongs to a scrap?" PC Townsend said, "Ok I will admit, I am being blackmailed." I said, "you what?" He said, "some guy on the internet." I said, "'stop with your excuses dude, if you want to cross dress, and be a transvestite, stop making excuses dude. Just come out and say it." He said, "Okay, I am a transvestite" Next thing you know, Seaburn casuals and us stopped fighting. And we were all laughing and cheering. And going. "Whey, PC Townsend, ballsack the size of two peas." PC Townsend said, "your mistaken, they are the size of two grapes."

I said, "you're exaggerating mate, you got brass bollocks up here man. Don't come here like this. Stop cramping my style. This was further shenanigans with The Police.

PC Townsend shouts, "I can't take it anymore, I am having a nervous breakdown." I threw water over him and said. "Oh shut up, now please, we have a fight to carry on with." PC Rufus arrives, he says, "lads, if you are going to fight, please don't throw coins, you could blind someone." I said, "yeah, don't throw coins man, you could blind someone. I mean Regan over here, has a whole coin collection." Regan said, "I do indeed, and what do you make of it?"

PC Townsend scampers away into a police van for emotional support. And PC Rufus shouts, "look lads, you are making me have a nervous breakdown. You can't even fight." I said, "with all due respect constable, I doubt you can fight either." PC Rufus said, "ah you want to go down this road do you? You want to go down this road." I said, "we are in the subway, there are no roads."

Seaburn casual, skinhead shouts, "Yeah man, shut the fuck up." I shouted, "listen, all of you have got to realise, this is what is happening. We are fighting to prove a point. This is all we are trying to do. This is all we are trying to achieve. This is what we can see.

It's just a load of bollocks and we start scrapping again. PC Rufus falls over. I help him up. I said, "listen, stop ordering us about." Tactical support police turn up. Showing no empathy. "Get out the way, move, move, move." They were very ruthless.

Chapter 25

My mind wasn't clear. Don't think anything was. I look back at my life. I look at this whole set up we have. The violence on the streets erupted. Blood everywhere. It soon became a case of every cop was corrupt. We armed ourselves with shotguns, and we walked the streets. It was time to pay PC Townsend a visit. The corrupt piece of shit.

We walked into The Police station, all armed with shotguns. And I said, "where is PC Townsend?" The receptionist said, "have you got an appointment?" I said, "can you see the shot guns?" She said, "yeah but you still need an appointment." Marko shot her dead, and said, "shut up bitch, we don't need one." We walk in, and find PC Townsend. All armed with shotguns. I have a pistol. I said, "look, you piece of shit, you are to blame for letting the streets go to waste, you are to blame. What's going to happen now?"

He said, "you go to prison, that is what." I said, "Marko, tie some duct tape around his mouth." I shouted, "this is vigilante justice." We tie him up really well. The station alarm goes off.

Nothing was stopping us, our whole defence system had gone. It was being back in the military all over again. When you look over the horizon, over the watershed. When you look at people in a way that makes a difference. You wander what difference it will make. Wether you are biting from the hand that feeds, or doing what the corrupt Police wanted. Immunity. They had immunity. But not from us. A Sargent shouts, "Get out of The Police station." I said, "never heard such poetic words." And we never hear such poetic words. All of the time."

We hear The Police speaking these poetic words, they creative write so many things. But in their minds they are strong. They are interfering. They are part of the capitalist government. They kiss the bottoms of banks. And that is what they do. Once was a public servant, is now a corporate servant. Then you turn into a corporate slave. People were consumers. That's all people were. It didn't matter on the numbers. How many people visited Ikea. And tried to fit the table whilst drunk. Or why these shit companies exist in the first place. Is it for reward? *The whole idea, in the first place. Is to create something.* Where we are aware. The Yid Army does not want any beef, yet if people give us the beef. We will retaliate We are like a rattle snake.

The more you find yourself in no mans land, with nothing really left to think of. All of the over swearing, the violence, and the corrupt system. Leaning down on you, like a heavy bowling ball. Just wanting to squeeze you from head to toe. Or the over riding meaning of self destruction. Wasn't so defiant or un rewarding anymore. You had defeated your ideology, and you were back with existence. This was contained in your self knowledge. And became something of a narrative. Of thought policing, weaponised control, shooting disabled people, and elderly people. That's what some police officers did.

Before I joined the military, this one cop. Shot a disabled man in the head. The disabled man. Was in a wheelchair. The cop, he vanished. It's like I had never seen anything like it. He ran away, there were warrants out for his arrest. And the police were looking for him. So he fled the country. He went to The USA. Then he went to Mexico. Then he just stayed there, then he travelled to Brazil. Slept with a lot of hookers over there. Then he killed himself in the mouth of a 9mm magnum pistol. Now I can't clarify all of this happened. Because I was very blurry eyed before starting the military. Because we were basically getting drunk every night. And doing cocaine. So we weren't sure what was reality and what wasn't.

Yet, what led from my existence, and the existence of other people. Is we realise. Pain is suffering. Life is suffering. We live, we die, we end. Our brains, malnourished, we are alone in a world that doesn't understand us. We are alone in a world, that is quick to judge us. Then turn it's back. Every infraction, every ticket, every thing you would see on the news. Every wrong doing. Every righteous act of the military, was thrown out and dismissed like you would never have guessed. We were born in a broken society, and we will die in a broken society. The only thing we can keep sacred is our hearts. And right now, they are on fire. Fuming, anxious, angry, and realising.

There are some people who treat the world like one big soap opera. Spreading lies, and stirring things up. Some people, simply don't care. You get it all of the time. You know the ones. The tradesmen, the people who come over. Only to give you no quote, and no service. Or the times you wanted to really excel, but needed someone to come over. We got these shotguns because they meant something to us. Not because we just liked them. There was a difference, and that difference. Along with all of the information you can find. Is a shit way of looking at the world.

A detective doesn't find clues in fiction books, these police officers. At this police station. Were reading Harry Potter books. And trying to link that to evidence. I could see in the background. And it surprised me, because I wasn't really sure what narrative they were going with. The means to the end. Became the means. The end became the end. The people we meet in our lives. The pure, the innocent people. Who need our protection. And you expect The Police to protect The Public. So this is why we are here. With our shotguns, and waiting for some news. From our chief. We had a manager. For the first time ever. His name was Mr Ralph Barnes. He was English. He was in an underground basement. In an undisclosed location in London. And he had everything with him. All of the dossiers. All of the equipment. Everything. You see him, you don't. He's there. He's not. He's alive. He's dead. He's welcome. He's dismissed. He lives in the world full of hatred, and ignorance. Full of the shattered souls of the world today. Trying to find progress. In every little bit of minor detail. That comes your way.

You wander around paradise beach too

long, you will find a nice woman. Maybe she will sleep with you for one night. But never two. That is the problem all of us men face. And it's time to say that in this police station. In Belgravia. We were here for purposes. Yet we had shotguns. And we had PC Townsend, right by the balls. We had elastic around his balls. We were going to shoot his dick off. We hated the guy. We seized all of his equipment. We locked the door. A whole army of police were outside. Now I can't guarantee this is in Belgravia. But it probably was. Yet the narrative remains the same. You poke at someone too much, they are going to bleed. You find someone too hard to energise. Or plead with. Or try something. All of the people who have turned their back on me. All of the people who have raised their fists and meant something to me. Have been an inspiration. The colossal mess of society and the way we go. With worlds apart. The mess we create. The undiagnosed mental health issues, some people face. As they try to climb the social ladder. And get nothing but hatred, love, fear, and respect. This was a time, for us to realise something. Through spirit, through armour. You can never forget.

We had seen people for who they were, and noticed people for who they weren't. We had them now. We had the cops by the balls. And we had no intentions on letting go. They were interfering with our operations, and they needed to stop. They were corrupt as shit. That is why, we were there. Trying our best. To find out. Why this society is in a mess in the first place. The values of respect and decency. The underlying repercussions, of serving to the crown.

And the impregnation of women. That they had been on one night stands with. And met at night clubs. Only to find out. They would never see their son. Their daughter. Because their policing job. Carried them, to a new level of corruption. They saw their children. Once a month. The woman cooked and baked, and did all of the work. Whilst they went out, volatile, angry. Working over time to put people's heads in the concrete. Their loathe of the detestable, and their love of the worthy. Became something of a miracle that was shunned before it was ever so bright. They were nothing without their pride. Virtue or signal, or to even begin to imagine. The way we believe. In a world that can pretend to like you. But swallow you, and take you under it's wing. Life wasn't secure, or valued. We weren't living in a place of safety. We were living in this burnt out police station. With grenades, waiting to be thrown outside. With machine guns at our disposal. Ralph Barnes. Had a ton of equipment. He was able to hack into the police national computers. He had a ton of things on his computer. He had a list of every corrupt cop, convicted. He had 30 shot guns per cupboard. And he had 20 cupboards. He had pistols, grenades. Rocket launchers, AK47's, and albeit. Sometimes you would look at him. And wander why.

Why in this tiny island, we have so much armour and shells nowadays. So many machines. In the age of 'paranoia', and worship. We begin to lose our sense of integrity. It leads us down a path of destruction. Evil awaited us at the gates. God couldn't save us, and that truly meant nobody could. We were slaves to a system much bigger than us. Yet we were taking control. We had PC Townsend there. Sweating like a pig, all wound up, crying for his life. All bloody, and sweaty, and you would wander. You would wander why.

Life, sometimes, was like a whirlwind, looking at this big sweaty guy. Looking at his jaw line, looking at his behaviour. Looking at every nuance of his character. Realising who he was. We knew, we were going to get caught. We knew, the ending was bad. But we wanted to try vigilantism, after the football hooligan era started to fade. Fighting became old. It was old news. Throwing coins at the coaches. Was old news. We knew, we were heading for hell. Or heaven. Or maybe both. Yet we knew that we had him. At this moment in time. The sweating pig roast of a police officer. So sweaty. He looked like a swimming pool of sweat. Just waiting to self terminate, and start a new life. Away from this sense of char grilled false justice.

I could see his blue eyes, looking back at me. Through the times he was alive. There was no way this was happening slowly. Marko reached for the chainsaw. Then we knew we had business to attend to. We knew, that through cutting his legs off. Once his cock and balls were shot. We knew we could, and we did. With the searing sound of the chainsaw. We had barricaded the door. Put extra locks on it. We had did everything we could. Armed police were trying to break the door down. Yet the door was made of the toughest material you could imagine. And we made it that way. Because two weeks ago, we got something sorted.

We got a fake engineer to go in, and say that he was from corporate And he said that he was instructed to fit a bullet proof, chainsaw proof, grenade proof. Door. To the room of PC Townsend. When The Police asked why. They said it was for every police officer's protection. And they were rolling it out across all stations. We paid this "corporate Dave man" a million pounds. And if you want to know how we got this money. Then let's just say we hacked the accounts of wealthy people. And took the money and didn't look back. We meant business. We had front row seats. Yet. I knew it was only a matter of time before The Police. Found some form of entry. It was just the door that we made secure.

We could hear them digging away at the bricks, demolishing their own police station. To save the life of a police officer who was in no fit shape for work now. When Regan got the tattoo machine out, and tattooed "twat" across his forehead. Saying, "keep still I have never done this before." Gone before dusk, gone before dawn.

Another sense that the Seaburn casuals had got to us. Another sense of reality that we once would dismiss. Another sense of justice, we would find nigh on impossible. It was us with the answers. We just didn't have the key. For all of the police stations. This one was under lock and bolt. I get an email from Ralph Barnes, who has just stolen a billion pounds from this wealthy poker player. And we are looking at Arsenal now. As the next team to scrap with, ironically, we do have a lot of Arsenal ourselves. You know why they call themselves that? You know why? Because they can't kick a ball to save their lives. They need that name, pretending they are god's gift. Pretending they have cannon balls. They offended me. They were a rival firm. We were going to fight with them. To the death. We were going to scrap with them.

We were bringing machine guns. Whilst they were bringing bb guns. We were bringing shot guns, whilst they were bringing coins to throw. We had advanced our power. And everyone knew it. Yet, a sense of what next?

It was around the corner for everyone to see. Around the corner for everyone to realise. Around the corner for people to know. This world. I knew what it was like. Women only want one night stands. That was the problem we had. We became inflicted with this idea, that people would judge us, and we became enemies of ourselves. Full of the same things you would like to think of.

Full of jealousy, hatred, you name it. It was people who stood in our way. The sense of compliance. Or the sense of wrong. Right. This. That. Wrong doing or not. It was nothing but a minor infraction. A minor wrong doing. To fulfil our purpose.

We still had him where we wanted him, we still had lift off. It wasn't perfect by any stretch of the imagination. But it was something we wanted to see. Beyond the horizon. Beyond something you would think was magical. Was a broken dream filled with hypocrisy. Too many lies and too many dreams going to waste. Cool one minute, hot the next. Hit and miss, trailer parks, car parks, long drives. Business as usual or not at all. Useless nights and nights in front of the TV. Removing yourself from The Police. In every direction and even then it would give you something to go on. If you wanted to be honest and trade your thoughts for a while. You would find your home. A safe place on a council estate. Just to be taken away. This sense of decay in my head. And left me just bitter, and not leaving anything to reconcile with. My thoughts were my thoughts. My word was my bond. My mind was made up.

I was lost and found. I was found, and then lost. I was looking to finish PC Townsend off. Finish him for good. This wasn't Lost, or Harry Potter. Or Game of Thrones, or something you wanted to watch one of Reegan's shit movies, then be your guest. This wasn't an adventure on some kind of magical hill top, with some bunny rabbit at the top, trying to sail down a chimney pipe. This wasn't new years eve, with the shudders, and cold. Of another tomorrow, that the hooligan firm didn't want. We wanted to see what life was made of. And this was what it was.

It was emotional with us now. It was personal with us. And it was something we knew. Something we felt inside, and something that we got riled up and realised. We understand that the main concern was the problems themselves. PC Townsend. Whilst Police break down the door. That was to come. Yet rewind for a second. Whilst I tell you what happened before. Marko is looking nervous, he is looking like he is defeated. PC Townsend has turned to mush. He is not even recognisable as a man. We look around and we see these people.

He was the hot shot for us, he was the target for us. He was the man that was in charge of the corruption. He was the guy we had to take out. He was the guy we had to destroy. Everything else, and all of this aside. We had to come to some kind of agreement. Yeah right, fuck that. He was sweltering, then he was dead. We chopped his head off, and his head/face, mouth, he was talking, for 30 seconds. It was quite surreal. He was just talking non stop. "Our father in heart in heaven, hello be thy name, thy kingdom come, thy will be done, as earth as it is in heaven. Give us our daily bread." He just kept reciting the lords prayer. Then the head dropped to the floor. All bloody and cold, and you would like to think this was okay.

You would like to think we had progress. Maybe we did, but deep down. We didn't really feel anything.. the marginal errors in society. The feeling of erosion on our feet. The feeling of proverbial quick sand, and you wanted to know why this is how we feel. Because the hooligan firm had been demolished. Everything had fallen to pieces. Our friends were our enemies. Our enemies were our friends. Our family were our enemies, and our enemies were our family. Life was full of contradictions, false alarms, lying, cheating, working for the state and working for the government.

They must have had some intelligence. Townsend was going to corrupt them. But we didn't know who else was working for him. Maybe a fisher man on a boat. We have no idea. We wanted clearance, and we wanted closure. We didn't want just a colossal mess. Waiting for us to be torn limb from limb. When the Police finally burst through the door. It was going to be my shot gun killing them all.

When the police burst through the door. It was going to be our Arsenal at the ready. Our weapons. Our shotguns. Our grenades, our way, our highway. Their lives, and then you think about a time. When you see them. Kicking the door down, imagination runs wild, and in slow motion. It wasn't going anywhere. The bricks were being chipped away. And we were just waiting like a waiting game was waiting. For maybe a chess piece. An activation A think tank. Someone with some integrity. We had been ruined, destroyed, corrupted, left, ran wild and left our friends, and self destructed to a proverbial island known as shit town. And before you even think to yourself about this. You become challenged, and lodged in some form of disclosure. It was us who wanted to know. Where we were. Where our life was. Our own memories. Our own times.

    We could not know, and we didn't want to. We left everything aside. We left everything aside. And we dreamed. Dreamed for freedom. Freedom was a better name for the mass colossal shit stains. You would see on TV. With brazen eyes, and a white washed finish. A nervous disposition. An error in ways. A purpose in numbers. A challenge to be met. A loss to be formed. A nightmare to be achieved. Or a wrong doing to be fulfilled. A life to be lived. A life to be acknowledged. A time to be engrossed in. With this erosion *you knew.* Everyone knew. And before you could.

    The chipping blocks, and the breeze blocks would consume you. We knew we had lift off. But we didn't have landing. We knew we had everything at our disposal. Yet we couldn't find any shred of information relating to the fact that Townsend was ruining things for the firms. His dead body lying on the floor. Looking like he had better days. And he definitely wasn't making any beauty magazines like Vogue. In state of affairs he was in.

You could imagine, before you, as the Police still chip away at the bricks. Seconds turned into smaller seconds. And me, Marko and Regan were stuck on what to do next. It was taking The Police a long time. To break through the building. And Ralph Barnes was playing online poker because he was so bored. I said, "Ralph Barnes, also known as a piece of shit, what the fuck are you doing playing online poker? We have an operation here." He said, "operation what?" I said, "I don't know, operation pork chop, how the fuck should I know what operation?" He said, "operation Windsor?" I said, "what ever feller, stop trying to act hard with these operation names. We don't need them. Yeah that's right, we don't need anybody.

Everything built on evidence. Valleys, lies, and even then in a corrupt place. And death was just a step from a time, when you knew it was no newer than life. Yet you counted your steps." You knew the coins keep changing. People were dealing with their problems. In their own way. They were knowing what was available. Knowing what to say, look at the world. Become what we knew.

Only to find out where we would go. In reality. When the final brick caved in, and shotguns were at the ready. Rapid fire was firing towards us. And we knew we had a battle on our hands. If only Ralph could cease with these stupid names. And get back to work.

Instead he was with us. Trying to do something. Trying to go somewhere. Trying to be someone. Trying to do something proactive. Yeah right. If only. And you wander why people like him work for us. It's because we had to know. Time and time again, when the penny drops and you realise where your island is. Were you realise where your home is. On cloud ten or five, you realise that life. Was built on some kind of interpretation.

Life was nothing but a show, of what you could see around you. Mindless faces, mindless names. Left over times, left over faces. Left over integrity. You would want to know, how far these things would go. Yet the more you looked at things, the more you realised. That life itself was to blame. And we were being treated the same to anyone. If only this was the first attempt. To pull over something you wanted to see. But it wasn't. Shotguns at the ready and you want to know something. We weren't afraid. Not one bit. We were doing something important. Stopped even believing the lies. The deceit The challenges that led in our wake. That left just destructed. Left to bury our minds. Just like what we had to see.

Our own home, and left over takeaway meals in pizza boxes. Would now became a stand off with The Police. Our shot guns pointing at them. Their guns pointing at us. A helicopter above. And a loudspeaker shouting. "Surrender, give yourself up." Marko grabs a poem, and reads it. He says, "surrender, surrender, never a dull day with a surrender.

Pretend to remember, it's like November. Stab me in the heart. I bleed." The cop in the helicopter shouted. "What the fuck is this!?"

He said it with such certainty also. I looked at Marko and I said, "to be fair Marko, you really shouldn't be reciting poems to The Police. You know that's kind of awkward for us." Marko said, "yeah I mean, it's something I have written." I said, "well tone it down." The man in the helicopter said, "put your hands on your head and drop your weapons." Marko, me and Regan. It was lucky Regan had a sniper, and was pointing it at the helicopter. Next thing you knew the police start shooting.

The helicopter starts shooting at us, and so do the cops. We climb underneath the table. We kill ten cops, and we get injured in the process. We are out numbered. And before we know it. We are arrested, and taken into the cells, to be processed. But that was yet to come. Right now, we were still fighting. I shouted, "grenade", and launched a grenade. As it landed nowhere near a Police officer. Military got involved and were shooting at us. In the end we were captured. Taken to private cells. This was the end of The Chip Shop Crew. We probably were going to all serve life without parole. This was in Belgravia police station. Getting checked into the police station. And going to the cells. Yet, albeit The Police didn't realise that my hitman I hired. Two weeks ago. He made some alterations to the cell bricks.

And had hidden chisels, everywhere. This was not over. The arrogant desk Sargent, before we were in cells. Just to rewind. He shouted, "right, your name." I said, "Steve Smith." He said, "Allergies?" I said, "you what?" He said, "do you have any allergies?" I said, "yes pork and bacon, next?" The desk Sargent Sargent Gary Gasser shouted, "are you trying to be a wise crack? You have killed my officers. Military surrounding the place. Even though we were captured, we kind of felt like it wasn't the best idea to be in Belgravia. But that was the place we were. Business men outside protesting for us to be released. For some strange reason. Only to know that Ralph Barnes, he was behind this whole thing. As our manager. And he had decided that the business men, they did have shares in the Yid Army. And we knew that now.

This was the Chip Shop Crew. And to know, this kind of altercation here. With this fire just everywhere in the background. Was bread and butter for us. We were violent, but it was going to show the matter for better or for worse. It wasn't poetry but reality. For every opinionated school teacher, who had marked you down subjects. For every opinionated person, who had took you off some kind of random adventure.

To scurry into the background and realise that we knew what to say. That hatred was amongst us, and things had escalated Only to realise that we had a lot of work to do. To finally know. Where we stood. We saw the police as a barrier to our hooliganism. That's why we hated the police, because they stopped us from fighting. They were an inconvenience to us.

Then, the more we got to know them. The more they started to issue us warnings. Like letters through the post. Like Dear John letters. Asking us to cease. And then we said, "this was further shenanigans with The Police." Which to be fair, it probably was. Put it in a book, stamp it up. Do no good, do some good. Do work, do no work. Be the best, do your worst, be your own person. But reality was shaken by this mass hatred. And the empire of lies we had seen around us. We had buried ourselves in our own self deprecation. We were nothing but faceless souls looking for ways to avenue our destruction. With the type of life now left. With the type of clearance now produced. We had nothing. Life was just something to marvel at. Like a comic book waiting to excite. Or some kind of hero just waiting to come over and save everyone from harm.

You could fight all day but realise when the penny drops. It really does drop. It goes down and trickles down your face. It makes you realise where you are going. And you find yourself without a home. Or a life. So with us all processed and in the cells. We were sure more problems would arise.

Sure the world would be a sacred place. Yet we had yet to fight Arsenal. Which was a shame. Because we were going to fight them. The Seaburn casuals had really caused us so much pain. As we tried to fight them. We were in a police station that was in tatters. The police officers were in ruins. The military were in ruins. Everything was in ruins. My thoughts were in ruins. The world is in ruins. The cell block/prison cell/custody suite I was in. Was in ruins. And that was the state of affairs I had to live with, until some overzealous nameless cop. Starts guarding my cell like it means something to him.

So yet again we would see. Timeless classics, and times you wanted to see. To see good hope and good dreams. Of people who meant something to others. All just thrown away on whims and empty stories. Nothing but memories just waiting to decay. We were nothing but our own destruction. We were nothing but our own ideas. We had nothing but our own hearts. And that was something I could see. Yet this was not justice to us, or the police. We had felt some kind of feeling. Where we had realised. That time was just taking us. To achieve, where we wanted to go. The times we had seen. The times that arrived. Life was nothing but some kind of idea. Once, twice, maybe. But this was too much, too soon. In our own times. We had seen. Now was too much. Now was left.

Escapades, shenanigans, violence, rows, loss of patience. You know where you stand in the world. The world needed someone to know. What kind of life you valued. And left you with nothing. And in some kind of way. It made sense. As we became to know. How our life was. Our life was taken on an adventure.

That sadly I would know. Would give you some kind of dream. Far away from home. Whilst being in the custody block. When away from the home that mattered the most to us. Fractured with this sense of guilt that everything was destroyed. Torn away from the life we were living. We were not creating anything but scenarios. That were there. Left on the table.

The Sun magazine, cocaine, Lexi Belle, night clubs, people who meant something. Gossip. And things, just, kept going. Like everything in life. We had value. We had hope. Not in this world but somewhere. When you take a trip down this world. And you know your home half the time is a custody suite. You will imagine the gravity of what was dealt with. No longer were you in charge of life. *In charge of deals being made.* In charge of life itself. Wrong, right, this, that, times, gone, remember, left to rot. This. And the other. Left to see everything fall into place. Like life had left us. Remember our names and turn us away. Leave us to nothing and remember. We had everything we had to see.

We had lift off and we were about to know. That being in these cell blocks. These prison cells. These custody suites. And knowing the geezer guarding you is a bit of a twat. It would pay credence to this fact. Even then, if you could engineer some pity from them. Get some biscuits, and maybe then they would help. But for all of the times we knew. Ten officers is ten too many. But it had to be done for the safety of the Yid Army, which was growing by numbers. And we wanted to take over the Seaburn Casuals.

That's what we wanted to do. This is our kind of life we life. And most of the time we can know.

That times we see, and times we know. Of course are valued. But you are missing the fine print. You are missing things which have become stuck. Left, open, and then nothing.

Like a flock of birds, maybe it meant something then. Maybe it means something in some kind of way. Maybe there was a memory behind all of this. Maybe this meant something. But with all of the machinery left, and with everything at our disposal, there was nothing but snakes in the grass. People trying to see what we could do. What we could focus with. We had to know how hard it was working, and even then we had to make sure life was tough.

We wanted to make sure we knew. The confines of our mind relied on it. So of course wanted to know. Through this kind of cell. I knew. That a military guard was walking down the corridor, walking like he needed a shit or something. Yet he wanted to speak, and he did. He said, "you worthless piece of shit." I said, "I am on the inside looking out at you, and what you are doing. This is interesting. You want to know. Why we want to have a row with the Seaburn casuals. Yet you won't let us, for safety. So we had to go to Belgravia. And we had to go into Belgravia. And it was the right thing to do. And we had to do it. And we had to do it feller. It was the right thing. And you had everything you could see just waiting for you. Just waiting for your own life. To become almost obsolete Or finished in some way. You were never the person you wanted to see. Or never the person, you wanted to know about. Our own time, our own life. Our own premise. Our own challenges. We had to see some kind of division. Yet, you knew. That life itself. You fool people, and you get. What comes your way. But this wasn't something we could see.

As much as you wanted to pretend life was okay. You could see yourself just in line. With the same narrative. The same problems. The same times we had seen. This was what this was. The Chip Shop Crew. This was what this was. This was our adventure. This was what it meant to us. It wasn't some just get out clause or some night shift where you meant to do something. And left your way with the world. On some cruise ship with nothing in sight but your peace of mind and maybe something to know. Or maybe you were found just alive somewhere. But you meant what you knew, and your life was just created. Before your eyes. Only for the destruction to wake up. This wasn't bridge or chess. This wasn't a game we could win or lose.

This was our own passion behind fighting, and the old bill got in our way. Plain and simple. They should have just let us fight. If they had let us fight. All of this would be over. All of the violence would be over. All of the violence would be left. This is what is happening. In this day. Where you look at the world. And see the world evolving. You are left with shards of the imagination. Just waiting to caress the inner feelings of doubt. You are nothing but a spec of dust on a radar so out far surpassed your own intelligence. Even your own mind, was a shadow of yourself. And even then you were leaving yourself open. But nobody seemed to care.

Communities failed, people lost, people lived just to see. That the finals, and the cups, and the fights. Only for this to be just something you would see. Life is just full of these grains of courage you once knew. Only for us to see for ourselves. What we could see.

We often accepted things, we often saw things how they were. We often knew, where life was. We could see their reactions. We could know how it meant. We knew what was happening. But life was lost in these values. You create, and the sheer man power behind the government. To stop the military operation of the Yid Army, and even then people's paranoia levels went from 0 to a 100 really quickly. Everything was a threat. If someone let out a fart. They would call the riot squad. It was not just physical, it was psychological warfare. Even though at times, you see. From your own point of view. Staying on the same confines of your own home. Mastering your own intelligence. Doing something with your life.

Only to find yourself, just a bit closer.

With things just left. As you entered a world of question marks. Questions after questions, after reality kicked in. It was what that stemmed from. So you could understand. So you could realise. This firm was what was keeping us going, and we were angry. Of course we were. Yet that something was to come later. In the mess we once created. The firms were going to fight and the police couldn't stop us. Or even try to. It wasn't until then you would realise your home. On this proverb of an island in some unknown location. When you realise about the truth. Is a far cry from knowing it also.

Things just get blurry. Things fade out. Things leave. Times change. People are quick to anger. It all happens like that. Maybe, after a while. You can see. Some kind of resilience. Some kind of hope. But eventually. We were locked in this cell. And the weight of anything we had to divulge in, was left with the current thoughts of knowing. Where our true value lies. We were building an army, yet this war on the streets. Was not going to stop.

Just because we were locked up, didn't mean it was ending anything. We had to become what we hated. We had to find a way to know. All about this. This was the end to an end, to a beginning. To some kind of less understanding you once would dream of. You would position yourself in the front row. Wait for lift off. You would know all about timing. You would feel some insecurity, as you took the plane to France for a holiday. Only for an argument with The French. Hotel. Over the state of the kitchen. And that was just the start of what was to be, in our wake. Travelling around Europe. Knowing, that we could bring the Yid Army to a full step in the right direction. Whilst other people were from Miami, Diablo, was live on screen. Chanting, and saying he wants affiliation with the Seaburn casuals, or he wants some kind of confirmation with the Seaburn casuals.

That he wants some kind of hope with them. That Miami Casuals were growing in numbers, and we knew this from the Diablo video links. Something was going to kick off soon, as the peace agreement between the firms seemed to fade. And with that became a depressing memory, of something so far away. The hopeless and empty dreams washed and drowned your ambition, of another dream or another moment. Left with some kind of summary. Would soon wash out your memory. You once knew, from time to time. What it was like. As your gazed in the direction of people you once knew. It was something that I could see inside. Something I wanted to see. Something I knew. Something I wanted to explain. And even then, something people knew was the right thing to do. To be locked up was not an option and we knew this now. This wasn't throwing caution to the wind, and you knew it.

Belgravia, the whole mess, and chaos of it now. And with everything you would accept, the challenges that were in your wake. You would find yourself just in a dream, just waiting to wake up from the only thing that mattered the most. Was salvation away from the peasants that crossed your mind. This was simply a convoy, of a memo, or a dossier. We once had to know. This could not continue. This could not begin to make sense right now. Because we had not known something like this. Our resistance, and our hope. Of building something we once knew. From the pitiless ground and the empty shards of realisation. And the bitter hope that left in your wake. You would once become just a reflection of the past. If people wanted to know, if you really wanted to go down the rabbit hole. And understand the pure intelligence we had. Fully known, and fully aware. Of times where people could continue. It was alive and with our reckoning. Beginning to become just left. With what we had in our wake.

We had to see, what we knew. So before anything was there. We could see. I didn't mind who guarded me. I didn't mind at all. I didn't mind what happened. I couldn't care less. Yet it all remained the same. The mass hysterical moments of a living so far away from the truth.

And a memory of things to come. Was just the beginning of a trilogy of disappointment just waiting to be flushed. Down the toilet. And once you knew that, maybe you were getting somewhere. It was the dreams where you once knew resilience. And bordering on the aggression of the Yid Army. We once knew so much, of what had to become. Lost, and afraid. And beginning to see. What we had to see. In our own mind. You once became just left. Hopes, dreams, lies, minutes, times. Beginnings, ends, waiting, waiting, still waiting. Collections, deliveries, hopes, dreams, hospitals, cells. Talks, homes, sleep, walks, towns, villages. Seas. Capitals. Moments. Ties being severed, and ties being cut. Only to find out your dreams were washed away. You meant to thing in your own mind, that you meant no malice. But the only thing I wanted to do, was to say the destruction of what was to become. And you could see now that being inside these walls. Was not a deterrent for me. Was simply just a time block, and something in which I had to wait.

Wait some more. Maybe something would crop up. Maybe something would be funny. Maybe something would crop up in our memories and cause us some kind of motivation. To excel towards the football grounds. The failings, the lies, the truth, the amount of avenues. Just digressing forward, at a state where you didn't know. When I look back at the past. I just realise. I realise that what I had, and what I have now. Is worlds apart. I couldn't convince myself even further. Time was of the essence, yet I didn't know why time went so slowly. Belgravia police station corrupted me. The police station corrupted everyone I used to know. London was the only place we could express ourselves whilst being locked up at the same time. We weren't allowed to express ourselves. We got into fights, so what, everyone was doing the same thing. And getting into fights galore. And that wasn't stopping anyone. I am starting to think this whole thing is a set up and people are getting involved. Like the Miami casuals, and I am starting to think this whole thing is not right, right now.

When you start to look at things. Yeah it's growing in numbers. So maybe we can do some work with them. Book a hotel and maybe do some talking for a bit. But then you know where the subway is. We are invading our own minds with this conspiracy theory of hope. Which by and large becomes an emotion of loss. When you finally can achieve any well being. Victory. Left over from the wreckage. Left over from your mind. Your own tyranny, that you had, was left from the wreckage of the gasoline you once wanted to know. You felt like you could become just lost. In some time zone. Before you were afraid to make it. In some short space of time. Too afraid to speak your mind. Too afraid to know. To stand up and be counted. To stand up for yourself, because you had to. You realised. You knew, and it was the right thing to do. To stand up and be counted. And stand up for yourself. This was the time we had to see. Throughout our history, and our lies. The truth of what we could see. Through the same motivation you once knew.

It was just lies after lies. After lies. You would know, that for all I knew. When I could know. The police officer guarding me. Refusing to give his name. Burly guy, looked like The Terminator. Looked like a bodybuilder. How the fuck could I forget these times. And you look at him, like he means something. This whole thing was bullshit, from the start to finish. And even then was something of a nightmare to finish that was what we were dealing with. Our own items Our own memories. Our own existence. Your own freedom. Only for us to know. One step at a time wasn't the answer we wanted. But maybe needed. In our own time in life. It became a fluent reminder we had something to say. Only for people to know. Through our lives. Past, present and future, we had to know that this guard. He finally told me his name was Dave. I said, "so Dave." He said, "Dave, nah that ain't my name." I said, "so why did you say it was my name?"

He said, "to fuck with you obviously, you ain't getting my name you piece of shit." I said, "right that's it, I want a copy of your code of ethics." Low and behold I don't get one. I said, "where are the code of ethics?" The copper, changing his name every five minutes. He was the reason why I was here in the first place. All of the silly jokes, and wet behind the ears new officers with nothing better to do. All of the things you could say. When push came to shove it was the only way.

This was not a time to begin to think, any different, than what you knew. It was a time to reflect and say you meant every word. You meant everything. Yet in these cells. When push came to shove and more armed guards started to arrive. One opened the cage, and started beating me to a pulp. I then returned to the cell. With porridge for lunch, dinner, breakfast. That was it. That was what we were dealing with. That was that was happening. We only realise this once was reflect. We know. Or maybe don't. I don't know. Yet times we see around us. Have changed. We all have.

We once knew, now we don't. We once find our freedom. Now we have any. We once have hope. Then we see. To be able to see what life is giving us. To see where life is going. To be able to see the same scenarios.

It was just a pipe dream. That was what it was. Nothing to be really concerned about. All it was, was a pipe dream. Going down the toilet. Being flushed up, into tiny pieces. Going nowhere. Worrying about the things that meant the most. And even then we had nothing to go on. You could cast your mind back as far as you wanted. You could go as far into the future as you wanted. You could deliver the same minds, and the same life you had.

You left yourself open, every day I was realising this, and every day, you could make a difference. So why I was getting involved in this lifestyle? When you have officers who just want to beat you to the ground. This is what we could see around us. The same principles staring at us. Waiting for us to make judgements. Or anything. To cast our minds away, and hope that our bad days would be good days all along. To know all about the swings of life, and the times where you got stuck. And found yourself without any freedom.

Being beaten up by the cops. It was times like these where no medic was on the scene. And we wander now, why, I was given a copy of The Sun. I was reading it, and reading it. And in this cell. In this custody suite. With the arrogant desk Sargent singing one of The Smith's songs. "Oh, panic on the streets of London, panic on the streets of Birmingham. I wander to myself..." I shouted. "That song is old, but it goes on." The Sargent went over and he said, "bigmouth strikes again." I said, "I was only joking when I said I wanted to smash every tooth inside your head." He said, "Oh sweetness, sweetness I was only joking when I said you should be butchered in your bed."

I said, "you made that line up, I think you need to listen to them more man, get some red wine, and just relax. Because your attitude right now. You won't even give me your name. Desk Sargent, and this is what you have done. Throwing everything but the kitchen sink at this whole thing. Listening to The Smiths.

Yet you won't listen to The Cure. Next thing you know. In the background, you can hear this lady screaming. And it was another prisoner. I said, "fuck all of you, fuck the lot of you." Desk Sargent, Michael Gray. He said, his name. That was his name. I said, "listen, we have a bit of trust going on, we share the same type of hobbies, and the same types of music you know. So that is the thing. That is what we are doing right now. And you realise why this is going wrong. All of the time. Because you know you have some kind of reason. Or some kind of light at the end of the tunnel. Where you just like to believe. Then again, you would see within yourself. Some kind of change. You would see, some kind of emotion. You would see something. You would know this was the end of the road. You would know this was how it was. Then before just hours ago, you could enter your mind. Then you were alone. Then you were gone. Then you were forgotten. Then you were alone. Then you had no freedom. Then you had no hope. Then you were a wolf amongst sheep. Then you knew what it all meant. Belgravia was never meant to be like this. And I couldn't believe I was incarcerated, just for killing 10 cops. I mean, you can do that on Grand Theft Auto, and nobody cares then. So now you know what this was. Yes, it was a game, that's what it was. That's exactly what it was. A game. That we like to play. Yes, get real, of course, this is more than a game. Of course this is more than anyone could ever imagine. And then you get into the kind of things we look at here. Like we had no choice. Or something was interfering in their line of work. It could be anything.

Yet the war on the streets wasn't going to stop, and until it did, we get the same things happening. Over and over again. Feeling like we had no options. The only emotions we had to say once evaporated. And people you used to love once threw you away. Only for times to become the only thing you once knew. The only times you can become the true heroes of your life. Something, was in your way. Someone was plotting against you. Someone was out there with a giant vendetta, just waiting for you to screw up. And it happens all of the time. It happens more times than you think. It happens most of the time.

But this jerk off who has me in custody. And he is a jerk off. It was just how it was. At that time. At that moment. At that time. No time like the present. For something I wanted to achieve. Which was the same thing anyone would do. I would try and achieve some kind of achievement.

Worthy of what they could see. Worth of what you wanted to know. Worthy of anything lying in your wake your dreams. Everything. They just left you, and wide awake. Your soul awake, with nothing but this dickhead of a custody Sargent. My arse cheeks. Only for a new guy to arrive. And what was this, changing rooms or some shit? Some other guy just turns up. And we realise what we are dealing with here. A police officer arrives. Sargent Tompkins. Rookie Sargent. He isn't playing The Smiths. He walks over. He points at his baton. He says, "you see this, shut your rabbit and pork." I said, "Sargent Tompkins." He said, "shut it, just shut it will you, you think you're hard don't ya. Well you're not. So keep it that way. Yeah."

I said, "I don't think I am hard at all." He said, "you killed ten of my officers. You know how much paperwork that is going to take?" I said, "you are only worried about paperwork?" He said, "yes." I said, "not anything else?" He said, "listen, I never liked you. I never did. I never did like you. And this is the response I get. That's fine. But you can say what you want. Just to let you know. I know all about the Yid Army. And I know all about their games, and your games. And this is going absolutely nowhere, and you know it. You cheat and lie just like the rest of them..you talk out of your bollocks being handed to ya." I said, "you snake in the grass, that is what you are, roaming around the place, with your belly hanging out ordering Greggs. Who do you think you are?"

I mean, this wasn't going to end well. You think of the typical place. The typical times you can believe. Even then, it becomes a nightmare. Then you start living. Start believing. In something. Some kind of hope. Yet in reality. You are left with something you can't dig out. The loopholes you have in life are left in some kind of distance. The people who once trusted you didn't realise how life was. And it was times where you could explain. How life just twisted you, from a state of realisation, to a state of not knowing.

Not knowing where you were. Not knowing the way you felt. Not knowing your own emotion. Not knowing this. It was, just how it was. You became to see. Where life was. The times you could, and the times available to you. I mean, something had to give. Belgravia was going to rot. I could sense it coming. The whole campaign. And this whole journey had gone to waste. And you were left with Sargent Tompkins, he was a bit of a twat. But maybe that's why he's in the job in the first place. Pie in hands. And that is what you get. To anyone who knows him. He is mad enough to believe he has shares in Harrods. Crazy enough to believe he has so many shares in all of the companies. Including British Gas. Unknown to him, this is a myth, and a delusion. Oh right, well he's there and he isn't. And he can become just left behind. Scattered on the floor. Left to rot. For all I knew. Then something else was around the corner. Something else was happening. You could see for yourself, how life was. How life was following you. In some dream, in some place. In some avenue. Down some stairs. To a place we all call home.

To a place we all knew. To a place everyone did. To the over reactions to the half nots. To the police not doing their job. Sargent Tompkins wanted to explain. He wanted to have trust, but with that trust. Became a wreckage of doubt. He didn't know about football's finest. He didn't know about the war on the streets. He didn't know about the vendetta we had against the Seaburn casuals, and the red army from Manchester. And Arsenal. All trying to collaborate together. And people think, oh "I know what this guy is doing." Then what is it going to be? When they have pasties at the cell custody suite. But all of this, all of that. Over just ten cops. And we get some kind of conversation going. The burly figure looking over me. Almost like his eyes would melt into the skin he was re living.

This as a mere fragment of the same corruption, or the same times you could see. Always knowing that life could become. The skill set. You once knew. And even then you were able to stand your ground. Be counted. Do something.

Yet it wasn't the same. It never was. He handed me a pistol. I cocked and loaded the gun.

No wait, that wasn't the end. It didn't have to be like this. Sargent Thompkins. The man of the hour. The man of the achievements. The guy who I wanted to speak to. It just went to show what was happening. With our escape out of custody. It was time to fight Arsenal. Local match. Arsenal away. And for the life of me. We dug out of the Belgravia police station.

Chapter 26

I was starting to imagine things, like if you could look closer. And look at things in the mirror. Or realise this. On the occasion we knew. Then maybe we meant something. To someone. When you have your whole life in front of you. And you have Jacky, still working in the Chip Shop. But that was all that it was. You wandered what it all meant. What everything meant.

And you wandered about yourself. You became to realise this was about the fighting. This was about knowing what you could do. For all I knew, this was the start. I mean of course it was. Yet this was all going to be on TV. Us kicking the shit out of the Arsenal fans. Because that's what it meant to us. So pissed down watered lager. Some kind of hot dogs, and Reegan munching on a burger. We felt like we had to say. What we felt. What we believed. And this was something that we found. Something similar.

A reality where something mattered. I am not playing the hard man, life goes around in circles. And sometimes you want to believe in something. But sometimes you can't believe in what you used to know. Your whole life becomes nourished by opportunity to say. In your world. In your kingdom. Behind all of these false news stories. And these idiots. Trying to sell the papers. The fact that we were the most wanted men in Britain, and still allowed to go to the game. Was a great privilege. It was just a shame PC Townsend was dead, yet out of nowhere he comes back to life again.

He said, "alright fellers." I said. "Wait, we killed you." He said, "mate you couldn't kill a fucking wasp, what the fuck are you on about?" I said, "Belgravia." He said, "yeah I know the place, I work there." I said, "we came in and tortured you." He said, "oh right, haha, yeah you dreamt that. We brought you in for public order, and you were chanting it all in your sleep. It was quite funny actually. You couldn't get two inches close to me if you tried."

I said, "it was a dream." He said, "well I am still alive aren't I?" I said, "Reegan, what is going on, why this is this idiot still alive?" PC Townsend looks at Reegan. Reegan said, "ur, because you dreamt of killing him you daft twat, he's not dead, look at him. His hearts still beating."

I said, "yeah alright, alright, so I dreamt it. Yeah right, who the fuck do you think you are mate? Just coming in here like this!"

He did, and that's who he was. It wasn't something to be proud of anymore. It wasn't something you wanted to explain. It wasn't something you wanted to feel. You explain yourself in ways you want to explain. Your own thoughts. Your own minds. Your own feelings. That I had this guy. Then, a dream. I cannot believe this to be a reality. I cannot believe this to be true. I cannot believe this to be happening right now because obviously it's not. So this isn't something I am willing to entertain, yet the sheer seconds just keep passing away.

The more you think about it, the worser it gets. You start to think about the memories, but realising it was a dream. That wasn't something I wanted to know or see. Or a reality you could understand. Just how we know. Life, our own eyes. And our own dreams.

Like a moth to a flame, we once were fighting. Now we are just left to this ambition of freedom. Fighting Arsenal was yet to come. This could have been over more and more times ago. Yet fighting was in our blood. We had eyes of blood, and we wanted to fight. Not knowing that Reegan was sniffing cocaine on some debit card he nicked.

There was nothing left. Nothing you could see really. It became just arbitrary.

Bloody Tony Fucking Blair, that's what you got now. What happened with him. He's the reason and Thatcher, both of them. Are the fucking reason we are fighting on the streets. The times have changed. Everything has. When you look at the small print. And you realise, that it's not just pie and chips you want. On a night out, with your mates. If that was what was happening. Even if you did understand. You would know. It wasn't too late. Yet it may have been.

Times had left you with some times even more feelings. You became just at a loss with the world. Feeling your self worth was just something you wanted to see. Knowing all of the time. What had happened to you, when you took yourself off this time.

You once knew the score, you once knew how to fight. With your knuckles bruised. We were scrapping. PC Townsend was alive. And that was the times we wanted to say. Where we were. And times we are going to explain. The same things always. The same changes you would explain. The same contradictions. You have to explain. The same reasons. Why. In some life or other. The people around you. Would become your enemies. That were once your friends.

That was the world we were living in. Nothing else mattered. Fighting became redundant. That was what was going on, you could look people in the eyes. But it was all the same. And even then that was something. And even then you would become just this fan. Having a scrap. Trying your best to get your last punch in. Your last word in. That was the whole point of this. So to know what goes on in this world. When obviously I have known. From time to time. Where life is going. I have known. Where life is. From just scrapping at a football match. It was times like these you wanted to feel. Like you could explain. Time and time again. Your own reasons. Or your own reasons of life.

Like there were reasons. Or people would say, "ah no, I know this geezer, he was with the best of us." Yet Reegan wasn't buying the nice guy act of The Police. He wasn't. And the more I think about it. The more I realise he's just different. In every way possible. Every excuse you could ever give him. Every excuse you would ever know. All down to this one thing, that I never knew made sense. Yeah we all fought in the marines.

We all did. But that was something to be proud of. This was street fighting. It was different. It was a different kettle of fish all together. That was the main reason all of the this fighting was happening in the first place.

This was the reason why I was trying my best to keep a straight face. This was the reason why I was trying my best to even achieve what I wanted to see.

This is where we belong. We are an island race. This is the whole point of this.

To bring attention to this fact. The whole point that we were fighting. It was the fight's that counted. Nothing else. Not that anything else mattered. Yet I was still there. Just in case. And even then things died down. Things changed. People changed. People left. People were just changing all of the time. Like the tides. It was only until we got stuck into Arsenal away. That we realised what it was like to be part of this fighting network. Where for once, the coppers didn't give a flying fuck about the rights. And some were joining in. Yet for the life of me. It all happened so quickly but I was punching Arsenal fans all the time. Brass knuckles. And then it just ended like, almost. Like they wanted a reaction, and that is what they were going to get.

To know the full extent, to know what's been happening. To know the whole places you leave behind. In a daze, and in some kind of confusion, you can find your safe place. Behind all of this banter. That you knew. But for once, you couldn't find out. Why on earth you were scrapping. When there were other things to do.

Other things to be sorted out. Other

people to talk to. Other things to look at. That was the whole point. And that's what never stopped. It became just alone in a world. Where we were fighting. Sure we were. But that alone wasn't enough.

That alone was just one part of the jigsaw puzzle. That was where I was going wrong. That was the line you had to cross. That was what you wanted. Then so be it. I didn't mind.

Yet we were an island race, and that is something we have to see. Something I want to say. Time and time again. The fighting, and all of this. It was never going to stop. Never going to end. Maybe I did dream some stuff but so what? You know where you are, when life hits you. Square in the face. Like a bus. Then you know how life is going. Where life is. And where you have to see your life in times to come. Things often build up until you get nowhere. Times often build up until you find yourself untouchable. Unbeatable.

Yeah right, in my fucking dreams. This was it. This was bandit country, and this was what this fucking was. This was south London. This is what was going on. I was expecting a cornetto, and a quick massage. But instead I get a blade in my face. This when all of this all started.

Reegan said, "Oi Soppy Bollocks, are you going to fight or just stand there." I said, "I have just been stabbed in the face." Reegan said, "looks like a paper cut, don't give up you silly cunt, you want to show some more respect." To be fair, it was a superficial cut.

That someone did with a pocket knife. But that was what it was like with scrapping with Arsenal. Get your head around that. If you work together, but then you want to kick them around. When you have the chance. And even then a kilo of cocaine was enough for us to realise what was making sense. All of this banter aside. You wanted something to mean something.

Down the frog and toad, they had something like the pie and mash. It was waiting on ice, and someone wouldn't shut their rabbit and pork. As I knock this one geezer out, and I said, "listen, you want to be careful." We start headbutting them, and it won't stop. PC Townsend, he reappears, how many lives does this guy have, 10, is he a cat or something. This time my visions blurry. It's blurry all of the time, and you want to know what's going on. Even then you don't want to know. When you are in bandit country. That was what was going on. As I sniffed some more cocaine, and that is when it started. And you wanted to slow down. And wether your hoover was broken or not. We wanted to fight Arsenal, because they were our rivals. And we were lucky. And this was an FA Cup, match by the way. Because we wanted to show them a good fight. And it was only the third round, we wanted to make sure they knew we meant business. That we meant something. Tottenham all of the way. Yid Army. We hated Chelsea. And we did call them out. On a lot of occasions and that was what you knew from time to time.

All of this time, you lived and realised, what you wanted to see in front of you. When you knew. It was living with this crap. Beating each other up for a quick laugh. When you know. The noise. Is just went onto the next point. And it didn't stop. So even then we wanted to know when this whole thing was starting.

Marko was chatting absolute shit to me, and the more the fighting continued, the more The Police started scrapping with the Yid Army. "Arsenal always ends up in murders." If I had listened to my instincts and watched strictly, and laid low for a bit. None of this would have happened. But meanwhile we were scrapping. And I knew Reegan had a mate down the frog and toad, down the pub. Who was going down nicking pizzas for a laugh. And that was the only start we knew.

In the end, we get into the game, and it's the same routine, except we get seated. And the game starts, and I start invading the pitch. And I shout, "Oi oi." And that is when you want to know what is going down, when Arsenal start booing. Mind you Reegan and Marko invade the pitch, and we land in the net. And then for all you know we start to think of something. Just something. Could be anything. But the more you think of it. The less you could know. Fighting for us was a release. It was a way out of this cage nightmare. That fled us away from scenes of murders, and investigations. Even then on our feet looking the part. With enough Burberry to last a life time. There was no way this was not going to end in murders. Only for people to think that I was going to become left alone. In the world where people cared. Yeah right, and I am pissed off, these cunts are fucking winning. Whilst we are running up the walls and evade the Police. And we still are scrapping. Whilst Terry picks us up on the coach. And we all shout. "Whey!"

This is the thing. This is what is happening. This isn't getting old. Nothing is getting old. You want to begin to see things clearly. And life is becoming even more clear. That you can begin to see. Where you are knowing in your life. Where you can see, where life, is going. You know where anyone is going. And you know the ring tones. So we are fighting, we are scrapping.

Thatcher ruined this country, and this coach driver thinks he's James Bond. What a prick, and the worst is yet to come. Fuck. This had ended badly. With this fat prick driving the coach. Nah fuck that guy. Don't like him at all. This is where it never gets old.

This is where it happens from time to time. You start to realise things. The same things happen all of the time, and you can't stop them. People running their mouths like it means something. And even then the soppy pricks just went to go back to Tottenham. Back to the Council Estate. Back to the council flat. 11A, this is what you knew. With the coach driver calling us silly bollocks. Yet this was how it was. And the coach driver couldn't touch us, so we couldn't fall out. We went on the motorway, and it was time to start chanting songs. Like they meant something to us. This was the only time you would think. The chip shop, this was what was going on. You wanted respect. You wanted to say. No fighting whatsoever, because you knew there was going to be a scrap on your hands. Yet it started slowly and for what you knew. You had to see how life was just thinking what you knew.

From time to time, we once knew. How life we can do the business down at Cardiff. Even though we have already been there.

Cardiff away. And this is really stretching it. Because all of this fighting is doing my fucking head in. I want to punch those sheep shaggers all of the time so that is what is going on. Then we get the beer, and then we are throwing beer bottles at them. That is what happened.

The Police turn up. But it's too late by now, and we want to scrap. We have to. *Cardiff away was something you would never have see before.* I think back to the dreams I was having. The things that I was achieving. And the people I was meeting. It all came as a surprise to me for so many reasons. I just wanted to know when the fighting was going to stop. But it came at a price, and nobody knew what the end result was. All of this towing and throwing. And all of the things we had witnessed. Had just gone to waste. Down the river. Like nothing had happened. Meanwhile we would wander why we were there. Just trying to pretend everything was okay. It was times like these we wanted to explain. From day to day. I didn't want to know. Didn't want to explain. Or didn't want to find out. The sheer size of the Cardiff fans and even then it was just by and large too much to handle. You could give yourself any excuse. Any. Then what would happen!?

This trip was fucking killing me. And the Cardiff fans were fucking animals. And even when we start getting Stanley out. That is when they start running. So fuck them, they can think what they want, and that is the main point here. and with their Burberry caps, and I am saying from time to time. Thinking their flash when they ain't. This wasn't rival but this was personal due to last time. We had to hit them where it hurts, and in the bollocks was a good start. Nicked all of their money, and went on the fruit machines. The game was yet to start, and I started to think to myself all of the time. Started to wander this would be it. This island race. We were the UK. There was something about this tiny island, we knew a little thing. And going to Wales. Obviously you get some of them who are so nationalistic, but we were too. So didn't make any difference. And the point to that, is fighting Cardiff was the biggest challenge we ever had. As Reegan was punching them left right and centre. With no Police in sight. Mind you. Reegan had a knuckle duster and was punching away. I grab out a flare gun, and sparks fly. And everyone starts running.

I leg it towards the Cardiff fans, and start scrapping with them. And start saying what I want to say to them. Saying they are all cunts. That is what you want to say, from times like these. It's times you always knew. Times you can see around you. Basically nothing that would make you think any different.

Some days were better than others. Some times you could just see into the distance. The Cardiff fans. This was one day alone and it was killing me. Unable to stand on your own two feet again. Wanting a helping hand. Looking over. Wanting to know where life was going to take you. Going through obstacles, knowing what was going to happen along the way. Knowing where people were.

That in the end, all of this was just nothing but a lie, and if we knew about it. Then we could find out more about the times we shared. To go out there and actually achieve something. Maybe something more valuable than something I knew. It would mean something. But the flares aside. I just knew what was happening. You keep yourself together, and remember what you want to remember. That our lives depend, on the very things, that we live to see.

We want to see life as something as something worthwhile. Something you look at. Enough of this fucking dance. We start kicking some heads in. That is the point. *It wasn't a dance so much*. It was a scrap. To anyone who knows what a scrap is. And even then we were thinking along the lines of just punching our way through the crowd. Able to get some kind of evening. Where everything simmered down. Time to get somewhere. Have your Sunday dinner. Have your pork pies, have something worthwhile. Know something you want to know. And all of a sudden become something you want to see. It was pointless arguing, and even pointless just being there. And times were just alone, and our moments in life. Just became as almost a militia of fans just coming towards us. We look at the world differently. We look at the world. As life was.

This was our own lives, this is what we wanted to see. How our life was. When we went about and took time to say. In our life we knew, at the end of the day what life was about. We wanted to know what scrapping meant. We wanted to know the fights were real. We wanted to know that people wanted to see us scrap. Yet the timing was endless like the fruit machines. So no longer were you in a position just to be there. At the right time. Knowing what you can do. Being who you can be. Knowing that your intentions are good, but you can't fucking stop yourself some times, from kicking someone's skull in two. And even then that is saying something.

You just want the whole world to be able to crumble. But it's not. And all we have is that fat fuck Terry on the coach. Whilst we are scrapping with the Cardiff fans. Whilst this is happening. And then we can begin to experience what life is. Because it wasn't just a second guess, or something you could see in the car parks. Or people going dogging. Even though that did happen for a change.

You just wanted to feel life was heading in the right direction. But you never knew how. That was the thing. The only way to make any consideration. Seek consultation with Terry. The fat fuck waiting for us in the coach. Like we needed his help. As the fighting was starting. Fuck. All I wanted was pie and chips, and now I get this. Fighting against Cardiff fans, that was the end of what I had to see. From what I wanted to know. Was the start of my adventures. And the end.

No news of that PC Townsend. I just wanted a good scrap. That would change things. That would make people see where life was going. Instead, nothing.

Wait a minute. Did I actually think that for one second. Throughout all of this pain. It was worth it. Worth something. Or maybe not. Yet people find excuses any where. People find excuses, and that is the part of what you know. You see, you can look someone in the face. And know what time around you are knowing. Yet time and push comes to shove. And you are left with Fat Terry, the coach driver. Getting involved and all, the fat prick. It didn't make sense why he was getting involved.

All I wanted was a say in the matter. Wanted to go back to fighting the Seaburn Casuals. Wanted to go back to fighting a firm that knew how to scrap. Yet Cardiff away, they didn't know how to scrap at all. And that was the part of what they did. On a week day. You always find yourself just guessing, and then guessing again. Your time on this planet. It's always the people that know full well if that time was up. You knew the silent type. The type that wouldn't say anything during a scrap. Or hint anything.

Life had it's twists and turns, and maybe I was just thinking too much. But that was how life was. You wanted to see. I knew what people thought about me. And I just felt like in some cases. Some times. Some avenues, shouldn't be crossed. I mean it was dangerous waters. All of the time. And that wasn't going to change. People could think that the Stanley blade wouldn't cut through someone's face but it did. And even then you can see yourself just knowing. That as a matter of fact. I knew who I was. And I knew what I was trying to achieve. And that was a scrap. Anyone could realise this, and you have to see it clearly. You have to see it throughout history. You have to see what you can see. Not the rest of it. Thinking out loud and pretending you are someone you are not. Or even then just thinking about the worst case scenario. It just made things even more just twisted in your mind.

The main theme here was knowing about your environment. The more Cardiff fans we knocked over. The more we thought we were in charge. Yet something along the lines of hope, or *anything*. Could not begin to imagine how life was going. Just to think we had a hold over some of these people. Leaving the rest to rot. Leaving everyone else to run around like headless chickens. Whilst we tried to get some meaning in life. Those values were hard to entertain. Yet it still happened on a daily basis.

You begin to notice all kinds of things. Mostly. As you want to see. As times you felt stuck. You can think what you want. Even then it just is something you want to see. Even when you know. Sure, I knew fully, what life was. I knew fully where life was going. Cardiff away was mental. I can't believe I dreamt all of that stuff before, dreamt of all of it. For what reason I don't know. And for some reason I have no idea. You just imagine things.

I can't understand some times what things mean. What people mean. What this state of affairs. These shenanigans aside. Nothing else mattered. You just wanted to fight. That's what you wanted to do. You wanted to scrap.

All of this aside however, I knew a man about a dog, who knew this lady across the road. Who knew what was going down a couple of hours ago. And we sure knew the times you knew. One minute you just start thinking You want to be fighting the local firms. Then you start realising when you go to Cardiff away. That is when you start fighting them, and it ain't local. But we still are going in and fighting them. Because that is what it's going to happen. Then so be it. A snickers bar apart and I wasn't bothered. Just to know I had Reegan and Marko to back me up.

Even then just to explain to them, that

things were a bit in the air at the moment. Things had changed. *People* were changing. Values were changing. People were living people were dying. People were knowing. Then we realise. Terry the fat fuck, started to scrap with the Cardiff fans. And we ain't even in the fucking stand yet. The geezer needs to calm down because it's getting heated. And I know it is.

You want to see things clearly how you wanted to see things. In a way which makes sense. As life was going on. Even then you were left with nothing. The fighting was what mattered.

The fighting was what we lived for. Yet we had to go down the pub before the game. And my phone was ringing in my pocket and at first. I wasn't even sure who it was from. Then we realise. Jacky is having a meltdown. "Where the fuck are you!?" She shouts, she says, "I am having to run this chip shop single handedly now. Due to you cunts. This is not okay. We can't continue like this." I give her honesty where honesty is due. I give her that. And I give her the respect she once knew. And that was something I could see quite clearly. But life wasn't about just this that or the other. You wanted to take control, of course you did. But she was getting on my nerves. Jacky was in a state. And we had more work to do beating the crap into The Cardiff lads the better.

You just wanted something to make sense. Something that was happening. Then all of this fighting was going to stop. Then you knew. All worlds apart. If someone knew me, fine. But it wasn't always about trust. Or maybe it was. Yet you became inflicted with this. This whole system. On the front of collapse. And people warning you to lay low. To trust your instincts, yet you keep running all over town. Just to make a point that you are worth something. It could have meant fuck all to me to say something but I had to. And this day I was saying the beat down of some of the Cardiff fans. Trying to get them involved. I had no time for The Chip Shop. Not now. So this was how it was going and until we know what's around the corner. It's a guessing game. So we just stand there and wait do we? Wait for what exactly? Someone just to explain to us what is happening? Like I already knew. Go back to thinking something is new. Something is different. Something is worth your while.

    Then you know what's going down. Even though at times you feel like your back is against the wall. That was the whole point. But when Jacky starts nagging me to go back to the chip shop. It's something I had to do. Yet I didn't want the aggravation. When push came to shove I returned. Jacky, with ketchup down her top. Was saying. "Listen you idiot, you know what time this is, you need to help me with the chip shop. We have got work to do. Haven't we? You are just sitting there, and it's not helping the situation now is it?" I said, "nothing helps the situation. That's the whole point. That's what I have to say. You can talk all day about this. Doesn't mean anything to me. So what? You have had a bit of aggravation from the customers." That it didn't mean anything to her. She was the same person she always was. And that didn't fucking change.

Meanwhile, for the thousandth time, I see PC Townsend in a thong. With people videoing. He said, "my mrs has thrown me out the house, all I have is this." I said, "mate this time I ain't helping you, your mrs is one evil person man." PC Townsend said, "have you got any clothes I can borrow, because otherwise, I am going to have to wear a traffic cone around my cock and bollocks."

I said, "you know, this is what happens, I will give you some clothes, yet this is further problems. I don't want right now. My dreams aside. Come inside dude." He comes inside. And I give him a change of clothes. Even give him cod and chips. Sit him down, talk to him. Was even ok talking to him now all this shit was aside. That we had buried the hatchet. That we had made friends again. Yet his mrs was evil.

I said, "are you a cross dresser?" He said, "No I am not, what it is, is basically, what is happening. Is my mrs keeps throwing me out the house. And all I could find was her thong on the floor." I said, "couldn't you find any underwear dude? Any of your own? Like this is seriously a problem. Are you a transvestite?" PC Townsend said, "believe me I am not, it's my mrs." I said, "let me speak to her." He said, "what?" I said, "let me talk to her." So I phoned her up. On his Samsung phone. And I get this. "Hello." I said, "hi, who am I talking to?" She said, "Lorraine." I said, "oh nice name." She said, "thanks, who is this?" I said, "I am a friend of PC Townsend, PC Brian Townsend. Totsworth, or what ever the fuck his name is." Lorraine said, "yes I know he's a bellend and all, I don't like him." I said, "did you chuck him out the house?" She said, "yeah." I said, "did you chuck him out the house with no clothes on except one of your thongs?" She said, "yeah." I said, "do you think this is acceptable?" Lorraine said, "no it won't happen again."

End of phone call and you start to wander. You start to second guess yourself. You start to believe what you want to believe. Even though at times you can't even see straight. You just wanted some times, to over think a situation. That was all it was. You didn't want things to go on for too long. Even then you are left stranded.

I knew PC Townsend well. I knew him well and I knew what it meant. I knew what happens. Some times. You just find yourself. At a loss. Worried. Maybe. But this guy. He knew how to talk to Jacky. In a way which I understood. It just came as a shock to me as some times Jacky would snap. Didn't like it. Didn't know what to say. Didn't know when she would stop snapping. The cod and chips were ready.

I didn't even know where Marko and Reegan were. *I didn't know,* and I didn't seem to be able to find out. Everything was just leaving me confused. Anxious, yeah sure thing. But when push came to shove. I am just sitting here. Just waiting. When Reegan bounces in. He starts saying. "Look dude, this is what is happening, is that you go all the way down here, you left Cardiff. That is what happened?" I said, "yeah." He said, "that was the thing, time and time again, until you understand. This ain't the first time this has happened either. So I am not surprised. I don't even know why these things matter. And then it comes along the same time. Just like everyone would see what it means. What everything means. What we can see. In front of our eyes. That was meaning something. To someone. To people who want to believe.

Then by virtue you just want to see. Of course. Life isn't perfect. Never said it was. Yet some times you become just confused. I could never find out some things in my life. I could never find out what it meant. I could never really understand. Yet it became something that we knew was right. So by this time. You can become, just what you knew.

The Yid Army would never be the same. The Yid Army would collapse. The Yid Army would never, ever be how it was. Not for a long time. Not with this going on. You dream of hope. You dream of something. Yet, some times or not. When the anger builds up. You don't know where it's going to go.

You don't know what it's going to achieve. You want your life conclude to that fact. And then you become, just, significant, in some times. You don't want to begin to realise. That life just passes you by. One after another. Just like you had some kind of information. Facts. Present. Then nothing. You just want to pretend. Even then. You don't know what's going on inside people's heads. Not that you want to know.

Some things never change, and I say this now. The sheer passion behind the Chip Shop Crew. Getting it up and running and getting it moving again. Only for this to happen. This was the results we are looking at. And for once, you look at the world differently. Sure, we get into fights galore, but that was the whole meaning behind anything you once would approach. Some things never change. And some people never change. Some people just drift apart, and become attracted to how the football is. Not that I can see it coming. When I realise where life is. We have to see ourselves, as what we have. Not that we can become anything.

Yet in that resolve things change. But for better or for worse. We don't know. You just could see things clear enough. As long as you wanted to.

Even then it was a close call. With people by your side to cheer you on. And it wasn't always about calling someone a cunt either but it did help. The chip shop crew, will always be in my heart. It's not something that we did lightly. It ain't something we thought of lightly. That is what we have been doing. That is what we have been saying all along. So what, if we run around the streets like mad men. It's the same approach you know. So you want to be counted. You want to stand up and be counted. You want to do something that's going to help.

You want to be there when the chips are down. And that is the whole purpose of what we are trying to achieve here. To be able to call people out. At the best of times. It was going to work like that.

To know, that throughout the fighting. There was some closure. To know some bellend of a copper, always had his mrs throwing him out the house with a thong. And he finds a traffic cone until I give him clothes. Some things never change. Well he did, after he got changed. But all of this cross dressing.

You wander. Why he is doing it. Why he would pick it up. And I know at times. Marko, *his mrs chucks him out the house*. And he once had to try and fit into her jeans before falling into a car, and his arse cheek landed on the front mirror. It was really a pain in the arse for him. That was what was going on.

So you can say what you want about the Seaburn casuals. You can say what you want about Millwall verses Stoke. We had it sorted. But we were going back. To this council estate. No more sniffing glue or taking viagra. Not that I was sniffing viagra. But took it, as Jacky walked in. I said, "have you closed the chip shop?" She said, "yeah." I said, "alright then sound." I said, "this viagra is useless" She said, "why do you take it then." I said, "no idea, you ain't giving me any fun, you just want to tell me what this means right. What all of this means."

    She sits down. Pint in hand. And Reegan is sipping some milk. And Marko is sniffing some glue. PC Townsend again..he knocks on our door. The local busy body. He said, "alright lads, how's it going?" Jacky shouted, "do I look like a fucking man!?" He walks in, I said, "mate, this is a private party." He said, "I have had reports someone is running a brothel." I said, "get out of here, do you really think that?" He said, "well I saw her over there, your Jacky." I said, "leave my Jacky out of this, what has she ever done to you?"

    That was the thing. They were so quick to latch onto Jacky. And blame her, and call her a whore. Like she was at fault. And I didn't know why this was all to blame. It didn't lie with her alone. So I didn't know why he was basically saying she was a hooker. Which wasn't nice. Considering it's only her weekend job. I said, "PC Townsend, can you leave." He leaves. But you can hear him walking down the stairs. Should have taken the lift. There's numbers for adultwork hookers in there. All that is on the stairs is the smell of piss and the stench, as he walks down. And he goes and meets. Low and behold Sargent Thompkins. I have mentioned him before.

    They do some freemasonry handshake. And everything is a laugh, everything is funny. Well I am not even pretending anymore. With your back against the wall you want to see something. With your back against the wall. You could see something was clear. You could see something, that all along. I could see that my life. What I know. You can know all along. You want to find out the truth. For once. You once to find out, what you really want to know.

You want to find things out. So you become just a number. A statistic. And then nothing happens again. And then you can believe what is happening. You can believe yourself. In every step of the way. You know. This madness had to stop. This madness was the same thing anyone saw. And we all believe that one day. We can see. Our life. And it's values.

Private party or not. Some things don't get old. Some things stay the same. Some things do. With your legs like jelly.

Chapter 27

With Chelsea around the corner. We had work to do. I have honestly lost track of which fucking game this was. It's a lonely road. You don't want to mug anyone off or play the hard man. I did it all the time. Terry, the fat prick. Picked us up from flat. Council estate. I said, "prick". He said, "alright, listen, just listen, it's all about me, this coach. You can fucking jog on."

I was right. Times were changing. All of

the time. I wanted to believe in something. But we had nothing really to believe in.

Chelsea at home was something that we wanted to see. I could see my enemy Dave. A Chelsea supporter. Looking lively. Looking like he could pack a punch or two. I said, "alright, long time no see, what the fuck are you doing here?"

He said, "I support Chelsea, you fucking mug." To be fair, he had a point. He did support Chelsea, and that was a valid statement. It's just something wasn't right. Along the way. You look at life, and you look at the differences. You look at the moments you just want to find. It's always about your life. Your help, your ambition. Your dreams. Something. Yet, it's an ambition we all have. An ambition you always like to see. You always want to know that deep down. Dave was just trying to mug me off. He looked like a Chelsea mug and all. I said, "games about to start." He said, "it's the under 21's you fucking idiot, don't think it will be as lively." I said, "you fucking what? Do you want to have a fight?" He said, "yeah." I said, "funny, you are supposed to eat chicken wings, and you are doing business with a prostitute." He said, "what the fuck did you say you fucking wrongun." I said, "you fucking prick, look at the state of ya. Look at ya, you think you can go around with all of this bullshit. Not a chance. It always comes down to the game. This ain't the under 21's you fat prick." He said, "why does it say it on the ticket then?" I had a look at the ticket. I said, "that's from ten years ago, you soppy bollocks, where did you buy that." He said, "from some geezer down the road." I said, "I will be fucking honest with you, I don't even know if we are playing Chelsea. You want to get your facts straight. And no more prostitutes. You will get VD. And then you will need treatment."

It's true, when you have VD, it's not the same, it really isn't. You kind of think of yourself, as invincible. You sleep with a bird. And you end up catching what she has. Then you have to go to the STD clinic. And you have to be tested for everything she could have possibly given you. At the same time the STD clinic would run you through tests. That was it. Yet, there was something about Dave that didn't make sense. Behind his lust for talking. And his ambition to do the right thing at the worst time. I could just end up knowing. Something was around the corner. Something. By and large what I am trying to say. Is the geezer was a cunt. And he always has been. And the more I think about it. The more I realise. That when you look at things clearly.

When you understand, in life. People change. Or you give some people sympathy. With Dave. Chelsea was his dream world. He fucking loved them. Me, it was a rival firm, and the Chelsea Headhunters, were by and large going to fight with us. He wasn't the main bowling pin to knock over. Just some dickhead with too much time on his hands. I said, "hey mate, *you are a dickhead, with too much time on your hands."* He said, "listen, you have been talking too much, you come and say what you have been saying about me on facebook to my face."

I said, "all I called you was ugly."
He said, "say it to my face then."
I said, "your face then."

I run over and we start scrapping. Marko and Reegan show up. And by and large what I am trying to say is right now. Right now this second. It just seems bizarre. Not saying it's perfect. Not saying that at all. But it's different. You like to think as people as what they wanted to say inside. Or you think life is running around in circles. You never know, or you never wanted to find out.

The same things apply, and the same things can make sense. And even then you have people to say. Marko meant no harm.

Yet the more you wanted to think about it. The more you wanted to see. The more you wanted to realise. The more you wanted to think. That time, to start again, to think differently. To do something differently. Then again, it was always about something new. Something you always wanted to see.

Chelsea at home, when I am snorting cocaine, and Dave ain't having any. The fat fucking prick. I brought Terry along and he's punching him about. Mind you Reegan looks like he's about to solicit a prostitute. When he's opening his mouth. Mind you, all of the time we can think about this. We realise where these things go. You take your time out of the

day, and you realise what life has become.
  Some people should know better, maybe I was one of them. But I didn't realise. It was something you could think. From time to time. Something you wanted to see. Something that you wanted to believe. It was something I knew. Or something other people did. I don't know. Every day was different. Getting into the ground wasn't hard work. But the past of all the scraps we have had. Getting texts from Jacky spamming my phone.
  Then you wander what it's about half the time. Don't know, couldn't figure it out. Wouldn't know or too much time on your hands. Wouldn't give it a miss. Yet watching the game, and knowing there was going to be fighting soon. Everything flashed before my eyes. All of the games we could see. And this was one of them you didn't want to miss. Yet you had to believe that Dave was in the opposite stand. Looking over. Just wandering. Wandering what's happening but even still. Knowing what he's going to do after the game. Open someone up. Yeah right, he's in bandit country, and I am going to open him up like a cannister. That was the thing. Time and time again. You look forward and you see things, and times. Where you could believe. But times have changed.
  I don't know why, or how. I just feel like, somewhere along the line. Things just end. Life is just one, after another. Life, it goes fast. But this game was fucking boring. I could see John Terry in one of the stands. Next thing I

know I just wander what's left of this game. We end up drawing nil nil, and that adds to the aggravation. So I meet up with Dave, and he's really pushing his luck. When he's coming around the corner.

When we can see what is happening. We can see, what is going on. We can see the resentment. We can see things clearly. Of course I resented him but that was the whole point.

He couldn't see where I was coming from. He wanted to live in his suburban lifestyle. He didn't understand, from time to time. Things change. Things get old. Things end up frustrating you. I don't know. But the Chelsea Headhunters remained firm. Solid in the ground. And I knew that we had work to do. With Police horses to punch. We knew we had business. So we start kicking police horses, and PC Townsend. For the third time. He comes up, and he says, "listen mate, I know, that you and Dave don't come along, it's breach of the peace if it carries on."

I said, "nah it's not, don't say that." Dave said, "you want to be honest, then fine, but by and large what I am going through right now." PC Townsend said, "I feel like getting my truncheon out." I said, "for the last time, stop, hows your mrs anyway?" He said, "yeah she's alright." I said, "has she kicked you out of the house?" He said, "yeah again."

That was the thing. Kicking people out the house. For no reason whatsoever. That was the kind of thing you got to hear. But with all of this fighting aside, and all of the dreams. About Belgravia. What the fuck happened there? Just dreamt it did I? What I even know is something I knew all along. Is that some times you just have to be realistic here, and say we have to be honest. In some kind of conflict. I didn't want to know or didn't find anything amusing from this.

You get into stages, where life passes you. And you wait. And wait for something to become just fascinating. Amazing. Left. You wander around. And then you wait for something to happen. Anything. But it's too late. It's way too late, and you wander why. All of this time. I could see where it was going.

I knew, by now. All of this aside. The dreams. The conversations. The talks. Watching the game, and the fights galore. The police officers you would meet along the way. Only to find yourself in bandit country. It just wasn't the same. So I couldn't really know.

Part of me wanted to feel everything was okay. Part of me wanted to believe that we could watch the game. But I didn't know anymore. I didn't know what to think. All I knew is that, the fights were getting longer. And then you wanted to find something worth doing. Scrapping, and going to the magistrates. Telling them about Chelsea Headhunters. You would be serious. You would want to believe it was how it was. With everything around the corner. You would believe it was the same.

You never could stop yourself, from

believing. Some fat fuckers in the stands have conquered all of the chip shops. I knew that. When it came down to things, all you are left with is old friends. People have gone out of your life. And then nothing. It all comes back to this kind of moment. In your life where everyone always had to be right. We got into scraps and then we found ourselves. Just, you know.

With your back against the wall, you seek consult from the only person who you think can help. With Reegan coming my way to offer me advice. About which hookers were about. I didn't know either.

Life wasn't like darts. Life wasn't like that whatsoever. This was how it always was. You wanted to see people differently. Who knew you differently to others. But it was never going to stop. The violence were never going to stop. The crazy dreams weren't going to stop, you never knew what was around the corner. For once, you just wanted closure. You wanted to feel things were moving in the right direction. You wanted to feel that was the case. But it never seemed to warrant that kind of thing. Chelsea Headhunters were ruthless. The Yid Army remained firm. That was the whole point to things. And you think of life as something you could see. Moving forward, and you could know. That we would be able to see how the world progressed. Throughout your life, or your times.

It was always the same things. And always the same fights you would get into. Always the same people or the same attitudes. You wanted to believe in. Fine.

But something wasn't sitting right, and I didn't know what it was. The clock was ticking but I didn't know about the end results. You want to see things perfectly. You want to see where life is going. You want to see where life is. On and on, and the things you can see. The things we want to be able to achieve. It was what we achieved. What we could see in front of us. Chelsea Headhunters. They were ruthless animals. That was how it was. How we started to think, in simple terms. How they were acting. Behaving.

Then you know. You want to know these things. You want to be able to see. Throughout life. Yeah. Fine. Been with it. Done it. Been with Jacky. She gave me VD. But apart from that. It wasn't the same.

You always want to believe in something, but knowing Marko has been scrapping. And we are just sitting eating pie and chips. You never know what to think. You never know exactly what you want to believe. Yet, we can believe in things. Sure. Yet, the resounding truth is. I don't know.

I refuse to believe in this life where, you just, you just don't agree. Or don't believe, don't want to see things. You want to be able to know. The fights. This is what is happening. This is how these fights were. Did I really kill ten officers? Ten police officers. I really don't know. It just goes around in circles. You want to think, that they are there to protect. But half of the time. They are not.

So, you can become, just left, in some kind of time. Where life, was going, from worst and then even times again. You want to believe, and want to think. You just do. Yet we didn't know what was happening next. We didn't know. We didn't want to know. Or we didn't have to see things clearly. The truth was out there. I mean I know that. Yet at times when you want to be serious. You have work to do. Yet, all of the time you just want to feel secure. For the life of me. I just didn't want to know. Yet one thing was for certain. The Chelsea Headhunters really had a grip. Of what was to become. Then nothing else.

Nothing else even mattered at this point. Back to the council estate. Back to the crazy dreams of killing coppers. Back to all of that.

You know, PC Townsend isn't that bad anyway. It is funny when his mrs kicks him out the house. Yet, in a way. The amount of times I have had to help him out. Like it was my civil duty to.

I look at him now. A crazed man, with a crazy attitude. He was, working single crewed. That's how it was going to stay. If I wanted to speak to him. I could. Yet with all of this going along. The best thing to do was just to pretend. Pretend that life was perfect.

Chelsea, vs Tottenham ended. Back to the council estate. Back to the busy body police officers. Back to the VD, viagra, cocaine, and prostitutes. The stupid Sun magazines stuck to your arse cheeks. Mr Singh at the local corner shop.

One thing was for certain, all of this aside. The fighting, even though we knew it had to stop. We continued. We made a name for ourselves. The Chip Shop Crew, it's not just a Chip Shop Feller. Part of the Yid Army. And Thatcher did put us through some rough times.

Reegan yells, "pass me the remote." That is when you know, things are slightly getting back to normal.

THE END